[signature]

RICHARD KADREY

THIS SPECIAL SIGNED EDITION
IS LIMITED TO
1000 NUMBERED COPIES.

THIS IS COPY **681**.

THE
SECRETS
OF
INSECTS

Richard Kadrey

Subterranean Press 2023

The Secrets of Insects Copyright © 2023
by Richard Kadrey. All rights reserved.

Dust jacket illustration Copyright © 2023
by Christopher Shy. All rights reserved.

Interior design Copyright © 2023
by Desert Isle Design, LLC. All rights reserved.

See pages 285-286 for individual story copyrights.

First Edition

ISBN
978-1-64524-128-7

Subterranean Press
PO Box 190106
Burton, MI 48519

subterraneanpress.com

Manufactured in the United States of America

TABLE OF CONTENTS

Ambitious Boys Like You........................7

The Secrets of Insects......................29

Razor Pig...................................47

A Trip to Paris.............................85

A Hinterlands Haunting....................103

Suspect Zero..............................115

Black Neurology—A Love Story............143

Flayed Ed.................................147

A Sandman Slim Christmas Carol..........151

The Air Is Chalk..........................161

The Tunguska Event........................183

Horse Latitudes...........................189

Snuff in Six Scenes.......................205

What Is Love but the Quiet Moments
After Dinner?.............................215

Devil in the Dollhouse...................237

Candy Among the Jades....................269

Ambitious Boys Like You

Witt pulled his father's '71 Malibu to a stop down the block from the derelict house. The car coughed a couple of times. It wasn't vintage. It was just old.

Sonny was riding shotgun. He said, "There it is."

"I've been driving by this place my whole life," said Witt. "Didn't ever think I'd have a reason to go inside. Didn't ever want to."

"Why's that?"

"When we was young, we figured it was haunted."

"Haunted? How come?" asked Sonny.

"Well, look."

"At what?"

"The bodies."

"Jesus fucking Christ."

Sonny, his cousin, was from Houston, but being from the city wasn't why Witt found him interesting. It was that while Witt believed in everything—God, the Devil, spooks, not spilling salt without throwing some over your shoulder—Sonny believed in absolutely nothing. Not

9/11 or the Kennedy assassination, not Heaven or Hell. The way he talked, Witt sometimes wondered if Sonny believed in him.

"Those are dolls, you psycho hillbilly."

"They don't look it at night," said Witt. "At night it looks like a whole cemetery in those trees."

Sonny had to give him that. There were at least a hundred small dolls nailed to the apple trees around the old man's yard. There were even a few on the porch and the low picket fence that surrounded the property.

"It's called hoarding," said Sonny. "These old assholes, their dog, or their wife dies and their brains turn to Swiss cheese. They can't let go of anything. That's why we're here, right?"

Witt nodded.

"I know. I'm just all of a sudden amused that after all these years, I'll finally see inside the place for real. You know, we wouldn't ride our bikes by here at night. We'd go clear around the block to avoid it."

"What a great story. Promise me you'll write a memoir. You ready to go?"

"Hell yeah," said Witt, trying to sound more ready than he was.

It was just after two a.m. Witt had set the interior light on the Malibu to not come on when they opened the doors. Sonny carried the bag with their tools. They wore sneakers and latex gloves from the Walmart by the freeway. Sonny pulled on his ski mask. Witt kept his in his windbreaker's pocket. The night was hot and humid and the mask itched like a son of a bitch when he tried it on in the store. He'd put it on once they got inside.

Sonny was the first through the picket fence. He held the gate open for Witt, not because he was polite, but because he didn't want it to slam shut. That was the other thing Witt liked about Sonny. He was a thinker.

It was only about thirty feet from the fence to the porch, and even though it was night and he was wearing a mask, Sonny kept his head down. Witt followed him, covering the side of his face with his hand.

Ambitious Boys Like You

Witt stepped onto the front porch gently. He didn't want the old boards to squeak. Sonny turned and looked at him.

"Where's your fucking mask?"

"In my pocket."

"Put it on."

"There's no one here."

"What if he has automatic lights or security cameras?"

"Cameras? You think this old son of a bitch is James Bond?"

Sonny sighed.

"Just put the damned mask on."

While Sonny got out his lock pick tools, Witt took the mask from his pocket and pulled it down over his face. He was sweating and itching in seconds. *There better be something inside worth stealing,* he thought. Gold coins or silver candlesticks or a goddamn treasure map from back when the hovel had been the nicest house in town, eighty some odd years ago. The old man had lived there by himself for as long as Witt could remember. No one had ever seen him take anything but the trash out, and even that was a rare thing. Witt hoped it was cash inside. He wasn't a pirate. He wouldn't know what the hell to do with a bunch of gold. When it was over, maybe he could buy his dad's Malibu and get it fixed up. That would be sweet. He was about to ask Sonny what he thought about the idea when Sonny said, "Well, damn."

"What?"

"You were right. The old man isn't exactly security-minded."

Sonny put the picks back in the bag and turned the knob on the door. It opened.

"The hayseed doesn't even lock the place."

"I told you," said Witt. "Folks don't like it here. There's no reason they'd want to go inside."

"But we're not just folks, are we?"

Witt smiled. Sonny reached up and pulled down a doll held with wire over the doorframe. He handed it to Witt. The doll was about eight inches long. Its body was straw and the head was made of rough, untanned leather, with button eyes.

"Toss it," said Sonny. "Time to grow up. This is no cemetery. It's a flophouse."

Witt threw the doll into the yard and it felt like a hundred pounds of bullshit lifted off his back. He'd been afraid of the house for so long, he took it for granted that he'd be spooked forever. And now he wasn't. The old wreck, with its rotten gables and broken windows covered with cardboard, wasn't *Dr. Terror's House of Horrors*. It was just a prison for a pathetic old man. Witt all of a sudden sort of felt kind of sorry for him, but sorry didn't mean that he and Sonny weren't down for business.

Sonny pushed the front door open and Witt followed him inside.

The stink hit Witt hard, an overpowering combination of mildew, spoiled meat, and something like copper, with a sour sting that brought tears to his eyes.

"Jesus. Does this old fuck ever flush his toilet?" said Sonny.

"Sometimes in these old places, rats or raccoons will get in the walls and die there."

"Smells like it was Noah's whole goddamn ark."

Sonny flicked on a small LED flashlight and Witt did the same as they went deeper into the place.

They were in a wide foyer. The floor was covered with a carpet turned black with grime and mold. To the left was a parlor. Wallpaper peeled from the walls like burned skin. To the right was a dining room. A hallway led off from the foyer. A door to the kitchen in the distance. A closet. Another door under the stairs that Witt was sure led to a basement. The place was even worse than he imagined.

"You sure there's anything left in here worth taking?" he said. "I mean it smells like the damned dump."

"Spend a lot of time out there, do you?" said Sonny. "You said the family were bankers. People like that, they know what to squirrel away for a rainy day."

Ambitious Boys Like You

"I suppose."

"Damn right you do. Now, let's get to work. Don't forget what I told you. Slow and steady wins the race. Take your time, but don't get lazy. Don't make noise, but don't go so fast you're going to miss valuables."

Witt nodded. He wanted to breathe through his mouth, but he didn't want to look like a pussy in front of Sonny. He swung his light into the parlor.

"As good a place to start as any," Sonny said and they went inside.

They went to opposite ends of the room. The plan was to work their way in and meet in the middle. It sounded good when they'd talked it over, but now Witt wasn't so sure. What the hell was he looking for exactly? He was sure they weren't going to find a pile of hundreds just lying around the place.

He looked at the dusty paintings. Generations of the old man's family, each more mean and joyless than the last. It eased Witt's conscience a little.

Witt checked the bookcase and drawers on rickety old end tables. Picking up some old books, he wondered if they were worth something. Or one of the lamps. His grandma had an old gilt lamp from France that she swore was worth more than his granddad's soul. Witt shook his head. No. They weren't there for lamps or shit like that. He checked around the cushions on a sofa that kicked up enough dust that it looked like a west Texas sandstorm.

"What are you doing?" said Sonny.

"Searching. What do you think?"

"What are you looking for, bus fare? Leave the sofa alone."

Sonny played his light over the room. Witt checked his watch. They'd been in the room for fifteen minutes, but it felt like an hour. *I might not be cut out for this life,* he thought, but he kept his mouth shut.

Sonny pursed his lips like he was going to spit.

"There's nothing in here. Let's check the dining room."

They went across the hall and inspected the room the same way they'd done the other. The dining room was even less interesting than the parlor. Just a big table, some chairs, and a sideboard. There was a crystal chandelier in the center of the room, covered in cobwebs. That was probably worth something, thought Witt, but how would they get it out of there?

"Nice."

It was Sonny's voice. Witt went and looked over his shoulder. He had one of the sideboard drawers open and was holding up a shiny butter knife. Sonny handed it to Witt.

"You know what that is?"

Witt shook his head.

"Gold-plated silver. Old too."

Witt turned the knife over. It was pretty and it reflected a buttery light onto his jacket where the flashlight caught it. It was nice, but it didn't seem like a fortune.

"Is this what we came for?" he asked.

Sonny took the knife back and shook his head.

"It's a start. We've got a few thousand dollars here easy. I know people who love this kind of shit. They sell it to antique dealers and designer fags for a fortune."

Sonny put the knife back in the drawer.

"Aren't we going to take it?" said Witt.

"It's heavy. We'll get it on the way out. But this is exactly what we're looking for right now. Smalls. The old man will know where the big ticket stuff is, but for now remember to keep your eyes out for cash or watches or rings. We'll finish down here and go upstairs to roust granddad."

A few thousand dollars already, thought Witt. *Maybe I am cut out for this after all.*

Sonny went ahead down the hall and Witt followed him inside an office. There was a heavy wooden desk with an old-fashioned typewriter on top. To the side, an office chair with bad springs. It sat low and leaned back at a funny angle. There was a hat rack with a moldy fedora and ancient lacquered file cabinets so swollen with moisture that some of the drawers were twisted and wedged tight. Sonny started to work on them while Witt looked through the desk.

It was one of those old kind you see in movies, with lots of cubbyholes on top. He shone his light in each one and stuck a finger in the holes where he saw something. All he found were a few dead roaches, some rusted paperclips, and mouse turds. The drawers weren't any better. Letterhead stationery, old pens, and a rusty letter opener. In one of the bottom drawers he found a dusty bottle of bourbon. He was tempted to take it until he saw that the seal had been broken. Did whiskey go bad like beer? He didn't want to take a chance, so he put the bottle back and opened the top middle drawer.

There was a doll inside, like the ones in the trees. *A goddamn funny place for one,* Witt thought. He reached in the drawer and picked it up. It hung for a second, like it was caught on a nail, but it came free with a little tug.

Something black boiled out from the drawer, spread across the desktop, up the walls and down onto the floor. Witt almost shouted, but kept himself under control. Some of what writhed on the desk hopped off and landed on the legs of his jeans. He pointed his light down.

There were spiders pouring out of the desk and trying to crawl up his legs.

"Fuck!" he yelled, and shook his legs like he was barefoot dancing on coals. Someone grabbed his jacket collar and pulled him into the hall.

Sonny turned him around and looked him over.

"Spiders," whispered Witt.

Without missing a beat, Sonny bent and brushed the spiders away with his sleeve. When they hit the floor, he stepped on them like it wasn't anything at all.

"Thanks," said Witt. "I'm scared shitless of those things."

Sonny slapped him across the face.

"Don't you make another goddamn noise, you hear me?" he said.

Witt was still trying to catch his breath. His cheek stung, but he nodded. Sonny walked over and closed the office door. Seeing the spiders locked inside, Witt relaxed a little.

"You got a thing about those bugs?" said Sonny.

Witt nodded.

"So did my old man. Turned to jelly at the sight of 'em. That's okay. You just better hope the old man didn't hear you and call the cops."

"Maybe we should leave?" said Witt.

Sonny shook his head. They were quiet for a minute, listening for footsteps or a phone.

"No. We're just getting started," Sonny said.

Witt looked around.

"This place is huge," he said. "It could take all night."

"No. When you've got a big place like this what you do is hurt somebody. In this case, the old man."

"Why?"

"Because he's obviously crazy and we're going to want him back on planet Earth for a while. Don't sweat it. I'll handle things. You just watch and learn."

Witt waited while Sonny walked down the hall. He wasn't sure how he felt about what Sonny wanted to do. Witt had been in plenty of fights over the years, but they were always stand up man-to-man things, not slapping an old cuss around. Still, the gold up front was awfully pretty and he didn't think Sonny was the kind of man who was going to be talked out of a plan once he'd set his mind to it. Witt knuckled his cheek where Sonny slapped him. Better the old man getting hurt than him.

He realized that he was still holding the doll. It was like the others. A few inches long and with a leather head. There was a piece of string around its waist, trailing off to a frayed end. Witt remembered the feeling of the doll getting snagged on something in the drawer. Then he thought something else.

Sonny was halfway down the hall, headed for the kitchen. Witt came up behind him and grabbed his shoulder.

AMBITIOUS BOYS LIKE YOU

"I think it was a trick," he said.

"What?"

"The spiders. Look." He held up the doll so Sonny could see the string. "They could have been in a bag or a net or something and when I picked up the doll it let 'em loose."

Sonny looked at him and a smile crept across his face.

"Be cool, man. You're just spooked. We're about done down here. We've got the kitchen and if there's a basement, maybe give the downstairs a quick once over. Then we go upstairs and we're out. Okay?"

Witt wanted to agree. He didn't want Sonny mad at him, but he didn't want spiders even more.

"I still think it was a trick," he said. "Something the old man set up."

Sonny glanced upstairs.

"I doubt this old guy can find his way down to the shitter. Stay focused and do the job."

Sonny started away and Witt wanted to say something, but knew it wouldn't do any good. He played his flashlight over the walls and floor.

"Stop," he said.

Up ahead, Sonny did. He dropped his head a little. His shoulders were tense like he was about to hit something.

"What?" he said.

Witt didn't get any closer to him. He kept his light pointed at the floor a few feet in front of Sonny.

"Look down there."

Sonny took a couple of steps forward and stood for a moment, then went down on one knee.

"I'll be goddamned," he said.

Witt came to where Sonny knelt. Their lights illuminated a length of monofilament fishing line across the hall about six inches off the ground. Sonny grinned up at Witt.

"What do you think? More spiders? Maybe ninjas'll fall from the ceiling?"

"Don't touch it," said Witt as Sonny hooked a finger around the wire and pulled. It snapped. Witt froze. Nothing happened. Sonny looked up at him, then stood.

"I've got to give you points, man. You were right. Grandpa has been up to some funny games. But he's still an addled old man. This one didn't work."

Witt looked around the hall, expecting more spiders to come raining down. But nothing happened. He pointed at something shiny near the ceiling.

"What's that?" he said.

Sonny saw it too. He moved closer, pulling a pistol from his jeans. He used the barrel to brush the tiny specks of light above his head. They made a small sound swinging against each other, like tiny wind chimes. It was fishhooks. Dozens of them hanging at eye level on more monofilament.

Sonny swept the gun barrel through the hooks, sending them swinging.

"This is good news. Know why?"

Witt shook his head.

"Because it means there's something in this house worth protecting. We're going to make ourselves some money tonight."

Sonny ducked under the hooks and stood when he reached the other side. He turned all the way around, checking the floor and walls for wires. When he was done, he motioned for Witt to follow him.

Witt hated creeping under the hooks almost as much as the spiders. He darted through and didn't stand again until he was past Sonny.

"We do the job just like we planned," Sonny said. "Just keep your eyes open for any more pranks."

"Yeah. Okay," said Witt.

"And get rid of that fucking doll. You look like an idiot."

Witt looked down. He was still holding the doll with the string. He tossed it back down the hall the way they'd come and flinched, afraid it might set off another trap. But nothing happened.

Ambitious Boys Like You

"There's another wire up ahead," said Sonny. "I'll go that way. You check the closet."

As Sonny moved off, Witt checked the closet door for hooks, and moved his light slowly over, around, and below the frame. He ran his fingers around the doorknob feeling for a tripwire, but didn't find one. He looked over at Sonny, wondering if he could just say he'd checked the closet. But Witt knew he wasn't a good liar. There was nothing he could do.

He put his hand on the closet doorknob and turned. It opened. Nothing happened. He swung the door open the rest of the way and shone his flashlight inside.

The closet was full of rotting coats and rain boots, some umbrellas and a couple of canes with silver tops. *Those could be worth something,* he thought. There were boxes on the floor and more on a shelf above the coats. He checked around for more lines, but didn't see any signs of them. *The canes first,* he thought, and reached for one.

A board under his foot sank a couple of inches. Witt froze. There was a metal-on-metal squeak. He pointed his flashlight at the floor. A board with long butcher knives pushed through it hung a foot away from his legs. It was supposed to swing out when he stepped on the board and hit him in the knees, but the house had betrayed the old man. The hinge the board hung from was caked with rust. Witt was so happy he wanted to laugh, but he didn't want to piss Sonny off by making noise. He grabbed one of the canes and stepped back. The board under his foot rose back up into place.

And another board swung out, this one chest-high. Witt jumped back, slamming his head into the wall opposite the closet. He went blind for a second as light exploded behind his eyes. When it cleared, he saw the second knife board, embedded in the closet door. It missed him by a few inches. The doll he'd thrown away earlier lay by his side. He kicked it into the closet.

Footsteps pounded down the hall.

Sonny pushed him out of the way. He looked over the scene and then at Witt.

"You okay?"

Witt nodded, but he was still a little light-headed from the fall. Sonny grabbed his shoulders and pulled him to his feet.

"Fuck this," said Sonny. "Let's find him."

He was already on the stairs when Witt saw it.

"Stop!" he yelled.

Too late.

He ducked as Sonny's foot broke the fishing line.

A shotgun blast ripped across the hall, right by Sonny's head. It looked like an old sawed-off was inside the wall, hidden behind a flap of wallpaper, now scorched and torn by the blast. Sonny stumbled down the stairs, holding a hand over one ear. He pulled his hand away and checked it. There was blood on the palm.

Witt came over.

"You okay?" he said.

Sonny looked at him for a second, then snapped out of it.

"I think I'm fucking deaf in this ear. I think that fucker blew out my ear drum."

"Maybe we should get the knives and forks and just go," said Witt.

Sonny took out his pistol.

"We're not going anywhere. I'm going to find out what that old fuck has and kill him."

Under normal circumstances, Witt would argue about something like killing a person, but these circumstances were damned far from normal and the old bastard was kind of asking for it, Witt thought. He followed Sonny up the stairs. They weren't quiet as they went. The old man had to have heard the shotgun. There wasn't any point in being quiet anymore.

"Careful," Witt said.

A few steps up Sonny said, "There's another doll and another wire. Duck."

Sonny bent over and when he was through, Witt followed him. As Sonny stood Witt saw the other line, the one strung so if you missed the first, you'd hit the second. Witt closed his eyes and what felt like a thousand pounds crashed down on them.

They were pinned to the steps. Sonny cursed and thrashed. Witt tried to push the weight off, but every time he moved the net ripped into his skin. He managed to get his flashlight turned around and finally understood what had happened. The net they were trapped in was made of barbed wire. And they weren't alone. There was a body with them. A bag of bones and rags. Some other poor asshole who'd wandered into the old man's house and never left. Behind him, Sonny cursed and growled about all the ways he was going to murder the old man.

"Hold it," said Witt. "Stop moving a minute."

Sonny thrashed for a few seconds more and stopped.

"Barbed wire don't weigh much, but this net has got big weights on the ends," Witt said. "We keep thrashing, we're going to wrap ourselves up and die here like Mr. Bones."

"Who the fuck?" said Sonny.

"Turn your head."

Sonny did. The net dug into Witt's skin again as Sonny jerked back from the body.

"Fuck me," said Sonny.

"What are we going to do?"

"One of us has got to get out. Then he can hold the net up for the other to get out."

"So who does what?" said Witt.

"I hate to admit it, and if you repeat it I'll deny it, but I think you're stronger. I can't lift for shit flat on my back here. You get me out and I can help you."

"Okay," said Witt. "Can you help push a little?"

"I'll do what I can. Just keep those goddamn bones away from me."

"How am I supposed to do that?"

"I don't know. Forget it. Just push."

Witt got hold of one of the weights holding the net in place. The problem was that it was wrapped in barbed wire. Each time he grabbed it, the metal barbs tore into his fingers and palms. On his first try, he moved the weight up about six inches before the pain got to be too much. The good news was that it allowed Sonny to turn and wriggle up next to him. They both got ahold of the weight and lifted it just high enough for Sonny to crawl out. Witt dropped the net back where it was. Sonny lay on the stairs, panting.

"Sonny?"

"Yeah."

"Think you can start helping me out of here? I don't want to spend the night with this dead boy."

Sonny got to his knees and came up a step to where the weight lay. He put his hands on it and yanked them away.

"What's wrong?" said Witt.

"That dead fucker touched me."

"Use your jacket," said Witt. "It'll help with the barbs and you won't feel the bones."

Sonny looked at him like Witt was speaking Chinese. Then he took his jacket off and wrapped it around his hands. Taking hold of the weight, he pulled up, leaning back against the staircase railing for support.

There was a spark and a thump. The weight came down, almost smashing into Witt's hand. Sonny flopped on the stairs next to it.

"Sonny," said Witt. "You all right?"

Sonny opened his eyes and looked at the banister.

"The railing is electrified. Zapped me good," he said.

"Can you lift the weight without touching it?"

Sonny reached up and pulled off his ski mask. His face was slick with sweat. He wiped it out of his eyes with his jacket sleeve.

"No, I can't," he said. He looked over. Witt knew Sonny was staring at the bones more than looking at him. Sonny frowned.

"I think I'm about done here, Hoss," he said.

"What do you mean?"

Sonny put his jacket back on.

"I'm done. I'm over. The old fucker won."

Ambitious Boys Like You

Sonny stood and pulled his ski mask back on. He jerked back when he almost touched the railing and shook his head.

"I'm sorry, man. I can't help you."

He turned and started down the stairs.

"Sonny," yelled Witt. "Please."

Sonny kept walking. Witt yelled after him.

"You can keep my share of the forks and stuff. Just don't leave me."

Sonny stopped at the bottom of the stairs. Witt waited for him to come back up. Sonny said, "Sorry, man." He turned and headed for the door.

"Sonny!"

Down in the dark, Sonny cursed.

"What is it?" said Witt.

"The goddamned door. It's locked."

Witt listened to Sonny walk around downstairs, cursing and punching things.

He came back into the hall.

"The windows are barred from the inside. What the hell kind of house did you bring me to? This is your fault, you hayseed prick. I hope you fucking rot up there with your dead pal."

Witt watched as the circle of Sonny's flashlight disappeared down the hall.

"Sonny?"

Silence.

"Sonny?"

Nothing.

Witt lay on the stairs sweating. He pulled his ski mask off too. He tried wrapping it around his hand to keep the wire from tearing into his palms, but when he lifted the net, the barbs cut into him and he couldn't hold on. His hands were ragged and bleeding. He lay there, breathing hard and trying not to completely lose his mind. Sonny was a thinker, but he lost it. *Be a better thinker. What would a better thinker do?*

Witt's elbow brushed against the skeleton. He reached over and twisted one of the bone hands and with some sweating and swearing, snapped it off at the wrist. He'd torn up his shoulders doing it, but it was worth it. He found the dead man's other arm and snapped off the second hand. That's when he noticed a doll duct taped into the dead man's mouth. Witt elbowed him away and turned back to the weight.

Balancing the skeleton hands over his palms, he grabbed the weight. When he pulled, the barbs dug into the bones, but didn't touch his hands. It took three tries, but he finally got the weight high enough to set it on the step above him. Slowly, he crawled forward, using the skeleton's hands to hold up as much of the net as possible.

He cut his legs up wiggling, but finally, he was out. Witt lay on the stairs facing the dead man. *Another thief?* he wondered. It couldn't be the old man. Maybe his family were embezzlers and it was someone from the bank come to confront him. That meant Sonny was right all along. There was a treasure somewhere in the house, and now neither one of them was going to get it.

Witt stood and started down, careful not to touch the railing. A gunshot boomed through the house. He went down the stairs as fast as he could, and crouched by the wall, keeping low. The place was quiet now.

"Sonny?" whispered Witt. "Sonny?"

He looked down the hall and saw an open door. Warm light, like dawn over a river, lit up the walls and floor. Yeah, he thought, Sonny was a yellow dog piece of coward shit, but if he left now, that would make him just as bad. Witt started down the hall. He'd lost his flashlight on the stairs, so he went slowly, looking for any tripwires he might have missed earlier.

The basement door was open. A doll was perched on the top step, nailed in place through the stomach. Witt looked at it for a good long while, searching for monofilament, funny floorboards, or electric wires. He didn't find any, but he couldn't make himself step past the doll. Maybe Sonny wasn't close enough family to go searching this crazyass dump after all.

A voice echoed up the stairwell. Witt looked downstairs.

"Sonny?"

Ambitious Boys Like You

Something hit him in the back of the head and the building seemed to tilt, swing around, and hit him in the face. His vision collapsed to a tunnel and went out.

WITT AWOKE handcuffed to a rough stone wall. His hands tingled with pins and needles and his face hurt like fire. He tried to say something but it hurt so much he screamed, only there wasn't any sound. His lips were sewn shut.

The basement stank. The moist reek of decay down here was why the rest of the house smelled like Death shitting in a dumpster. The blow to his head made it hard for Witt to see clearly. The glare from the bare bulbs strung along the ceiling hurt his eyes. He heard a splash, like someone was dragging wet laundry across the floor. Witt blinked, shook his head, and tried to focus.

Sonny hung on the wall like Jesus on the cross, held there with nails through his hands. A scrawny old man in overalls and a barbecue apron that read I LIKE MY PORK PULLED was gutting him with a long, curved butcher knife. The old man sawed his way up Sonny's stomach, stopping when he hit the breastbone. Then he made a cut across Sonny's belly, set down the knife, and reached inside, yanking out a long tangle of intestines. The old man let them flop into a plastic trashcan pushed up against the body. Sonny's head moved from side to side as the old man worked. His eyes opened, showing the whites. Witt's breath caught for a minute. Sonny was still alive. He wanted to scream, but remembered the pain.

The old man glanced at him, then turned back to his work.

"I'm not ignoring you, son," the old man said. "It's just that I'm a little busy right this second." His voice startled Witt. He expected an old coot, but the voice was strong and cultured, like someone in one of those ancient aliens documentaries on cable.

The old man pulled Sonny's stomach wide, pinning the folds of skin to the wall with hooks and monofilament line. Sonny's stomach was splayed open like a wet red flower. The old man took the knife and cut a couple of more things from Sonny's gut and dropped them into the trash. When he looked at Witt again, the old man's gaze lingered on him.

"I suppose you're wondering what's going on," he said, and smiled. "Since you're in no position to ask questions, I'll do my best to guess what you'd like to know."

The old man tossed the knife onto a worktable and pulled off bloody dishwashing gloves, dropping them next to Sonny's gun.

The man's face was creased and yellow, like a kid Witt remembered from grade school. The one with hepatitis, and they'd all had to get shots because of him. The man's knuckles were swollen and bent like he had rheumatism. His teeth were gray. Still, as beat up as he was, the closer the old man got, the more Witt saw something hard and ferocious in his eyes.

"First of all, nothing you see here tonight is about torture or cruelty, though lord knows you boys deserve a little of both. Showing up here with a gun," said the old man.

He turned and pointed to a couple of little dolls lying on his worktable.

"My eyes and ears," he said. "I saw you two coming a mile away." He looked at Witt. "Made all these dolls myself. A trick my *grand-mère* taught me long ago and far away. Made them out of ambitious boys like you and your friend."

The old man wiped sweat out of his eyes and pushed back wisps of thin white hair.

"On the other hand, I'm grateful you're here. If it wasn't for boys, and a few girls, like you two, I wouldn't be where I am today." He held out his arms like the filthy basement was Hollywood Boulevard. "That was a joke," he said. "Don't try to laugh. It'll hurt."

When he got close, the old man held open each of Witt's eyes and looked at them, like a doctor examining a patient. His breath smelled like a swamp and he wheezed a little. Witt tried to squirm from his hands.

The old man looked away for a moment, like he was lost in thought.

"Did you ever think about living forever?" he said. "I don't mean like fluttering off on angel wings and sipping tea with Jesus on a cloud, but living forever right here. Like a man. Well, I'm here to tell you, it can be done." He smiled wide, showing his rotten teeth. "Now, I know what you're thinking. If living forever looks like me, you're not interested. But you see me, this body, it's only a part of the story."

Sonny moaned and the old man walked back to him. He put on his gloves, picked up his knife, and got back to work, cutting into Sonny's stomach. He talked as he worked.

"Immortality isn't what you think it is. It's not like in movies where you stay young and pretty forever. It's harder than that and in a way it's more poetic. You live your life and grow old and when the time is right, you're reborn in new flesh. A bit like a phoenix." He turned to Witt. "You know what a phoenix is, don't you? Surely even a crude lad like you must know that."

Things from inside Sonny fell into the can.

"Your young friend here is my phoenix. When I shrug off this old meat, I'll be reborn in his. But first," he said, "I have to clear away the clutter."

He winked at Witt and pulled out more of Sonny's insides, until Witt could see his friend's spine.

"The heart and the brain. That's all I need. They're the only things I don't take out."

The old man stood, kicked off his work boots, and started to undress. He moved slowly, like each joint was stiff and painful.

When he struggled to get the apron up over his head, Witt pulled at the cuffs holding him to the wall. The ring that held the cuffs in place felt loose. He put slow, steady pressure on it, not wanting the old man to notice what he was doing.

Finally, the old man was naked. His skin sagged like it was melting off his bones. Patches of white, stiff tumbleweed hair bristled on his crotch and under his arms. He picked up the knife and looked over. Witt stopped moving.

"I know you think what I did to your friend hurt him, but consider this: at least he didn't have to do it to himself. Watch this."

The old man took the butcher knife and reached behind his head. He made a deep cut at the base of his skull, dragging the blade up and over his head to just above his eyebrows. This time, Witt screamed and the pain brought tears to his eyes.

The old man's hands were shaking when he set down the knife. He reached behind his head with both hands and pulled. The skin slid away from his skull like he was skinning a dead deer. He kept pulling and the flesh came down over his face, his neck, his chest, and down his legs. He moaned the whole time, but the old man's pain didn't give Witt any satisfaction. He pulled on the ring that held his handcuffs to the wall. It turned a little. He kept twisting, wondering how long it would take the old man to snake all the way out of his skin, and if it was enough time to get free.

It wasn't. Witt was still pinned tight when the last of the old man's skin hit the floor. He stepped out of it like he was kicking off dirty socks and fell against his worktable panting. A glistening wet mass of sagging muscle and bone, the old man reached over and picked up Sonny's pistol. He pointed it at Witt.

"Stop that wiggling or I'll do double worse to you what I did to your friend," he said. "Besides, you'll like this next part. Slithering out of my old skin isn't fun, but I'm used to it. This next part, is what really hurts."

He pushed a stool under Sonny's ass, then used a hammer to pull out the nails that held his hands to the wall. Sonny's body dropped onto the stool like someone cutting the strings of a marionette. The old man eyed the opening in Sonny's stomach like a Peeping Tom looking through a window, thought Witt.

The flayed man bent over, stiff and arthritic. When he was down as low as he could go, he grabbed his head and yanked it forward. Witt heard his neck snap. The old man screamed and his head hung like it was held in place by spaghetti. Then he reached his arms around in front, like he was trying to hug himself. He jerked hard, dislocating both of his arms at the shoulder. Another scream. Witt closed his eyes, afraid he might throw up and drown inside his sealed lips.

Ambitious Boys Like You

The old man continued with whatever it was he was doing, the ritual coming to Witt as a series of horrible sounds. A wet tearing of muscles and snapping of bones. The old man's screams. When the noise stopped, Witt opened his eyes a fraction of an inch. He couldn't believe what he saw.

The old man lay on the filthy floor. He'd folded himself up like a goddamned origami bird. His legs were up around his shoulders and his head was buried beneath his ankles. The only thing that still sort of worked were his arms, and even they were kind of loose and dangling. Groping blindly, the old man's skinless hands went up Sonny's body, finally stopping when they found the opening in his stomach. They got a good grip on the edges and hauled the rest of the old man's body up and into the hole.

Witt knew that what he was doing would never work. There was no way he could get his whole body into Sonny's stomach. And yet, as Witt watched, the old man did it. By whatever magic or skill or madness he'd learned over the years, the old man kept squeezing and squeezing his body tighter and tighter until he'd worked his way completely inside Sonny. Then he reached out and pulled the loose stomach flaps closed. The slits he'd cut into them healed seamlessly.

Sonny twitched. His body went stiff. His eyes fluttered. He relaxed and his head fell forward. He pissed himself. Then he laughed.

"That always cracks me up," Sonny said. "I start off each new life by pissing myself like an infant. It's all right. It's how I know all the plumbing is working."

Sonny stood, holding himself with his hand against the wall. He took a stiff step. Then another, his balance coming back to him. He breathed deeply, as if relishing this new younger flesh.

"*Que penses-tu de ma nouvelle poupée?*" he said, then, "What do you think of my new doll?"

As Sonny came over to him, Witt braced himself against the wall like maybe if he pushed hard enough he could pass through solid stone.

When Sonny reached him, he held Witt's head in his hands.

"The worst part is over. Don't worry about me gutting you like your friend. All I need from you is your head. I just pull out the skull, scrape the fat from the inside of the skin, and shrink the rest of it down for one of my dolls."

He looked around the basement.

"These dolls are old. I'll be moving on soon and I'll need new ones. You'll be the first in my new life. Try to relax. It'll hurt less if you're calm. Be extra good and I'll kill you quick with the gun."

The thing that used to be Sonny went and picked up the old man's skin from the floor. He dumped it into the garbage can with Sonny's insides. It took him a while to drag the can over to an ancient gas furnace. He didn't quite have the hang of the new body yet.

While Sonny had his back to him, Witt pulled as hard as he could on the ring holding the handcuffs. He picked his feet off the floor, using his body weight to pull down. The cuffs felt like hot metal digging into his wrists. He grit his teeth and swallowed so he wouldn't make any noise. He felt the ring move an inch. Then another. But the pain was too much. His vision started fogging again and he was afraid he might pass out. He put his feet on the floor and looked over. Sonny had the body parts in the furnace and was fiddling around with the controls. He touched handles and gauges randomly, like he was having trouble remembering how they worked. *Good,* thought Witt. He still had some time. If he could get to the table, he could get the gun. *That's all I need.*

Witt took a breath and raised his head, getting ready for the pain when he pulled his feet off the floor. Hanging there, his hands turning dark with trapped blood and feeling like they were going to pop off, he raised his head.

He stopped what he was doing when he saw the doll nailed to a beam a few feet above. That's why Sonny was taking his time. He knew everything Witt was doing. He wasn't going anywhere. And probably, he thought, he wasn't going to get that quick death after all.

The Secrets of Insects

Detectives Leonard Moore and Dale Komiski walked the prisoner to the car. With the killer cuffed and shackled, it took a few minutes to get him out of the elevator and put him into the backseat. Dale was careful not to strike the prisoner's head on the doorframe and to make sure that his hands and feet were safely inside before closing the door. Len nodded in approval. The prisoner was important and he wanted everything locked down, secure, and, above all, boring.

"Boring is always the best scenario," he liked to tell younger detectives. "It's like going to the doctor. If there's something wrong with you, you want it to be boring. If the doc gets too interested, you're fucked."

"Dull enough for you, boss?" said Dale, getting into the car. He smiled at the older man.

"So far so good," said Len. He got behind the wheel and steered them away from the San Francisco central holding facility. Ten minutes later they were on the freeway, heading south. The afternoon was clear and sunny. Hot even. Traffic on 101 was sparse. *A good beginning,* he thought.

Dale fiddled around with the air conditioner controls.

"How's that?"

Len nodded.

"Just fine."

He rapped on the cage separating the backseat from the front with his knuckle.

"Don't start," said Len.

"I'm being polite," Dale said. He half turned in his seat. "How's it for you back there, Looney Tunes? Comfy?"

The prisoner was thin and tall enough that his head grazed the car's ceiling. When he smiled, which he did now, his face was all teeth.

"Very. Thank you, Detective Dale," he said.

"That's Detective Komiski. And when you're referring to my partner, it's Detective Moore."

"Of course."

The prisoner pressed his face to the window and looked up into the cloudless sky.

"I wonder if it's going to rain."

Dale looked out his window.

"Are you kidding? It's never going to rain again."

"The drought. Some say it's the act of an angry God."

"Who says that?"

"Oh, you know. People."

"Sometimes people don't know shit."

"I agree completely. Still. It would be nice if it rained."

"That it would."

The prisoner didn't speak again for over an hour and they passed through San Jose.

"Ah. The happy hunting grounds," he said, then frowned. "That was a gruesome thing to say, wasn't it?"

"A little," said Len.

"Sorry. Still, it's interesting how definitions of acceptable versus unacceptable change, don't you think so, Detective Dale?"

"Change how?" said Dale.

The Secrets of Insects

The prisoner looked out the window.

"An older black man like Detective Leonard chauffeuring a young white man like you. Why, back in my daddy's day, people would have thought something of that. How the situation denoted who had status and privilege. But in these more enlightened times, no one bats an eye."

Dale looked at Len. Len shook his head.

"I told you not to start, didn't I?" he said.

Dale turned to the prisoner.

"That was an asshole thing to say, Asten," he said. "Through this whole thing, the trial and everything, you weren't an asshole. Don't start now."

"Of course. You're right," said the prisoner. "Detective Leonard, please accept my apologies. You too, Detective Dale."

Dale frowned and turned to the front.

"For the record, Detective Moore always drives because he likes it."

"And because you drive like my half-blind grandmother," said Len.

"That's what you keep telling me."

"Banter. How fun," said the prisoner.

Dale rapped the cage again.

"No more talking for a while. Let's do that, okay?"

"I've upset you again. It wasn't my intention. I'm tense. This is all new to me, you know."

"What did I just say?"

"No talking for a while. A very good idea."

Traffic was picking up as they headed south through San Jose. Len slowed the car, but worried that if the traffic kept piling up they'd be late making their delivery.

He gave Dale a quick glance. In some ways, his partner worried him as much as the cars crowding in around them. Dale was a good detective. He knew how to work a crime scene. He had a good feel for interrogations and he never went too rough on anyone they brought in for questioning. Len knew plenty of other detectives Dale's age who couldn't wait to play Dirty Harry with suspects. But Dale was more restrained,

31

more of a head guy than some of the other detectives he'd come up with. However, something had changed recently. The Nightcrawler case did something to him, though Len couldn't quite put his finger on what. And there were more obvious changes, like the chatter with Asten. That's not something he would have done a few weeks ago.

The prisoner didn't speak again until they drove through Gilroy and the pungent scent of the garlic fields filled the car.

"Thank you for using my name earlier, Detective Dale."

"Did I?"

"Yes. You said, 'That was an asshole thing to say, Asten.' No one has used my name since this whole ugly episode began. I wanted to thank you."

"You're welcome. Now let's circle back to the no talking rule, right?"

"Of course."

A delivery truck cut across two lanes of traffic, barely missing them. Len had to slam on the brakes. When he accelerated again he said, "Everyone all right?"

"I'm fine," said Dale.

He looked back at Asten.

"He looks all right too."

From the back, Asten began to hum. Something low and simple, in a peculiar pentatonic scale. It was almost pretty, which grated on Len. He'd played guitar in college. Free jazz mainly. Wild hours-long improvs with young hotshots all wanting to show off their chops. Len thought he'd heard every funny scale and chord pattern possible back in those days, but the humming was something different.

"Would you please stop that?" he said.

"Sorry," Asten said. Then he began to quietly sing the same strange melody.

Dale turned around.

"He said stop."

"He said to stop humming. I was singing. Sorry if I misunderstood."

Dale shook his head.

The Secrets of Insects

"And what was that exactly? It sounded like you were trying to play a cat's ass like a flute."

Asten smiled faintly.

"It was an old hymn, inspired by Detective Leonard's skid back there. It seemed like the time to get the angels on my side."

"The angels deserted you a long time ago, pal."

The prisoner scratched his nose, which wasn't easy in his tight cuffs. There was a lot of twisting of his wrists and head.

"It was also an ancient incantation," he said. "You know, historically, hymns and incantations are closely linked. For example, back in Sunday school, we used to sing Onward Christian Soldiers. Do you know it? An amazing little ditty. If it's not a war god chant then I'm the Big Bopper."

"Is that what you were thinking about when you killed all those people? War? God?" said Dale.

Asten shrugged.

"They're compelling topics, don't you think? But I have other interests."

He pointed to Dale's wrist.

"That's a sweet timepiece you have there, detective. Is it new?"

Dale glanced down at his watch.

"Brand new. You like watches?"

He held it up so Asten could get a good look at it. Len wasn't sure if Dale was being polite or taunting the prisoner. Either way, he didn't like it.

"I like all sorts of technology," said Asten. "You might even call me a technophile."

"I can think of a lot of things to call you, you fucking lunatic."

"Dale," said Len.

"Sorry."

"Technology. That's why I came to the Bay Area. High tech. Silicon Valley. I like being around smart people."

"Lucky us," said Dale.

"It was a compliment."

"On my planet, compliments from killers don't count for a lot."

"Don't talk to him," said Len.

Dale settled back in his seat.

Mist rolled in from the west, came tumbling over the hills like a slow motion avalanche. It was a bit early in the day, thought Len, but the drought had fucked up all the local weather patterns. This was just one more unwelcome gift from the sky.

The mist quickly turned to fog and blotted out the sun. The temperature dropped. Len reached down and turned off the air conditioner. Traffic slowed and cars began to turn on their headlights.

Len noticed that Dale was turned around in his seat again. From the look on his face, he could tell Dale was going to say something stupid and start an argument. He had to get in there first.

"Asten Set," said Len.

Asten sat up.

"That's my name. Don't wear it out."

"We know that's not your real name," said Len. "We found all your books."

"All of them? Are you sure?"

"You seem to really enjoy Egyptian mythology."

"Not really. I just like the pretty pictures."

"I don't believe you," said Len. "Your last name. Set. That was the Egyptian name for the Devil."

Asten laughed.

"Don't be thick, Detective Leonard. The Egyptians wouldn't know the Christian devil if he prodded them with a pitchfork. No, Set was merely the god of the realm of the dead."

"In your books, he also personified chaos, darkness, and drought. Calling yourself something like that sounds to me like a plea for attention."

"Are you accusing me of being mentally unstable, detective?"

Len nodded, looking at Asten in the rearview mirror.

The Secrets of Insects

"We'll find your real name. Who you really are."

"Well, you better hurry. From what I hear, I won't last much longer in jail. Something about me killing that police officer?"

"Shut up about that," yelled Dale.

Len reached out and put a hand on his shoulder. Dale settled back into his seat.

Traffic came to a stop. The fog had all but swallowed the freeway. Len couldn't see much of anything on either side of the road but headlights and taillights glowing in the mist.

"What the fuck is this?" he muttered.

"Looks like we're going to be late," said Dale.

"It does at that."

"Do you get a demerit for that?" said Asten. "Will this affect your final score? I'd hate to be the reason you had to repeat a grade."

"Hush," said Len.

The cars barely moved through the fog. Len didn't have to touch the accelerator. He'd just take his foot off the brake and the car would roll a few feet at a time all on its own. At this rate, they wouldn't be there until morning.

"What time is it?" he said.

"Nearly five," said Dale.

"Five?" Time had slipped by very quickly. And now, not only were they stuck in an opaque fog, but it was rush hour too, which meant that the traffic was only going to get worse.

"Nightcrawler," said Asten. "Nightcrawler. Do you like that name, Detective Dale?"

"What do I care? It's your name, not mine."

Asten sighed.

"I really preferred the Ravenswood Ripper. It had a charming Victorian ring. Why did you change it?"

"We didn't."

"The press did," said Len, cutting Dale off. "It changed because you only killed your first two out in the marsh."

"Still. Nightcrawler. It sounds like we're going down to the ole fishin' hole."

"We thought Nightcrawler was more appropriate too," said Dale.

Asten nodded.

"Because I like to work in the dark."

"Yes."

"And because of the insects."

"Yes. Plus, you're bug fuck crazy."

"And because you translated one of the words I left on the walls."

"That's right," said Len.

"Who did the translation?"

"Your code was good, I'll admit. No one in our department could figure it out. We had to send it to the FBI crypto squad."

Asten shook his head. Len looked at him in the mirror again. Maybe Dale was smart. Maybe if they kept Asten talking long enough, he'd say something incriminating and they could add on new charges. There were rumors he'd killed in other states, some with the death penalty.

Asten said, "You should have gone to an archaeologist or paleographer. They would have figured it out faster and been more accurate."

"How's that?"

"Your crypto guys and gals didn't get it quite right. It's not crawler. It's crawling."

"What's the other word?" said Dale.

Asten slumped back in the seat so he almost vanished in the dark.

"I forget," he said. He began to sing the quiet hymn again.

The car crept forward. The fog rolled in.

"While you're in a chatty mood, why don't you tell us why you killed all those people, Asten?" said Dale.

He laughed briefly.

"If I didn't talk about it at the trial, why would I now?"

"It passes the time. We have a long drive ahead of us."

"Is this little chat admissible in some future court hearing?"

"Of course not."

The Secrets of Insects

"I'm not sure I believe you, but I'm bored, so okay. I didn't kill anyone. They all just died."

An opening, thought Len. He looked at Dale thinking, *Don't press too hard. Don't blow this.* Dale didn't look at him, but Len couldn't worry about that now. It was hard enough keeping the car on the road.

"What do you mean that they just died?" said Dale. "You drilled holes in their heads. You put insects in their fucking brains."

Asten shrugged.

"I was looking for something."

"What?"

"I am the word. I am the messenger. But it's not an easy job. I could use an assistant."

Don't blow this, thought Len.

"What word? What kind of message?"

Something flashed on the dashboard. Len looked down.

"Shit," he said. "Who gave us this damned car?"

Dale braced a hand on the dashboard.

"What's wrong?"

"We're almost out of gas."

"Are you fucking kidding me?"

"Look for yourself."

Dale looked past Len. The gas gauge was almost on E.

"That's some detective work, detectives," said Asten.

"Shut up," shouted Dale.

Asten smiled and sat back, resting his head on the window.

Dale turned to Len.

"We can't stop. We have a prisoner."

"We don't have any choice. We're not going to make it without filling up."

"Shit. Okay. I'll keep an eye out for a station."

Len peered through the fog for the light from a station sign, a truck stop, something.

In the back, Asten began singing quietly.

37

"Stop that," shouted Len. He looked at the prisoner in the rearview mirror. Asten's face was lost in shadows. When they passed under a freeway light, it didn't illuminate the back. Asten was still a shadow. He leaned close to the cage separating the seats.

Len blinked.

Asten's face was gone. There was nothing but a man-shaped void filled with grinning, leering mouths.

The car lurched onto the freeway shoulder as Len jerked his head around to look at the backseat. Asten was there, staring at him, bored and sullen.

"Len," said Dale.

Len nodded, twisted the wheel, and the car bounced back onto the freeway.

"You all right?" said Dale.

"Fine. I just thought I saw something."

"What?"

Len shook his head.

"Keep looking for gas."

"There's some right ahead. See it?"

Len looked and just past the next exit was an Exxon station. He steered them off the freeway, across the empty feeder road, and up to the pumps.

"I'll pump," said Dale. "You watch him."

"All right," said Len.

"There's one more thing."

"What?"

A look of embarrassment played across Dale's face.

"I really have to piss."

"For god's sake. Can't it wait?"

Dale adjusted his position.

"I just need a minute."

Len breathed in and out, glanced at Asten in the back. The prisoner raised his eyebrows at him.

THE SECRETS OF INSECTS

"Fine. Go. But don't fuck around."

Dale smiled.

"Thanks. I'll be quick."

Dale got out. He fumbled with the gas cap in the fog, but got it off and put the hose in place. As the gas pumped, he headed toward the station, disappearing almost instantly into the mist.

Asten sighed.

"A-hunting we will go, a-hunting we will go, Heigh-ho, the derry-o, a-hunting we will go," he said.

"Hush," said Len.

"The insects are a test, detective. In case you were wondering."

Len looked at him.

"What kind of test?"

"I thought you wanted me to hush."

Len looked for Dale through the fog. He couldn't see a goddamned thing.

"I'm tired of your games, Asten. If you have something to say, say it."

The prisoner didn't say anything for a minute. Then, "Insects know secrets, but they don't have a true voice. I give them one."

"Through the people whose heads you put them in?"

"Through the worthy."

"Who's worthy, Asten?"

Asten put his head down. For a split second, Len saw the mouths again, but he shook off the image, refusing to be spooked.

"My companion is dying. He moves through the bodies of insects, but he needs something more. I've been looking for a vessel. I still am."

Len looked at Asten, trying to figure out if he was angling for some kind of psych plea to escape prison by way of a mental hospital.

"The Egyptians worshipped me once, Detective Leonard. They called me Dust Devil and the Black Pharaoh. But my followers turned against me. They destroyed my temples and statues. Do you know what it's like to be a god and then not?"

"It's not going to work," Len said.

"What's not going to work?"

"This insanity defense you're trying for. It's not going to work."

"Don't you believe in God, detective? Don't you believe in the wisdom of insects? Of anything greater than yourself?"

"I'll tell you what I believe," he said, but cut himself off.

A grasshopper landed on the windshield. Then another. And another. In a few seconds, they covered the glass.

"May I ask you a simple, honest question, Detective Leonard?"

Len rapped on the glass, hoping to scare the insects off. They ignored him.

"What?" he said.

"Where are you taking me?"

There was a subtle *thunk* outside. The gas pump had stopped. Now where the hell was Dale?

"Where are you taking me, Len?"

Len turned in his seat.

"The state holding facility in…" He realized at that moment he couldn't remember.

He hit the windshield again, but the grasshoppers weren't interested.

"Doesn't it strike you as odd that San Francisco PD would send two detectives to transport a prisoner out of town? They have whole squads and armored vans for that kind of thing, don't they?"

He was right, thought Len. Who had given him and Dale the assignment? The name was on the tip of his tongue.

"It's like a plague, isn't it?" said Asten. "You're pharaoh and Moses is somewhere out there in the fog calling down God's wrath on you."

"Who does that make you?"

"Guess the other half of my name and I'll tell you."

Something banged against the side of the car. Len turned and saw Dale putting the gas hose back on the pump. When he headed back to the car, the grasshoppers flew off. He was smiling when he got in.

"Thanks," Dale said. "I feel a lot better."

Len pointed out the windshield.

The Secrets of Insects

"Those bugs didn't bother you flying off like that?"

"What bugs?"

"On the windshield."

"I didn't see anything. But it was pretty bad out there. I couldn't find the car for a couple of minutes."

"But you must have heard them," said Len.

Dale held up his hands.

"I'm sorry, man. I didn't notice anything."

Len started the car.

"Forget it."

"Remind him where we're going, Detective Dale. In case he forgot."

He steered them out of the station and back onto the freeway.

"Asten is right," said Len. "I can't remember where exactly we're headed. What's the address?"

"Don't let him bother you. I know where we're going. Just keep us pointed south. It's not far now."

Len nodded. He wanted the subject gone and done with, so he didn't ask any questions.

"They divided up my domain, you see," said Asten. "They invented Thoth and Set to take my place because they were afraid of one god having all the power I possessed."

Dale looked at Len.

"He's been chattering the whole time I was gone?"

Len let out a breath.

"That he was."

"Anything interesting?"

"I was explaining about my fall from grace, Detective Dale. And about the false gods who took my place."

Dale nodded.

"I think I read about that. In those Egyptian books and the other one. The old one."

"De Vermis Mysteriis."

41

"That's it. About an old god replaced by two younger ones."

"That old book was in Latin," said Len. "You can read Latin?"

Dale shrugged.

"I studied a little in high school. The book talked about the all-seeing eye. The Crawling Chaos."

"Crawling? You knew about that word this whole time and you didn't say anything?" said Len.

"It didn't seem important. We're nearly there. It's the next exit," Dale said.

Len glanced at him, then turned back to the road, looking for the exit.

"What else did the book say?"

"That the Chaos is the soul of the old Outer Gods."

"And messenger," said Asten.

"Yeah, and messenger. He'll prepare the way for the Outer God's return."

"And you didn't think any of that was important to mention?" said Len.

Dale shook his head.

"Why would it be? It's just old stories, right?"

"A-hunting we will go, a-hunting we will go, Heigh-ho, the derry-o, a-hunting we will go," sang Asten.

"Quiet," said Len. When he looked in the mirror he didn't see Asten, but a mass of writhing tentacles. He ignored the sight and turned his eyes back to the road. Little by little, the fog began to dissipate. By the time he took the exit, the sky was almost clear.

"I don't see anything," Len said. "What's the address?"

"It's about a mile further up. There's a turnoff. You can't miss it."

"If you say so."

"The All-seeing eye. Crawling Chaos. Nyarlathotep. The Ravenswood Ripper. I'm sure you can see why I was so disappointed being known as the Nightcrawler."

"It isn't much of a name for a god," said Dale.

The Secrets of Insects

Len saw the sign and turned the car onto the side road. He scanned the sky above the trees, looking for the guard towers and stone walls of a prison.

"Where are we? I don't see a thing," he said.

"One more turn. Right up here," Dale said.

Len turned the car. A few hundred yards later he stopped. They were at a dead end, by a beach facing the Pacific.

"Where the hell are we, Dale? Did we take the wrong exit?"

"We're fine," said Asten. "Aren't we, Detective Dale?"

Dale rubbed the bridge of his nose with a finger.

"He was telling the truth before, Len. He didn't murder anyone. People just died."

Len looked through the windshield at the beach. He stayed calm and looked calm. Until Dale looked out the window too. Then he went for the pistol in his shoulder holster. He'd barely moved when he felt Dale's gun pressed against his temple. Len sat back and let Dale take his gun and toss it on the floor. Dale lowered his own pistol, but kept hold of it.

"We don't need these, Len. It's just you and me."

"And him," said Len inclining his head toward the backseat.

"Don't worry about him. This part is you and me."

Len ignored him. He turned to Asten.

"Why this game?" he said. "You have what you wanted. Someone as crazy as you to grovel at your godlike feet. Why bring me all the way out here?"

Asten leaned his forehead against the screen separating them.

"Do you have a laptop, Detective Leonard? Don't you back it up in case something happens to it?"

"Copies. Redundant systems," said Dale.

"I like all sorts of technology. And smart people," said Asten.

"Clearly I wasn't smart enough to see this coming," Len said.

"Don't think about it that way," said Dale. "I didn't see so many things until he showed me."

"I made your partner an offer," said Asten.

"What kind?"

"Don't you want to live forever, Len?" said Dale.

"Not really."

"Don't worry. If things don't work out you won't live much longer anyway," said Asten.

Len looked at him, then Dale. But Len didn't see him. What he saw had bulging, segmented eyes and barbed mandibles. Len looked down at his own hands, just to make sure he was real. That he was really there. Dale put a hand on his arm, and it was like the stick-leg of a centipede.

When Len looked up, Dale was himself again. He was holding a small battery-powered drill in his hand.

"Please, Len. It hurts so much less if you don't fight it."

"Listen to him, detective. He helped me out on a lot of hunts."

Len looked out the windshield. Something massive seemed to move across the night sky. The stars shifted in its wake. He didn't recognize the constellations anymore.

Grasshoppers massed on the car, covering the windows. Len looked at the floor. The gun was too far away to reach and Dale still had his.

"Where's the insect?" said Len.

"In my pocket. You don't want to see it."

Len thought about that. He could fight, but Dale would kill him for sure. He thought, *Where are you going to run when something overhead is moving the stars?*

Len closed his eyes.

The sound of the drill was loud in the car.

LATER, THE grasshoppers flew away. The car reversed and drove carefully up the road they'd come down half an hour earlier. They turned back onto the freeway and headed north.

The stars were back in their original positions. Or so it seemed. Len wasn't sure anymore. It didn't matter. He couldn't drive, couldn't even

The Secrets of Insects

hold the wheel, so Dale steered them home. From the backseat, Asten sang his quiet hymn.

Voices filled Len's head. Dale, the Crawling Chaos, and one that buzzed with mad secrets from somewhere infinitely cold and far away.

He touched his scalp, just above his right ear. No more blood. Dale was right. The drill hadn't hurt much and now, Len was certain, nothing would ever hurt again.

RAZOR PIG

The morning David O'Meara took a leave of absence from the junior college where he was head security guard, he loaded his Chevy Suburban with maps, protein bars, and a recent birthday photo of his daughter. He'd taken the picture out of the frame the day after Lucy disappeared and laid it in a drawer. Putting it in his pocket was the first time he'd seen her face in a week. He knew there might be trouble when he tracked her down, so he packed a Glock 9mm pistol in a holster that fit at the small of his back. That way, the gun would be hidden under his untucked shirt. No need to show the thing if he didn't have to. Besides, when he found Lucy, he didn't want her first sight of him to be packing heat. That, he knew, wouldn't help the situation at all.

O'Meara drove north from San Marcos, Texas, on I-35 toward Austin. He knew the road well. It was where, many years earlier, his secret, second heart had truly begun to grow. Following the route on the dusty map, he turned off onto highway 21 and sped through Uhland, heading north to Mustang Ridge. The carnival seemed to be sticking to the smaller towns along the narrow highways that snaked through that region of Texas.

He'd been rigid with tension ever since Lucy disappeared, unable to sleep or eat. A tap on the radio button in the Suburban brought up his favorite broadcast, an old-fashioned local San Marcos AM news and call-in show. Today, though, something was off. The host did his usual rants, going attack dog on "liberal gay humanists" while mixing in homespun redneck wisdom. But O'Meara found himself strangely bored. He listened to the call-in portion of the show, hoping for a UFO weirdo or conspiracy nut who'd go on and on about how the government was controlled by lizard people. No such luck. It was just the same tired Mexicans, Jews, and lesbians infiltrating the schools. After a few minutes, he turned the damn thing off.

Reaching into the plastic bag on the passenger seat, he pulled out a protein bar and tore it open with his teeth. It was a bad idea. The thing tasted like sugar on switchgrass, or at least his sleepless brain made it seem that way. O'Meara rolled down the window, spit out what was in his mouth and tossed the rest of the bar with it.

As the window rolled back up he wondered what Lucy was doing at that exact moment. His mind hopped from images of her laughing with friends to ones of her tied up in the back of a van, helpless and abused. He'd seen what that could do to people.

O'Meara had more than his share of strange encounters along this stretch of road. There was one before Uhland and two more on the empty stretch of road out of town. It bothered him when he couldn't remember who'd been first, the trucker or the Target cashier? The third was definitely the hippie boy heading to Dallas for a music festival. There had been enough of those brief, intense encounters by now that O'Meara was sometimes tempted to write them down. However, aside from it being dangerously foolish, it felt like cheating. Like he'd be diluting the experience. And if he did that, would he ever see the moon again?

He shook his head to clear it. None of that was important now. Bringing Lucy home safe and sound was all that mattered.

RAZOR PIG

THE DAY after his daughter disappeared, O'Meara called the police. Two uniformed officers arrived and asked a lot of stupid questions. Did Lucy take drugs? Did she have boyfriends? Had she and O'Meara been fighting? He practically had to drag them into her bedroom. They didn't even search it. After a half hour of pointless chatter, he knew they weren't going to be any help. When they asked for a photo, he didn't want to waste the birthday picture on them, so he tore a shot of her from her school yearbook. The officers said they'd do what they could, which O'Meara knew from experience meant they'd decided Lucy was a teenage deadbeat and unless she tried to rob a bank, they wouldn't do a damn thing.

After they left O'Meara, who'd barely been in Lucy's room since she disappeared, went to the small desk by the closet. The laptop was gone, which probably meant she wasn't planning on coming home anytime soon. He went through the papers on top of the desk and looked in and under every drawer. There was nothing but school work, printouts of photos with friends, and one of the silly tarot decks she collected. He went through her closet and looked under the bed. More nothing. It was when he stripped the sheets off the mattress that he found it: a dusty leaflet from a traveling carnival that had recently been on the outskirts of San Marcos. The front of the leaflet had pictures of clowns, a sword swallower, and acrobats. On the back was a map of highway 21 with the names of several towns highlighted. Across the bottom of the sheet was a handwritten phone number.

O'Meara almost dropped his phone, pulling it from his pocket. He quickly punched in the number and waited. It rang several times, and went to voicemail. When he tried to leave a message, the recorded voice said the mailbox was full. O'Meara thumbed off the phone and sat down on Lucy's bed, staring at the map on the back of the leaflet.

A moment later, his phone rang. Hoping it was the police, he said hello. There was a few seconds of silence before a deep male voice said, "Who is this?"

"Hello?" he said. "Is this the police?"

There was another stretch of silence, then he heard an intake of breath and, "Friend, how wrong can one man be?"

O'Meara looked at the phone. The number displayed was the same one on the leaflet. He put the phone back to his ear and said, "Is Lucy there? I'm her father. I want to talk to her."

It took him a moment to understand what he was listening to. The sounds were low and staccato. It was a laugh, he decided, but punctuated with grunting sounds like a hog might make.

"Who is this?" shouted O'Meara. "I've already called the cops. Hell, I am a cop."

"That's not what I hear," said the voice. "You're just a girls' school rent-a-pig. Not much more than a janitor with a badge."

"Let me talk to Lucy. Please."

"There's no one here by that name."

O'Meara knew the man was lying because the moment he said it he burst out with his pig grunt laugh. "I'll find you," he said.

"Don't call here again," said the man and the line went dead. O'Meara hit the button to dial the number back, but the call went straight to voicemail. He hung up and sat unmoving, playing the conversation over in his head. From outside came the sound of cars and dogs. A plane flying overhead. In a few minutes he took the leaflet downstairs and got out a map of Texas.

WHEN O'MEARA reached Mustang Ridge, he found the fairgrounds, but the carnival had already moved on. He got back on the highway and continued to the next stop on the leaflet—Garfield. A few miles outside of town, O'Meara spotted a large sign for the carnival in an orange grove along the highway. He spotted someone sitting on a tractor along the edge of the orchard, so he pulled the Suburban onto the highway shoulder and walked across the road.

"Hello!" he shouted as he ran to the orchard fence. An old man in a plaid shirt and well-worn Carhartt pants looked up from his phone and came to the fence. "Can I help you?" he said.

O'Meara pointed to the sign. "The carnival. Was it here? Did you see it?"

RAZOR PIG

The old man squinted. "Who are you?"

"I'm David O'Meara," he said, and put out his hand. They shook, though the old man looked at him warily. "I was wondering about the carnival. I think my daughter might have left with it."

"I'm Clemson," said the old man. "And I'm sorry for your loss."

"Did you see it?"

"The carnival? Sure. They gave me a handful of free tickets for putting up the sign. But I only went once and didn't stay all that long."

"Why? Did something happen?"

Clemson kicked at a dirt clod. "Nothing happened. It's just that I found the place a bit unsavory. There were lady acrobats, but they had tattoos all over. The clowns looked like something you'd see in an old horror movie on TV. There were games in the midway, only I think they were all rigged. But I didn't leave on account of any of that."

O'Meara took out Lucy's photo and handed it to Clemson. "Did you see her, by any chance?"

The old man pulled at his ear as he looked at the photo. "Maybe. It could be her. There was a young gal telling fortunes. Might be the one in the photo."

O'Meara flushed in the heat and excitement of the moment. He thought about Lucy's tarot decks. She'd left the one behind, but he knew she had others. He said, "I take it you didn't get your fortune told."

Clemson made a face. "'Course not. I'm not an idiot. I don't believe in that nonsense."

A part of O'Meara wanted to get in his car and floor it for Garfield, but another part of him wanted to know as much as he could before he tracked the carnival down. "You said you left the carnival early. Why?"

"Are you a cop?" said Clemson. "'Cause whatever that carnival was up to, all I did was let them put a sign up."

"Ex-cop," said O'Meara. "I just want to find my daughter and to know what she's gotten herself into."

"Oh. Well, if she's with that bunch, who knows?"

"You still didn't say why you left early."

Clemson glanced at his phone. "Really, it was the whole place. It just felt wrong. Sordid. But, I guess if there's one thing that drove me off, it was the metal man."

"Tell me about him."

"I thought he was just one of those sword swallower acts. I'd seen them before and I never knew how a man could do that. But this man was different. He didn't swallow the swords. He ate them."

A car sped by and someone threw a couple of beer cans onto the side of the road.

"What do you mean he ate them?"

"Just that," said Clemson. "Put one in his mouth like a regular swallower act, then yanked it out and bit it in half. He swallowed the pointy end and chewed up the rest. Did the same thing with some knives too. I never saw anything like it and I never want to again. There's something *wrong* with that man."

O'Meara looked back toward the Suburban. Maybe he'd been wasting his time with an old coot who got spooked by a carny magic act. Still, he might have seen Lucy and that was worth something. "If the carnival is gone and you thought it was so bad, why do you leave the sign up?"

Clemson shook his head. "I thought about taking it down, but touching it gives me the willies. I figure I'll just let it fall apart on its own and burn the pieces."

O'Meara looked back at the sign as a cloud passed overhead. For the briefest second, the letters seemed to squirm, like earthworms on the ground after a rain. He blinked and the sign was back to its original form.

"See what I mean?" said Clemson.

"See what? It was a trick of the light."

"Believe what you want." The old man nodded at his tractor. "I got to get back to work now."

"Of course," said O'Meara. "Thank you very much for your time."

When he'd climbed on the tractor Clemson shouted, "Find your daughter and don't take no for an answer. If she's with those people, get her away from there."

RAZOR PIG

As he slipped the photo into his pocket, O'Meara shouted back, "I can't kidnap her."

Clemson started the tractor's engine and said, "Then I'm sorry for you both." As he drove into the orchard, O'Meara went back to the Suburban and started again for Garfield.

But he'd missed the carnival there too.

As HE drove, Lucy's face drifted through his mind like a time-lapse photo on TV. Lucy from when she was an infant, morphing to a toddler, then a schoolgirl, then graduation and preparation for college. She hadn't wanted to go to the one where he ran security which, he supposed, was to be expected. But the school where she got a scholarship was all the way in New York. They'd fought about her going and, after a while, they fought about her staying. It felt like toward the end fighting was all that was left to them. At night he thought about her as a little girl, pulling her into his lap and telling her stories. *Winnie the Pooh*. *The Cat in the Hat*. What life would be like when they finally lived on the moon. His wife's disappearance had hit them both hard, especially Lucy, but the stories seemed to help.

An image of the squirming letters on the sign pushed its way into his thoughts for a few seconds.

Nothing, O'Meara thought, *in this world is right. Sometimes it seems like all that's left for a man is confusion and anger.*

He stopped for gas on the outskirts of the town of Manor. There wasn't any real need to fill up yet, but he wanted to walk around for a minute and, even though he swore he'd quit, have a smoke.

The gas station was the kind for long distance drivers and truckers, with a large grocery section attached. The sun was starting to go down, but there were no other vehicles in the parking lot other than a battered white and blue Camaro by the employees' entrance. O'Meara started the gas pumping and went inside to walk the aisles while the van filled.

A bored-looking young man sat behind the counter reading a motorcycle magazine. The interior of the grocery was cool and pleasant, but one of the overhead lights near the rear of the place winked and buzzed. The intermittent shadows almost looked like there was someone back there tailing him, but when he looked the aisles were empty.

At the counter, O'Meara set down a package of little chocolate donuts and a Coke. Before the kid rang him up, he also asked for a pack of American Spirits. As he got out his wallet to pay, he noticed a flyer for the carnival taped to the back of the glass door.

The bored young man told him how much he owed and O'Meara handed him the cash. He said, "The carnival over there. Did you go?"

The young man didn't look up as he counted the change from the till. "Sure did," he said. "Best night of my life."

O'Meara put the change in his pocket. "Really? Someone else told me that he hated it."

Grinning, the young man said, "Not me. It was like an Iron Maiden video in there. Fire. Monsters. Clowns that make Juggalos look like little bitches. This teacup ride that shook like it was going to fly apart. And the best part? Pussy. Lots of pussy."

O'Meara looked at him.

A nervous expression spread across the young man's face. "I'm sorry. That was disrespectful language to use."

It sure as hell was, O'Meara thought. But he wasn't going to let this idiot kid off that easily. "Tell me more about them," he said. "The girls."

"Yeah?" said the young man and he relaxed. He leaned closer to O'Meara and spoke quietly. "There were girls everywhere. Girls with the shows. And they'd do anything. I mean anything. And for free. You didn't have to buy them anything or give them weed. Not that I carry weed with me." He looked nervous again.

"That's good, son," said O'Meara. He quickly flashed his security guard badge. If you looked for more than a second it was obvious that it wasn't a police badge, but the kid behind the counter didn't strike him

RAZOR PIG

as bright enough to ask to examine it. "Keep talking. Don't scrimp on the details. I'm not shy."

Smiling lopsidedly, the young man continued. "Sure. I partied all night with those girls."

"Did you see anything or did anything unusual happen while you were partying?"

"There was one thing. These three girls and me were starting to get it on and when one got my pants off another got real excited and—I swear to god—bit my leg."

"Bit? What do you mean bit?"

"I mean the stupid slut *bit* me. Took a little chunk out of my thigh."

Maybe the kid was too high or too dumb to take seriously, thought O'Meara. He wondered if he would show him the leg wound if he asked. The buzzing light in the back of the store was giving him a headache. Maybe it was time to come at it from a different angle. "Did you go to a doctor?" he said.

"No," the kid said. "One of the other girls started blowing me and I forgot all about it."

O'Meara put his hands on the counter and looked the kid in the eyes. "Did it occur to you that the girl who bit you might have been sick? That any of the girls could have been sick?"

The young man went a little pale. "No sir. I just put some Bactine and gauze on it."

"Go see a doctor tomorrow. Get a blood test."

"If you think I should."

"I do." O'Meara put Lucy's photo on the counter and opened the American Spirits. "While you were at the carnival, did you see this girl?"

The kid stabbed the shot with a finger. "Fuck yeah. She's the one who bit me."

O'Meara quickly picked up the picture and held it in front of the kid's face. "Look again. Be careful how you answer. *Is this the girl you saw?*"

After blinking a couple of times, the kid seemed to deflate a little. "I mean it was dark and I was kind of messed up by then. I can't be a hundred percent sure."

He put the photo down and said, "But it's possible."

"Yes, sir."

O'Meara thought it over. The idiot kid had been high and getting all kinds of attention from pretty girls. Probably a group of pros working the carny circuit with the show. Instead of asking if the kid got bitten, he should find out if he still had his wallet after the party.

When O'Meara looked again, the kid was staring at the photo. "You have something else to say?"

The kid nodded. "The more I look the more it seems right. It was her. The whore bit me like a damn vampire."

It took all of O'Meara's self-control not to pull the kid over the counter and beat him bloody right then and there. His hand even twitched to where he kept the riot baton on his work belt. Instead of hitting the kid, he put away Lucy's photo and said, "Bag up my shit."

Outside, O'Meara took a few deep breaths and held the still hot, humid evening air in his lungs. He set the bag in the van and unhooked from the gas pump. His temper told him to go back inside and settle things, but he knew the time wasn't right. Too many lights. Too many cameras. Anyway, he knew where the kid worked and what his car looked like. He could settle up later. Still. He thought about the tools in his suitcase and everything he could do with them. Everything he *would* do. Once he found Lucy, he'd come back, take the boy's soul and give it to Mr. Umbra. Then they'd walk the pale light path to the moon. The thought calmed him and he could breathe again.

Driving onto the freeway he thought, *Lucy, where are you and what have you gotten yourself into? Is it drugs? Is it money? I'll fix it for you. Eat all their souls and spit them out on the moon path. But before then, I'll have my fun with them first.*

He lit one of the cigarettes.

Sure as hell, I'm going to get some enjoyment out of this madness.

RAZOR PIG

LATER, O'MEARA stopped at a highway cafe for dinner. His eyes were weary from the road and the donuts he'd bought earlier were inedible. He knew he needed food if he wanted to keep going. There were two empty stools at the far end of the counter. A highway patrol officer sat on the third stool quietly eating a burger. O'Meara took the last stool and ordered a cheeseburger, fries, and a strawberry milkshake. After the waitress left, he looked at his watch. It was later than he thought. His eyes burned and the headache he'd picked up at the gas station light refused to let go. He touched his napkin into the ice water the waitress had left and rubbed its coolness across his forehead hoping that would help.

Someone said, "Are you all right?"

O'Meara turned and saw the highway patrol man looking in his direction. He nodded to the man. "I'm okay. Just can't seem to shake this headache."

The officer took a small tin from his breast pocket and held it out. It was aspirin. O'Meara took three and dry swallowed before handing the tin back to the officer. "Is aspirin regular issue for the highway patrol these days?"

The officer smiled faintly. "No, but I always have some handy. It helps keep the drunks with hangovers quiet."

"Thank you for the pills."

"Thank you for not being drunk."

O'Meara laughed a little at that. The trip was so surreal that he'd felt a little drunk for a good part of the day. He knew he wasn't going to last much longer. "Are there any decent motels around here?" he said.

The officer thought for a minute. "On the highway? There's the Rancho Grande. Lot of truckers stay there. It's not much, but it's clean."

"Thank you." It was such a relief to talk to a sane man. "I'm David O'Meara."

The patrolman wiped his hand on his napkin and they shook. "Mal Jackson," he said. "You just passing through or are you staying a while, because there's nicer places than the Rancho Grande in town."

O'Meara shook his head. "I'm just passing through. Trying to catch up with a carnival that passed through here."

Jackson rolled his eyes. "That place. What a bunch of freaks. I can't say that anyone around here misses them."

He'd been wondering why the carnival moved from town to town so quickly. Maybe that was the reason. They pissed off people everywhere they went. "Did you have trouble with them? Any kids from around here get mixed up with the place?"

Leaning an elbow on the counter, Jackson said, "Are you on the job?"

He knew what the question meant and hearing it ruined the good mood he was working on since sitting down. "No," O'Meara said. "I was on the force for two years, but no more. I'm just a college security guard these days."

"There's no shame in that," said Jackson. "Why did you leave?"

O'Meara thought about his answer carefully. Lying was easy with most people, but this was a law enforcement officer. A seasoned one, too, by his look. He had to say it just right. "I couldn't take the politics. Crooked promotions. Who got assigned where for how long depending on who laughed at the brass's jokes. I don't mean to sound bitter, but I joined up to take care of people, not kiss ass." What O'Meara didn't say was how grateful he was for all he learned during those two years. He couldn't do his work without that knowledge. Moving quickly and randomly. Never taking the same kind of person twice in a row. And always taking them in different ways so it was hard for the authorities to zero in on a pattern. His secret heart wouldn't be nearly as dark as it was if he hadn't been careful all these years.

Jackson leaned across the stool that separated them and whispered, "I know what you mean. It's no different out here. I mean, my station is better than most, but we have the same problems. Maybe everywhere is like that if you dig deep enough."

"Thank you for saying that. Sometimes I'm ashamed for not sticking it out," said O'Meara, another careful lie.

RAZOR PIG

Jackson moved upright again and took a bite of his burger. After he swallowed he said, "You know, we arrested one of those carnies. Aaron something."

"Do you still have him?" said O'Meara.

"That," said Jackson. "No, we don't. Someone fucked up somewhere, somehow. I blame all the cutbacks the state's been doing. These days, we barely have enough people to file the paperwork."

"So, where is he?"

"God knows."

"You mean he escaped?"

"It baffles the hell out of me," said Jackson. "He wasn't that bright. He must have had help. Maybe someone on the inside."

"What did you arrest him for?"

Jackson wiped his mouth again, pushed the remains of his food away, and turned to face O'Meara. "The crazy son of a bitch killed and skinned a full-grown bull. No easy feat, as I'm sure you can imagine. Slit its throat from ear to ear. Ate pieces of the raw flesh. We found him in the morning wearing the bull's skin and horns. He was praying and crying before some kind of altar he'd set up in the woods. There were dolls all stuck through with nails, razors, and old saw blades."

Hearing that the carny had eaten the bull's flesh made O'Meara think of what the gas station kid said about being bitten. But it felt too early to pursue that. Instead, he said, "Did he say why he did it?"

Jackson signaled for his check. "He talked about the iron man."

That made O'Meara stop for a minute. "Like the guy in the movies?"

"That's what we thought at first too but, no, this is someone else. According to Aaron, someone a lot scarier."

First Clemson's metal man and now an iron man, O'Meara thought. *And a flesh-eating lunatic. My god, Lucy. Who have you fallen in with?*

"I wish I'd been the one to find him," said O'Meara. "I'd love to have questioned him."

Jackson said, "I can do the next best thing. I have a friend of his locked up right now. Want to talk to him?"

RICHARD KADREY

"You would do that?"

Jackson laid out the money for his dinner. The waitress took it and he said, "A favor. Cop to cop."

O'Meara smiled at him and said, "Thank you so much."

"Have Cindy box up your food and I'll meet you outside. You can follow me to the station."

"I'll be right out."

He signaled for the waitress to put his food in a to-go container and paid quickly. Whether it was the aspirins or the offer to talk to the prisoner, O'Meara's headache had vanished. When he got in the van, Jackson blinked his lights and they slid out onto the highway.

On another night, in another place, he thought that Jackson's soul might have been an interesting one to take. He'd taken a police woman once, but that was a long time ago and in another state. It might just be time to take a male officer's soul. Would it feel or taste different? Once he got Lucy home and dealt with the idiot at the gas station, it might be time to go hunting for someone in a uniform.

THE HIGHWAY patrol station was just a few miles up the road.

The place was larger than O'Meara had expected, but it was largely empty. A dozen desks sat vacant, the computer monitors dark. A woman in patrol uniform waved to Jackson from across the office and he raised his hat to her.

"Is it always this empty?" said O'Meara.

"Not always," Jackson said. "Like I mentioned, we're understaffed, but it's also shift change. Most of the new crew isn't here yet. A good time to go in the back. Follow me."

They went around the desks and down a corridor past offices, many of which were dark. Jackson nodded to a few more co-workers and then they were in the back area with the cells. The familiar smell hit O'Meara even before Jackson had opened the door. Sweat, shit, and bleach. *Jailhouse perfume*, he thought.

RAZOR PIG

Like the office, the cells were mostly unoccupied. The few prisoners O'Meara saw looked mostly like drunks sleeping one off, though down the row were a couple of large men with black eyes and split lips. *Bar brawlers. The bums look the same everywhere you go.*

They went to the last cell in the row. A man lay on a cot inside, but he wasn't asleep. "Get up, Flint," said Jackson firmly. O'Meara liked that the jailbird did what he was told. Jackson continued, "This is Mr. O'Meara. He wants to talk to you about Aaron."

"Why should I?" said Flint. His eyes were on O'Meara. "He don't look like a cop."

"You should do it because I asked you nicely," said Jackson. Flint's eyes moved back to him.

"You didn't really ask me at all."

"All right, then pretty please with sugar on top and I'll see you get an extra cup of coffee in the morning."

"Milk too?"

"Would you like me to stir it for you?"

Flint grinned, showing crooked yellow teeth. "That won't be necessary, sir," he said. He moved forward and leaned his whole body against the bars so his face was framed in dull metal. "Well, what is it you want to know?"

"Everything about Aaron and the carnival," said O'Meara.

Flint shrugged. "What's there to say? I don't know nothing about stuff he did to some cow."

"Bull," said Jackson.

"Could be a goddamn moose for all I care."

"I don't care about any of that," said O'Meara. "Tell me about the iron man."

The prisoner grunted. "Aaron was a crazy fucker. Always has been, since we were kids."

"What did he say?"

"He told me god lives at the carnival," said Flint. "The iron man. He said the guy was *the* God or *a* god. Some shit like that."

"Is that why he left the carnival?"

Flint made a face. "Hell no. He loved the guy. But he hated the place. Said he was scared all the time. Look, all that happened was that he got high and the carnival left without him. He said he tried to go home, but changed his mind. Only it was too late. The carnival didn't want him anymore."

"I see." O'Meara thought for a moment.

"Does any of that make sense to you?" said Jackson.

O'Meara saw the letters squirm on the farmer's sign. "I don't know."

"That carnival was spooky as fuck and the chicks were worse," Flint said. "If you're looking for it, you're dumber than Aaron. At least he had the brains to run the other way."

"How did he get out of here?" said Jackson.

Flint made a comical, imbecilic face and spoke in a childish voice. "Gosh, I don't rightly know, now do I, officer?"

"All right, calm down."

"Yes boss," said Flint in the same voice. He turned and spat into his cell. In his normal voice he said, "Are we done here?"

Jackson turned to O'Meara. "Are we?"

He shook his head and stepped closer to the bars. "The map on the leaflet said the next town on the tour was Weir. Did you see them here or up there?"

Flint laughed. "Oh, they're not on the map anymore, boss. Too many people in too many towns complained about them, so they had to change plans. That's why Aaron said he couldn't find them. They've gone commando. Wild in the country."

O'Meara felt a stab of cold inside. If the carnival really had left the map, how the hell was he going to find them? "Did your friend, Aaron, say where they were heading next?"

"Why do you care so much?" said Flint, frowning. "Why don't you go home and watch a fucking movie?"

"Be nice," said Jackson warily.

"Fuck this asshole. You offer me coffee. Okay. What's this shitheel got for me?"

"Listen to me," said O'Meara. "My daughter is missing. You said yourself that there were bad people in the carnival. Lucy might be with them."

Flint laughed hard and loud at that. "Oh man. Poor little Lucy hooked up with them? She must be one dumb bitch."

"That's it, Flint. No coffee for you." said Jackson.

O'Meara edged toward the prisoner. "You should watch your mouth."

In a split second, Flint had his hands around O'Meara's throat. He threw his body weight back from the cell door, slamming O'Meara's head into the bars. The next thing he knew, Flint had let go and was sliding to the floor. When his vision cleared, he saw Jackson with his riot baton in his hand.

"That's it, Flint. You fucked up." He pushed his way into the cell and cuffed both of Flint's hands to the bars. Jackson put a hand on O'Meara's shoulder. "You want to press charges?"

It took a moment for him to find his voice again. When he did, it came out raspy. O'Meara said, "Do you know where the carnival is now?"

Flint let his head loll back against the cell bars. "Of course. It's where Aaron went when they took him out of here."

"Who took him out?" said Jackson.

"I don't remember."

O'Meara said, "Where are they? What town?"

"Why, they're right up yonder in fuck youville."

Jackson tapped the baton against his hand and said to O'Meara, "What do you want to do here?"

For the first time, O'Meara was scared for himself. This man Flint— *this trash*—had hurt him and taken some of his power. But he needed to get moving if he was going to find Lucy. Trying to figure a way out of the situation, he said, "I don't think I can."

Flint laughed quietly to himself.

"You can't let a man like him off after doing that," said Jackson.

Torn, O'Meara said, "I just don't have time."

Jackson stepped out of the cell and handed O'Meara the riot baton. "Then take care of business now."

Flint's face flushed. "Wait a fucking minute, motherfucker."

O'Meara was frozen. This wasn't supposed to be how things worked. Jackson handing him power and a mere beating for the man on the floor, with no chance at all of finishing him and taking his soul. What would Mr. Umbra think? Still, the temptation to hurt Flint was deep and hot.

From behind him, Jackson said, "You're still a cop in your heart. A protector. You have a responsibility to the community."

Flint kicked at him awkwardly with one leg. "Get this fucker away from me," he yelled.

O'Meara said, "I don't know if I'm permitted to do this."

"I'm permitting you. That's enough in here."

"Can't you do it?"

"Then what would it mean? You're the one he attacked. If I did it, it wouldn't mean anything."

O'Meara felt the lunar light recede in his head. His secret heart itched like fire. He felt weak as he let the baton fall to his side. "All right. I'll press charges."

"Faggot," said Flint. "I'm going to call my lawyer and tell him about this. I'll be out of here tomorrow night and when I am? I'm going to find your little Lucy and fuck her right up her juicy ass. Tell her Daddy sent me while I'm doing it."

It was too much. Without thinking, O'Meara slammed the riot baton down on Flint, over and over until his face and chest were bloody and he lay curled in a ball on the cell floor. Finally, Jackson grabbed O'Meara's arm and took the baton away.

"Tell me where she is," O'Meara shouted.

"Tell him," said Jackson. "Or round two will be mine."

Flint uncurled painfully and looked up at the men. "Up north. Town called Sundown," he said.

"Are you sure?" said Jackson.

"Yeah," said Flint and his head fell back.

Jackson looked at O'Meara. "You got some blood on you. Go clean up in the officer's wash room right outside the cell room. Get out of here and find your daughter."

"What about him?"

"I'll put him in with one of those two tough guys up front. If anyone asks I'll say they got into a fight."

"I can't thank you enough."

"Go. The new shift will be coming in by now."

From the floor, Flint yelled, "I hope Aaron's god cuts you down, fucker."

Shaken, O'Meara left the cell area and went straight to the men's room. Indeed, when he looked in the mirror, there were streaks of blood across his face and on his hands. A few spots on his shirt too. He turned on a tap but stopped before putting his hands under the water. Blood dripped from his fingers into the bowl. Slowly, he put his index finger into his mouth and when he drew it out it was clean. The blood offering wasn't Flint's soul, but it was a small measure of his power. O'Meara closed his eyes and felt the lunar road open. His heart stopped itching. He washed his hands and face and left through a side exit.

When he got to the van, he took off his shirt and put on a new one from his bag. O'Meara drove away and didn't stop until he was ten miles from the patrol station. Pulling onto the side of the highway, he turned on the overhead light and took out his map. He looked north on every road he could find until he gave up. There wasn't a Sundown anywhere.

I need a new map. A bigger one. And I need to get somewhere I can study it.

O'Meara thought for a moment about going back to the highway patrol station, but he knew that he'd worn out his welcome. There was nothing to do but hope Flint had been telling the truth about the town being north. He pulled back onto the road, his stomach queasy.

SMOKE BILLOWED from under the Suburban's hood a few miles outside of Taylor. He had to call AAA and wait an hour for a tow truck to take him into town.

The tension and frustration were too much. Lucy was his priority, but he knew that if he didn't truly replenish his soul soon it would be too thin to save her when the time came. It couldn't be the tow truck driver. *I need him.* O'Meara knew the trick was to be patient. He'd had dry spells before. *Calm down,* he told himself. *Patience is a virtue.*

But not for long.

THE SERVICE station owner was a friendly, grease-stained man named Ray who told him as gently as he could, "I don't have the parts for some of these newer models on hand. I can get one in town, but the store is closed by now. I'm afraid I can't get you out of here until late morning or early afternoon tomorrow."

O'Meara wasn't angry when he got the news. Instead, a kind of weary numbness settled over him. He simply said, "I understand."

"The good news is that the Rodeside, a nice little motel, is right down the road. Just a five-minute walk. A block over is the Buzzard Nest, a cozy bar with decent food."

"I appreciate it," said O'Meara. "By the way, do you have any Texas maps? Ones that go all the north to the border?"

"Sure," said Ray. He handed one to O'Meara from a rack by the door. "On the house. Hardly anyone uses them anymore."

"Thank you."

O'Meara took his boxed meal from the diner, his shoulder bag, and a heavy suitcase and walked the short distance to the Rodeside. There was no one at the check-in counter when he went inside.

"Hello?" he called toward an inner office. "Is anyone there?"

"Hang on a minute," said a brusque voice. O'Meara could hear tinny conversation coming from inside. Quiet laughter and applause. It was the sound of a television. When the last of the laughter died away the manager—a frowning bearded man—came out of the office. He didn't look at O'Meara when he said, "Checking in?"

"Yes. Just for a night."

O'Meara raised his eyebrows a little when the manager told him the price. He obviously knew that a man carrying food and his bags was stranded and had no choice where to stay. O'Meara pulled out his credit card and slid it across the desk.

"We charge an extra day for key deposit."

"That's ridiculous."

The manager tapped a finger on the counter. "Folks lose them or drive off with them in their pocket. I have to pay to make new ones. Of course, you can always sleep in your car."

It was a cheat, but O'Meara knew he was stuck. There was no way he could do what he had to do curled up in the back of the Suburban.

"Well?" said the manger impatiently. He glanced back at the office. "Look, my show is on and I can't pause it like at home. Take it or leave it."

"Will I get the key deposit back when I return it?"

The sound of voices came from the office again. "Yes, yes, you'll get your money. Wait here while I run your card in the office." It was a good five minutes before the manager returned. O'Meara knew that he was watching the show again and wouldn't return until there was a commercial. He opened the box and ate a few French fries while he waited. His milkshake was warm by now, so he threw it away in a trashcan by the door.

When the manager returned he set a key to room seven and the credit card on the counter. "Thanks," said O'Meara, but the manager was back in the office again.

He went to his room and ate his lukewarm burger while studying the maps he had spread over the bed. There was a Sundown City, but it was way over by New Mexico. *That can't be right.* He even checked the parts of southern Oklahoma at the very top of the map. Still nothing. He tossed out the lukewarm remains of his food. O'Meara felt tired and weak. Nothing since Lucy's disappearance felt right. Home was unreal and the road felt tenuous, with each stop giving him something, but also taking away some of his certainty and power. He felt lucky that he'd taken a speck of Flint's soul back at the highway patrol station, otherwise he wasn't sure what state he'd be in.

He finally gave up on the map and walked along the road to the Buzzard Nest.

Inside, it was dark and cool. There were perhaps a dozen people, spread out among the tables and chairs. A few of the seats at the bar had lights above them. O'Meara settled into one of those and ordered a Corona. The bartender, a woman in a sleeveless Pendleton shirt, held up a glass. When he shook his head, she brought him the bottle. He thanked her, took out the map and began looking it over again. He drank the whole bottle without seeing a Sundown anywhere. The bartender was talking to a young man in a dirty John Deere hat down the bar a few seats. When O'Meara held up his empty bottle she took it away and gave him a fresh one. After she set it down, she lingered for a moment.

"You've been staring at that since you got in. Don't you have GPS on your phone?" she said.

"I do," he said. "But I prefer physical things. Things I can touch with my hands."

"You've been touching that map all night. Is it helping?"

"Not a bit. Someone gave me the name of a town. I need to get there, but I just can't find it."

"What's it called?"

"Sundown."

She shook her head. "I haven't heard of that around here."

"I'm not surprised," said O'Meara.

The bartender called down to the man in the John Deere hat. "Hey Claude. You ever heard of a town around here called Sundown?"

Claude strolled down to where O'Meara sat and dropped down onto the next stool. "Sundown? Nothing like that around here."

RAZOR PIG

The bartender looked back at O'Meara. "Sorry. Wish I could help."

"Thanks anyway." He gulped down half of his Corona and thought about ordering a third, but without much food in his stomach his head was already beginning to swim. "Maybe this whole thing was a mistake. I should check with the police back home."

The bartender gave him a sympathetic look. "You lost something, haven't you?"

"Indeed, I have."

"Wife or daughter?"

O'Meara thought about saying both, but it didn't feel like a moment to try and be clever. "Daughter," he said.

"I'm sorry. I'm Jillian, by the way."

"I'm David."

"Nice to meet you, David. Sorry we couldn't be more help."

"Get a room, you two," said Claude. They both looked at him. He beamed at them and said, "Jillie here is getting ahead of herself. She can't help you, but I bet I can."

"How?" said O'Meara.

"Give me that map."

O'Meara handed it to him and Claude opened it across the bar. "You're looking for Sundown, only there ain't one, right?"

"I think we established that," said Jillian.

"Not so fast. See over here? Puesta del Sol. That's Sundown in Spanish. Your friend was either dumb or fucking with you."

O'Meara shook his head. Of course Flint had given him the answer he wanted, but in the worst way possible. "I'll be damned."

"Won't we all," said Claude.

Jillian frowned. "You sure your daughter is up there?"

"I hope so. Why?"

"There's a lot of shady stuff in that area."

"Like what?"

"The only witch trials in the Southwest, for one thing," said Claude. "Bunch of gringo missionaries came in and put some local Mexican gals on trial. The women got off, but a few days later some old coot found them strung up on a tree on his land."

"Stop it," said Jillian sharply. "That's just fairy tales and you know it. Any killings up there nowadays are 'cause of tweakers cooking meth."

"What about the kids?" said Claude.

O'Meara looked at Jillian. "What happened to the kids?"

She crossed her arms and said, "Some kids disappeared. But that isn't all that uncommon around here. There's no work and kids today don't exactly find Taylor exciting."

"So, they're just runaways?"

"Of course."

"You're the expert on that, right Jillie?" said Claude.

"Shut up."

He looked at O'Meara. "I heard that some of those runaways wound up dead," he said, adding air quotes around "runaways."

"Will you stop it?" snapped Jillian. "Next thing you'll be saying a witch in a gingerbread house ate them."

"Just telling you what I heard. What everyone with an open mind knows about."

Jillian inclined her head at the door. "You're drunk, Claude. Time for you to go."

He got to his feet slowly, but instead of moving for the door he moved closer to O'Meara. Leaning an elbow on the bar, he said, "If I didn't give you the name of that town you'd never know where to look for your little girl. Don't you think that kind of favor deserves some kind of reward?"

O'Meara pulled a wad of bills from his pocket, peeled off a twenty and gave it to Claude. "I appreciate your help."

"Any time," Claude said, tucking the bill into his breast pocket.

"'Night Claude," said Jillian. He blew her a kiss on the way out. When he was gone she said, "Don't let him get to you. He's an asshole, but it looks like he's right about that town."

"Let's hope so," said O'Meara. Jillian gave him a sympathetic smile. Despite his earlier dark mood, he found himself liking her. He wondered what her soul would taste like. "I understand that you serve food here?"

"Sure do," she said. "The grill is closed now, but we open for breakfast at nine."

"That sounds great. I'll be back then." O'Meara paid for his beer, adding on a hefty tip.

Holding up the cash, she said, "Thank you very much. See you in the morning."

"Good night."

O'Meara was slightly annoyed as he walked back to the motel. His head was swimming, but a couple of beers shouldn't have hit him that hard. It felt like there was something squirming around in his head, something that wasn't him or Mr. Umbra. He tried to shake it off. *Probably just tired and worn out from worry,* he thought. Things would be better in the morning.

An unlit vacant lot sat between the bar and the motel. As he passed it, two men stepped from the darkness. One was Claude and the other was a bigger man O'Meara didn't recognize. "Howdy again," said Claude.

"Evening. Thanks again for the help earlier," O'Meara said.

O'Meara started to walk on by when Claude got in front of him. "It really is dangerous territory where you're headed. That info I gave you might save your daughter's life. Don't you think that's worth more than twenty dollars?"

"How much do you figure I owe you?"

Claude put a hand on his chin like he was thinking. O'Meara realized that he couldn't see the big man anymore. A fist slammed into the back of his head and he dropped down to his knees. Someone kicked him in his ribs and he fell onto his side, curled in a ball. After a few more kicks, he felt someone's hand pulling the cash from his pocket. Then nothing happened for a while. O'Meara blinked and it occurred to him that he might have passed out for a few minutes. When he looked around, he was alone in the vacant lot. He crawled painfully to his feet and stumbled the rest of the way to his motel room.

Inside, he slumped on the bed and probed his sides. It didn't feel like he had any broken ribs, but there was a throbbing knot at the back of his head. He looked at himself in the bathroom mirror. His shirt was torn and filthy. There were some bruises around his left eye and long scrapes on his right cheek. *Probably from when I fell.* Over all, he counted himself lucky. In the dark lot like that, and with two men working him over, he knew from experience that he could be a lot worse off. He wished he hadn't left his damn gun in the van.

He took off his shirt and splashed some water on his face, then lay down on the bed. Sleep came quickly, but it wasn't pleasant. In his dreams, Lucy was with him, but when he tried to hug her her face squirmed like the wormy letters on the farmer's sign. Something loomed behind her, black and pulsating. When he reached for her she wasn't there but far across a field, hung from a tree like the old witches. He looked into the sky and the moon seemed to drift away from him, growing smaller as it went. O'Meara knew that he'd disappointed Mr. Umbra. It felt like the whole day—Hell, everything in his life since Lucy left—had been about him losing power. He could see Mr. Umbra on the moon, tiny and mournful as he drifted away. The sadness that hit him came from deep inside. His fear was total and gut wrenching, like a child watching a parent turn their back on them.

O'Meara awoke suddenly with tears on his face. They stung where they touched his scraped cheek. He'd brought a towel with him from the bathroom and he used it to wipe his face. As he did it, the sadness and fear was replaced with the kind of anger that unnerved him. It was reckless. The kind where rash men did stupid things. He sat up and took deep breaths until he got control of himself.

Patience is a virtue, he thought, *until it's not.* He put on a new shirt, picked up his heavy suitcase and walked around the motel. From what he could see through the windows, most of the rooms were unoccupied. O'Meara tried five doors before he found one that wasn't locked. *Mr. Umbra hasn't left me. Not completely.* He opened the suitcase on the far side of the room and gazed down on his tools in the moonlight that filtered through the open windows. They glowed with a magical light all their own. After he pulled the curtains closed, he set a pair of heavy Kevlar gloves on the table. Then O'Meara called the office for the manager to come up and put on a set of brass knuckles.

LATER IN his room he took a long, hot shower. When he was completely clean, he toweled off and took a safety pin and bottle of India ink from the heavy suitcase. In the bathroom mirror, he darkened another black spot within the secret heart tattoo on his chest. There were dozens of other marks, filling over half of the heart. The sting of the needle was familiar and comforting. It brought back good memories. How Mr. Umbra had come to him as a child and encouraged his first fumbling attempts at the work. Later, as a teenager, he grew more confident and cleverer. Then, there were the sweet years on the force and now. All it took was the flash of a badge to make most people stand still. Even the ones who ran were no match. O'Meara kept himself in good shape and worked out regularly for just such occasions. It still made him sad that his wife had discovered his work. She was a lovely, funny woman and when he took her, her soul was as sweet as candy.

Afterwards, his sleep was deep and relaxing. Mr. Umbra was there in his dapper black and white striped suit, his white face shifting through the phases of the moon. He called O'Meara to him and they walked the lunar path to the edge of a crater, where they sat together. Mr. Umbra put a hand on O'Meara's leg and gently said, "I thought I'd lost you, David. You seemed to step off the path."

"It won't happen again," said O'Meara. "When I find Lucy, when I find who took her, I'll drag his soul up here and lay him at your feet."

Mr. Umbra looked wistful. "That sounds lovely. It made me so sad when I thought you were gone. Remember what I said about stepping off the path."

"That if I did I'd fall into the abyss. The filthy trough filled with swine."

"Good boy, David. You were always my favorite." Mr. Umbra put an arm around his shoulder. It was both cold and reassuring. "Because of the fine ending to your difficult day, you may spend the night with me here on the moon."

"Thank you, Mr. Umbra. Thank you."

"But I need more souls, and so do you. Keep up with the work and soon your heart will be full and you can stay here forever."

O'Meara was so grateful that he didn't have the words to respond. Instead, they went to the manor house Mr. Umbra was building with all the souls his children brought him. The walls moved gently as if in a breeze as the souls shifted in their suffering. "You have to find Lucy soon," Mr. Umbra said. "Take her back from her captors. Then your power will be fully restored."

With those words, O'Meara woke up again. He fumbled his phone off the nightstand and dialed the number he'd found on the carnival leaflet. The call went to voicemail, but instead of getting a message that the box was full, he heard, "Go home. She isn't here." The line went dead.

He checked the clock. It was four a.m. Ray said it would be late morning or early afternoon before he could get the van fixed. There wouldn't be food at the Buzzard Nest until nine. For now, he had time to rest and let some of his strength return. He'd feel better and stronger in the morning, and then he'd find Lucy. Tomorrow would be great. Tomorrow would be perfect.

HE MADE it to the bar at nine-thirty and Jillian served him very good scrambled eggs, toast, and bacon. There were other servers in the bar during the breakfast rush, so she hovered over him as he ate.

"Nice face," she said. "Looks like you got hit by a bus last night."

O'Meara took a sip of coffee and said, "I got hit by something. Your friend Claude and a big man he had with him."

"Randall," said Jillian in disgust. "Did you call the cops?"

RAZOR PIG

"I don't have time for that. The moment the van is ready, I have to hit the road. Besides, it's embarrassing for a man in law enforcement getting his money taken by a couple of morons. The last people I want to see me like this are the police."

"I can understand that," she said. Jillian laid her hands on the bar and leaned in closer. "You weren't the only one who got what for last night."

O'Meara looked up at her. "Someone else got hurt?"

She looked around to make sure none of the other customers were listening. "The motel manager. He got killed in one of his own rooms."

"Last night?"

Jillian nodded. "I heard they found him cut up and wrapped in barbed wire like a bug in a cocoon."

O'Meara put down his fork. "That's awful."

"And that's not the weirdest part. They found his head across the room watching TV with the sound off."

"I guess I got off easy then."

"Did you hear or see anything strange last night?"

O'Meara shook his head. "After the beating, I took a shower and fell right asleep."

"From the look of you I'm not surprised," said Jillian. "So, Claude and Randall jumped you." She seemed to think for a minute. "Those boys get wild sometimes. Still, it's hard to see them doing something like what happened at the motel."

O'Meara said, "I agree. They seemed like just another couple of punks. I've seen a thousand of them."

"Still. It makes you wonder."

He shrugged. "I mean, who really knows what's in another person's heart?"

Jillian stood back up straight again. "Have you checked on your car yet?"

"Ray said it would be ready in a couple of hours."

"Why do you think your daughter ended up in Puesta del Sol?"

"A carnival. I think she might have left with them."

Jillian looked around the room. "Breakfast rush will be over by then and lunch won't have started yet," she said. "What do you think about taking a passenger with you?"

O'Meara sat back in his seat. "You?"

Jillian looked down at the counter. "You might have noticed Claude giving me a hard time last night."

"I did. He seemed to imply that you might have a missing child too."

She half-smiled. "He ain't a child anymore. Just a big, reckless bundle of trouble," she said. "Abel isn't a bad boy, you understand, but I think he might have taken up with some bad people."

"Carnival people?"

"I don't know. The carnival passed through here recently. He went off right after that. The cops are supposed to be looking for him, but you know how useless they can be." Jillian caught herself and looked at him. "No offense."

"None taken. That's why I'm on the road. I doubt the police give a damn about Lucy."

"So, what do you think? I can leave the crew to run the place for a day or two. Take me with you?" She added, "There's an extra order of bacon in it for you."

O'Meara thought about it. Having Jillian along would complicate things, but it would be interesting. He sensed that her soul might be something special, something bigger and richer than the paltry thing he took last night. He said, "If bacon is part of the deal, how can I say no?"

Jillian looked happy and bright.

Yes, she is something special.

"Great. You let me know the moment Ray gets done with your car. That'll give me time to set things up here."

"It sounds perfect," O'Meara said. He sipped his coffee and thought, *Things are finally going my way.*

RAZOR PIG

Ray got the van working earlier than expected. When O'Meara told Jillian, she came straight from the bar and they set out for Puesta del Sol.

After a day's driving, when the setting sun was just hitting the tops of the trees, they found the carnival in a large field on the outskirts of town. Even from the parking lot, the place looked seedy and decrepit. Paint peeled from signs and the rides O'Meara could see beyond the fence looked like ones that were old when he was a boy.

He drove around for a while before finding a space for the van close to the carnival's entrance. "In case we have to get out of here fast," O'Meara said. He took his .9mm from the glove compartment and slipped it into the holster at the small of his back.

"Do you think we'll need that?" said Jillian.

"Better to have it and not need it than the other way around."

"Good point. Let's go."

O'Meara took out Lucy's picture and after Jillian reassured him that she'd keep an eye out for her too they split up.

The carnival was as crazy as the idiot kid at the gas station said it was. Girls in tank tops and skinny jeans gave him the eye. *Definitely pros.* The clowns were right out of a child's nightmare. The concession stands were filthy and the only people who went near them didn't buy anything, but left money on the counter and went around back. He wondered if the stands were dealing meth or weed. He'd heard that coke was making a comeback in some towns but it would be too expensive for a cheap setup like this.

The carnival acts weren't any better than the rides or clowns. There were half-assed magicians doing kiddie party tricks, a mangy petting zoo, and dancing girls who looked like they'd faint if they didn't get a fix in the next ten minutes.

The only real excitement he heard was near a tent at the far side of the carnival. A chipped, hand-painted placard nearby read RAZOR PIG— THE IRON MAN. The image on the sign was of a great black hog holding huge swords over its head. He thought it was like an ad for some old-time drive-in theater horror movie. Something for fifties teens to Ooo and Aah over. However, even the absurdity of the sign couldn't dampen O'Meara's excitement.

The Iron Man.

He pushed his way through to the front of the crowd.

Though Razor Pig wasn't quite the monster he'd been promised, he was still an imposing figure. He had a thick nose ring hanging from his septum, like something you'd see on an old cartoon pig. His skin glistened. It didn't look like sweat, but more like some kind of blue-black oil. Probably to darken him so that he looked more like the black hog on the placard. O'Meara was also sure the man was on steroids. Every one of his muscles bulged, but not like a bodybuilder. More like the giant weightlifters he'd seen during the Olympics.

To O'Meara's surprise, Clemson, the farmer, hadn't exaggerated Razor Pig's act. He invited people from the audience to examine the array of swords, straight razors, and daggers he had on stage. Each one nodded in agreement that they were real. Of course, it was just a carny trick. Mind readers did it all the time, he thought. Plant some people in the audience to convince the rubes that the act was on the up and up. Still, however Razor Pig was doing it, the act was impressive. He chewed up straight razors like candy bars and swallowed small knives whole. Someone from the crowd held up a rusty Civil War sabre. Razor Pig bit the thing in half and started eating it.

Now I know it's fake. No carnival, not even one this shabby and degenerate, would let someone walk through the crowd with a real sword.

But like any good magic act, O'Meara could understand how someone predisposed to foolishness might buy what they were seeing. All he really knew at that moment was that he was going to talk to Razor Pig and that no one was going to stop him.

Half an hour later, he met Jillian by the gate. She hadn't found any sign of her son or Lucy. He told her about finding the Iron Man. However, they still walked by the fortune-telling booths because he remembered that Clemson had said one of the girls might have been Lucy. But she wasn't there and all of the women in the booths claimed not to know her. They hung around the booths for another thirty minutes, hoping someone might spell the current fortune tellers, but none of them budged. When the sun set and the lights came on, they headed back to the van to wait for the carnival to close.

O'Meara was still sore from the previous night's beating, and the knot on the back of his neck felt hot. He and Jillian bought big cups of beer and drank them in the Suburban.

"I'm sorry you haven't found your boy," O'Meara said.

Jillian took a sip of beer. "This whole thing might be a wild goose chase. I was just guessing about the carnival. You know, Colleen, a friend of mine, her boy ran off and joined the Marines without telling her. I'd like to think that Abel ended up there rather than here. Unfortunately, this is more his speed."

"You know, when things thin out in there, you look again while I talk to Mr. Pig."

She shook her head. "No, I'll come with you for moral support. That way maybe one of us might get what we came for."

They finished their beers and smoked and chatted for another hour before the carnival closed. O'Meara found himself attracted to Jillian, more than he thought he could be after his wife. Of course, having to deal with Lucy at home, there was no way he could start up any kind of long-distance relationship. But there were other ways to keep Jillian close to him, and taste her in ways even more intimate than sex.

When the lights dimmed and the final patrons were ushered out of the carnival, they left the van. The entrance was just a row of turnstiles that someone had run a chain across. O'Meara stepped over it easily, then helped Jillian over. He checked the gun at his back one more time, pulled his shirt over it, and they went to Razor Pig's tent.

He was alone inside, still glistening with oil, smoking a cigarette. He looked up when O'Meara and Jillian came in.

"So, you're the famous Iron Man I've been hearing about," said Jillian.

He barely turned his head in their direction. "It's not my favorite name among the ones I've used, but it brings the crowds in. And now it's brought you. What do you want?"

"If you answered your phone and gave straight answers, we might not have to be here at all," said O'Meara.

"I don't like phones. I like face-to-face, and you still haven't told me what you want."

"My daughter."

Razor Pig dropped his cigarette and ground it out with his boot. When he came over, he loomed over them. O'Meara was happy that he'd brought his gun.

Razor Pig laughed. "We all want someone's daughter." He glanced at Jillian. "Or son. But there have been so many. You're going to have to be more specific."

O'Meara held up the photo. "Lucinda O'Meara."

Razor Pig grinned and pointed. "Lucy! Yes, she's here."

"I want to see her."

"And Abel Stone. Is he here?" said Jillian.

Razor Pig looked her up and down. "I know him too. Lovely children. Tasty, if you take my meaning."

"Stop talking and get them here," said O'Meara. The back of his neck was throbbing, and he was dizzy in the same unnerving way he was the night before. *Maybe the heat,* he thought. *Maybe the beer.*

"Sure," said Razor Pig. He dialed an ancient flip phone he took from his pocket. It was greasy with the oil he used on his body. "Are Lucy and Abel around? Good. Have them come to my tent. I have a surprise for them." He sat down on one of the sets of bleachers that took up half of the tent. "Sit down. Make yourselves comfortable. This might take a minute or two."

"No thanks. I'll stand," said Jillian.

"Me too," said O'Meara.

Razor Pig narrowed his eyes at him. "You sure about that, Hoss? You don't look so good. The heat getting to you? Be careful. You don't want to fall on your face and scare Lucy."

RAZOR PIG

"I'm fine." But he wasn't. The inside of his head squirmed. Razor Pig stared.

A flap opened at the far end of the tent. A young woman and man came through. "Daddy?" said the young woman. "What are you doing here?"

"Abel," shouted Jillian, but he didn't go to her. He went over and sat down next to Razor Pig.

"What are *you* doing here, Lucy?" said O'Meara. "Who are these people? What hold do they have on you? If it's drugs or something, I'll get you any help you want."

Lucy hugged him warmly and said, "It's nothing. It's just that I've found a home here. This is where I belong. Abel too. We're finally happy."

Jillian took a few steps in Abel's direction, but when he cowered behind Razor Pig she stopped. "Is what she says true? You're here of your own free will and happy?" she said.

"Yes," said Abel, barely more than a whisper.

"You'll have to forgive him," said Razor Pig. "He's really taken to us. If you're here to take him home you're too late. He is home."

"It's true, Mama, I am," said Abel.

Razor Pig put a big hand on his head and tousled his hair. "You see, mommy? He's with us now. If he was ever with you at all. Like dear Lucy over there, they felt their lives were on hold. They were waiting for something. They were waiting for me."

Jillian frowned and her face turned red. "What have you done to them?" she shouted. "Is this some kind of cult? This man is a police officer. He'll drag your ass to jail."

Razor Pig laughed and stood, pulling Abel with him. "He tried that line on me already. But I know he's not a cop, just as I know that Abel is mine now."

Jillian rushed to her son, but Razor Pig got in front and shoved her to the ground. She scrambled back to her feet and ran back to O'Meara. "Give me the gun."

O'Meara put up a hand. "Hold on. We have to be smart."

Jillian was weeping now. "You have your Lucy. I want my boy."

"We'll get him."

She looked at Razor Pig. "He won't let him go."

"You're right," said the big man. "I won't."

"Wait a minute," said O'Meara. This wasn't how things were supposed to go. But it was too late. Jillian rammed her shoulder into his sore ribs, sending him to the ground. While he was there, she grabbed the pistol from his holster and fired six rounds into Razor Pig's chest.

When the bullets struck him, the big man grunted deep, like a hog. He staggered back a few steps, but didn't fall. Instead, he put his fingers into the red holes and slowly pulled, ripping apart the flesh of his chest. Jillian let out a short scream. His skin stretched, but when it broke open there was no blood, and inside his body there were no bones. Instead, he gleamed with decades of knives, razors, and sword blades. Razor Pig took a couple of deep breaths and spoke. "Abel. Go say hi to Mommy. Show her why you're really here."

"Abel?" said Jillian. She dropped the gun and held open her arms. The boy ran to her, but when he embraced her, she began to scream. Abel kept his face close to her and shook his head back and forth like a dog trying to kill a rat. Finally, he broke free with a mouthful of flesh from her throat.

Jillian fell to the dirty floor of the tent, gasping and gaping, coughing up blood. She kept a hand over the wound and never took her eyes off of Abel, even as he swallowed her flesh.

On his hands and knees, O'Meara finally knew where he really was. He'd been tricked off the lunar path and was in the trough with the swine now. There was only one way back to Mr. Umbra. Still, he had to ask the question.

"Who are you?"

Even with his body torn open, Razor Pig stood tall. He said, "I am Bereft. Void. The Devourer. I know you know my brother, Umbra. He brings people to one side of the moon and I to the other— the black side like a hole in the dark. The endless abyss. You think

RAZOR PIG

you've known power through him, but I am the real power. Ask me how I know."

"*How?*" said O'Meara.

"Because Umbra called you to him as a child. I, on the other hand, have led you here as an adult. A grown, whining animal." He crouched so that he was on O'Meara's level. "You want Lucy? Crawl to me now. Crawl like a pig."

O'Meara spotted the gun just a few feet away. There were still a couple of shots left in the magazine. He might be able to grab it if he leapt for it. Jillian had shot this beast in the chest. He would aim for the head. However, before he could crawl more than a couple of feet, Lucy pulled him upright.

"This isn't necessary," Lucy said to Razor Pig. "Let me talk to him."

She took him by the arm and pulled him down onto the bleachers. They sat there together for a minute and she held his hand. "I know all about Mr. Umbra, Daddy. I let you think I didn't, but I've known the whole time."

He looked at her. "How?"

"You told me about him when I was a little girl."

"No, I didn't."

"Yes. After Mom disappeared, you just pushed it from your mind. I know all about him and the souls on the moon."

"I don't remember any of it."

She set a cool hand on his cheek. It didn't sting the scrapes. "You said that I would meet him too. When it never happened, you told me it was all right. You knew him well enough for the both of us."

O'Meara looked down. "I'm sorry it never happened for you. He's wonderful. All light and peace and joy forever."

"You also said that one day you'd take us to the moon together. Like the way you took Mom?"

He shook his head, holding her hand tight. "No. Never that way. Not you."

She laid her forehead against his. "When I was little and you told me about Mr. Umbra, you drew a heart on my chest in ballpoint pen. You told me it was my secret heart and that it would link us forever. But don't you remember what happened?"

"No, baby. What?"

"It washed off." She laughed. "I'm heartless. Like Pig."

The big man stood behind Lucy. "You bring souls to the moon for your god. But I don't wait. I'm here and I eat every soul I touch. Every one that comes unto me."

O'Meara looked at Lucy. "You too?"

She cocked her head slightly. "Do you mean have I given up my soul to Pig or that I eat souls for him?"

"Both. Neither. I don't know." O'Meara's head pounded as his strength ebbed away. All his work for nothing. But Pig was so close.

Maybe I can still reach my gun.

He tried to lurch away from Lucy, but she held him tight. Without looking, she reached back into Pig's chest, grabbed a knife, and plunged it deep into her father's secret heart.

O'Meara fell back against the bleachers and looked up. He could just make out the moon through a gap in the top of the tent. As Lucy, Pig, and Abel began tearing into his flesh, others closed in hungrily around him. The pretty girls in tank tops. The fortune tellers, ticket takers, clowns, and the men who ran the concession stands. He barely felt his devouring. O'Meara understood that he'd moved into Razor Pig's domain, a realm beyond ordinary pain—for the moment. He looked up again to see Mr. Umbra turn his back on him. The lunar path began to fade until it was gone. Then there was nothing but the sounds of animal grunts and a cold and endless fall.

A Trip to Paris

Houston, Texas 1963

Roxanne Hill cut her finger on a broken tea cup while finishing the dishes. She went into the bathroom and doused the injury with iodine, grimacing as it burned, but not making a sound. The pain was her penance for being clumsy enough to shatter one of her late mother's cups. When she was done, she returned to the kitchen, but left the rest of the dishes to soak rather than ruining the bandage she'd carefully wrapped around the wound. She would finish the cutlery and plates tomorrow, at the same time she would scour the wall clean where a small patch of mold was beginning to grow behind the faucet.

The house was quiet. It was always quiet now since Sean and the kids were gone. However, some days seemed heavier with silence than others and this was one of them. Glancing at the calendar on the cupboard door reminded her why. It had been exactly a year since her family had died. How could she possibly have forgotten a date like that, she wondered. But she forgave herself because there had been so much to think about since her husband and children had left her. The police, for instance. She'd worried about them every day, though the fear had diminished greatly over the last few months. If the authorities didn't know that she'd poisoned them by now, they weren't likely to ever know. It was thrilling to think. She was free. Roxanne said the word once.

"Free." And in filling the silence it felt as if she'd broken a dark spell that had surrounded her for the previous three hundred and sixty-five days. She took a long breath and turned on the burner under the kettle. There was time for a cup of tea before she had to be at church.

AFTER WEDNESDAY evening services, she went down into the church basement with four other women and began sorting boxes of donations for the parish's clothing drive. While the other women babbled, Roxanne noticed that their voices were more hushed than usual. It was clear that while she'd forgotten the significance of the day earlier, the other women had not. Jeanette Morgan tried to draw her into the conversation by asking Roxanne's opinion about an elegant evening dress she'd found in one of the boxes. There was no reason for the question, of course. Roxanne knew very little about fashion, much less about evening wear. It was an obvious attempt by the other women to draw her out. So, to break the tension mounting in the room she said, "It's beautiful. I wish I'd had something like that for my wedding."

As she'd guessed, mentioning her marriage quieted the other women and they worked most of the rest of the night in relative silence. That was until the end of the evening when Delilah Montgomery drew Roxanne aside and confided in her that she and the other women were worried.

She said, "You've been strong, honey, for a whole year. But we know it's been hard on you too."

"What do you mean?" said Roxanne, not liking the comment one bit.

"It's your skin, darling. It's so pale. And your eyes. We can tell you don't sleep."

In fact, Roxanne slept soundly every night. Still, she played along with the other women's worry just to get through the rest of the night.

A Trip to Paris

They'd become intolerable to her over the past year. Such tiny people with such tiny lives, wanting nothing more than a clean house and mowed lawn to complete them. But she held her tongue and gave Delilah a smile that could be taken for grateful.

"I suppose that it has been hard," Roxanne said, hoping that would end the discussion. But it didn't.

As if on cue, Jeanette approached her with a large aluminum pot covered with a lid.

"We didn't want you to have to cook tonight," she said. "So we got together and made you a beef stew. Enough to last for a few days. And you don't even have to return the pot. It's yours. Our gift to you."

Roxanne never dropped her grateful smile. She accepted the pot saying, "Thank you so much. You're such good friends."

That was all it took. The other women swooped down on her, hugging her and kissing her cheeks. Roxanne tolerated it knowing that soon enough, she'd never have to see any of them again.

After that, the other women shooed her from the basement, insisting she go home and rest. She didn't need to be told twice. With the cook pot on the passenger seat, she drove home and went straight to the kitchen. When she sniffed the stew, it actually smelled rather good, if a bit spicy. *That would be Delilah's doing,* she thought. The woman believed that a few jalapeno flakes in a dish made her a daring chef. Roxanne shook her head at the foolishness of it.

She put the stew on to warm and poured herself a glass of wine. What truly disgusted her about the other women in the church group was the thought that if she hadn't acted to save herself, she might have ended up just like them.

Idiots. Letting themselves be trapped by laziness and fate.

Roxanne remembered when the doctor had told her she was pregnant the first time. She thought she was going to faint. Dr. Powell had to help her into a chair so she wouldn't fall on her face. She was sure that Sean, her husband, had tricked her somehow. She wasn't ready for babies. Wasn't sure she even wanted them, yet there she was. It wasn't fair.

I was drowning, and when you're drowning, you'll do anything to keep from going under. You can't blame a drowning victim for simply wanting to live.

When the stew was ready, she heaped a good-size portion into a bowl and ate on the sofa while looking through travel brochures. She'd been collecting them for months and now that a year had passed it was time to move on. But to where?

An hour later, still as undecided as before, she put the rest of the stew away and the bowl in water to soak. That's when she was reminded of the thumb-sized patch of mold on the wall behind the sink. Roxanne got out the bleach from the pantry and scrubbed thoroughly until the wall was immaculate. Afterwards, she went upstairs to bed where she fell into a deep and pleasant sleep.

THURSDAY WAS always grocery day. Roxanne took the car to the Piggly Wiggly with a short shopping list in her pocket.

Living on her own these days, she never spent much time in the grocery store and seldom filled her cart more than a third full. Today was no different, especially since she was anxious to get home to her brochures. She'd been leaning toward moving to New York, but now she was thinking about Europe. She had plenty of time to decide. The house had to be sold before she could leave and that might take months. The idea of another summer in Houston depressed Roxanne, but she was determined to be patient. She'd been patient about dealing with the family. She just had to do it one more time.

There were few enough items in her cart today that Roxanne headed for the express lane. However, on her way over, Jeanette from church cut her off.

Jeanette smiled at Roxanne with surprised delight and she smiled back sunnily thinking, *Pack mule*, at the sight of the other woman's nearly full cart.

"Are you coming to Delilah's ladies-only lunch this Sunday?" said Jeanette excitedly. "Her roses are coming into bloom and it should be beautiful."

A Trip to Paris

Roxanne nodded. "She does love those roses."

"Then you'll be there?"

I would rather die than be there, Roxanne thought.

"I'll try to be."

"Did she ask you about the library book drive?"

Anxious to get out of the store and the inane chatter, Roxanne said, "Of course. I'll put a box or two together this week. Sean and the kids' books mostly."

"Oh," said Delilah, going quiet. "Will you be all right doing that?"

She took a breath and said, "It's healthy, don't you think? Time to let go and move on."

Jeanette shook her head. "You're so strong. I don't know if I could ever do it."

I am. I am stronger than you, thought Roxanne.

Bored and wanting to get out of the conversation, she glanced at her cart as if she'd forgotten something. "You know, I have some frozen things I should be getting home."

"Of course, dear. I'll see you Sunday."

"Good-bye."

When she arrived home, Roxanne put away the groceries, heated up some of the beef stew, and froze the rest. Later, when she went to wash her bowl the patch of mold was back on the wall. A larger patch this time, as big as the palm of her hand.

Annoyed, she wiped it away again, this time with ammonia.

To get away from the smell, she went into the living room and pulled books from the shelves, piling them on the sofa. She'd been in a foul mood since running into Jeanette. It was getting harder and harder to maintain a placid public face for these people. That's why the book drive was such a godsend. The books were one less thing to worry about when she finally escaped to wherever the brochures would take her.

THE NEXT morning, the mold patch was back on the wall, larger and thicker than ever. It spread out in all directions, like the branches of a tree. The mold was thickest where the branches separated, with bulges and little hillocks. Looking at the foul mess was like gazing at a toxic cloud in the sky. Roxanne could almost make out shapes in the filth. The sight of it made her feel queasy.

She pulled a bucket and scrub brush from under the sink and got the bleach from the pantry. She mixed it with scalding hot water and tried to wipe the mold off the wall. Where before it had come off easily, this time she had to scrub as hard as she could to dig down through the rancid tree trunk to the wall beneath. Eventually, the mold disappeared under her insistent brushing, but Roxanne saw that she'd damaged the wallpaper. Where two sections met, they now pulled apart trailing glue, like a scab coming off a wound. Worse yet, she found that some of the mold had worked its way into the drywall. Furious, she scraped at it with a butcher knife. When it didn't come off immediately, she threw open the cupboard looking for something stronger than the bleach and ammonia she'd tried earlier.

That's when she saw it.

It was a small glass spice bottle labeled "Garlic Salt." But what it contained was much stronger stuff. She stared at it and thought of Sean and the kids. She was certain that she'd disposed of the poison, yet here was the concoction she'd used that night, in a bottle of the one spice she wouldn't ever use in a million years. Roxanne took the bottle off the shelf and held it in her hand.

I forgot the date the other day and now this. Things have gone so well up to now. What is that people say? That some murderers want to be caught? No. I don't want that, she thought, wondering in a mild panic what else she might have forgotten.

She looked back at the wall, at the shapes in the mess, like silhouettes of animals and people. There were definitely faces forming in the moldy tree branches. Roxanne stared at one in particular.

Sean, she thought.

Now angry as well as scared, she twisted the top off the garlic salt. *Why won't you stay dead?*

A Trip to Paris

She shook the bottle, throwing some of the poison directly onto the moldy face. It bubbled briefly and began to shrink and dissolve. When it was almost gone, Roxanne scrubbed the spot with bleach again. When she was done, she carefully threw the bottle into the kitchen trash and shoved it all the way to the bottom of the bag. Exhausted and sick to her stomach, she went into the living room and pushed the books off the sofa so she could lie down.

She knew she had to be more careful from now on. She'd waited months for people's obsession with her tragic story to die down. She couldn't afford any more mistakes. Not when she was so close to making her final escape from this stupid town and these ridiculous people.

To relax, she looked through the brochures and decided on Paris as her first destination. Between the family's life insurance and what she would get when she sold the house, Roxanne was sure she'd be able to have a grand life there.

Feeling more relaxed, she went into the kitchen and made herself that cup of chamomile tea.

That night, she dreamed of the Eiffel Tower and the Champs-Élysées. As happy as Paris made her, dark skies dampened her mood. It always looked as if the city was on the verge of rain. Worse, she saw things in the scudding clouds overhead. Silhouettes of animals. A neighbor's dog. A horse she'd ridden as a child. Human faces too—some familiar—their features constantly changing in the roiling mist. Their mouths moved as if they were trying to speak, but all Roxanne heard was the rushing of the wind.

THE NEXT morning, mold covered almost the whole wall behind the sink, reaching to the ceiling. Twisted bodies and faces were clearly outlined in thick patches. Her children's faces. A gnarled mass at the lower corner thrust out like a hand reaching for her.

Her heart was beating so hard that she had to sit down at the kitchen table and catch her breath. She wanted to run from the wretched house.

Better yet, burn it to the ground. In her head, she calculated how much insurance she had left in the bank. It wasn't enough. If she simply left and abandoned the house, the money wouldn't last for more than a year or two. Besides, simply running would raise suspicions. She'd worked so hard to tamp down gossip, she didn't want it to start now. No, mold or not, she had to sell the house. Be patient and play the shattered widow and mother for a while longer. But to do that, she'd need a useable kitchen. Between the mold and the damage she'd done to the wall, that was impossible without help.

Roxanne spent half an hour leafing through the phone book before settling on a repairman named Jameson. She called and arranged for him to come by the next morning.

Before retreating to the living room, she reached up and tapped at the mold with a polished fingernail. A few wet bits of it fell away. She reached up and touched her son's face, then drew her fingernails across it until his features were unrecognizable. Sean and her daughter's faces were too high to reach, so she gave up on them. On her way to the sofa, she found bits of the mold stuck to her fingertips. She wiped them clean with a rag, threw it in the trash, and put the bag in the garbage can that sat at the end of the driveway.

Mr. Jameson arrived at nine the next morning. After a brief, polite greeting Roxanne led him straight into the kitchen. When he saw the wall, he set down his tool box and whistled. The mold now crept across the ceiling over the sink.

"I wish you'd called me earlier, ma'am, I might have been able to help before it got this bad."

"Can you fix it?" Roxanne said.

Jameson frowned for a moment, put on a pair of rubber gloves, and approached the wall. He pinched some of the mold between his fingers, tearing off of a narrow section of her son's corrupt leg, and letting the mess fall into the sink. He pressed his fingertips to the wall and pushed gently. It gave a little. Jameson shook his head.

A Trip to Paris

"I'm not sure I'm going to be able to save the wall right above the sink. It'll have to get replaced."

Roxanne swallowed a stab of panic. She didn't like the idea of a stranger creeping around her house, especially now that she could plainly see her family staring down on her. She wondered what Jameson saw in the mold.

"Are you sure?" she said. "Isn't there anything else you can do?"

"I can knock some of this down with a chemical wash I have in the truck. But that doesn't fix things. You see, ma'am, if the mold is this bad by the sink, it's likely it's spread. You might have to replace the whole wall."

No, no, no, no, no, she thought, but said, "How long would that take?"

"If I do it myself, a few days. If I call in a crew, one or two."

The panic returned, a cold wave that washed through her body. She looked at her dead family and said, "A crew? No. I can't have people trampling through the house. I need to think."

"Take your time," said Jameson. "I'll get some things from the truck. See if I can clear up some of the mess. You don't need to be breathing that stuff."

When he returned, Roxanne sat at the kitchen table and watched him work. Whatever cleaning supplies he had were much stronger than hers. The mold quickly disappeared under the mop he used on the wall and ceiling. Seeing her family vanish from the kitchen, she began to feel like herself again.

She said, "Oh my. That's much better. Maybe you won't have to do the whole wall."

Jameson looked around. "We'll see. Let's let this dry for now and I'll come back tomorrow. This stuff is strong. If anything is going to handle that mess, it's this."

Roxanne leaned her elbows on the table, suddenly tired. Still, the clear wall made her smile.

"What do I owe you for today?" she said.

Waving a hand at her, Jameson said, "Nothing. Let's see where things stand tomorrow."

"Do you do that with all of your customers?"

He shrugged. "It's a nice town. Why not?"

"Aren't you afraid someone will cheat you? I mean, you cleaned my wall already. What if it stays clean and I didn't let you in tomorrow?"

Jameson smiled for the first time since he'd entered the house.

"You wouldn't do something like that. You're a good person, Mrs. Hill."

She looked at the man, concerned.

"How do you know that? What do you mean?"

As he gathered up some tools, Jameson said, "You don't remember me, but we were in high school together. You, Sean, and me. That's how I know you're a good person. You were nice to me when you didn't have to be."

Roxanne wracked her memory and then it came to her. "You're not Billy Jameson, are you?"

He took off his hat and did a small bow. "Billidiot the Idiot," he said. "Dumbest kid in our year. I thought that's why you might have called me. You recognized the name."

"I didn't. I'm sorry," said Roxanne, relaxing. If he was the Billy she remembered, he was as thick as tar. "But now I'm glad it was you. If I'm going to have someone in my home, it should be an old friend."

Jameson nodded as he picked up his equipment. "See? A nice person."

Roxanne walked him outside and they agreed for him to come by the next morning.

"With luck, that will be the end of it," Jameson said.

She waved to him as he started the truck. "Thank you, Billy."

Back inside, she examined the kitchen. There were black smears here and there where the mop had wiped away the mold but, aside from that, the wall didn't look too bad at all.

She sat down at the table again and flipped through the phone book to the Realtors section until she found the company that had originally

A Trip to Paris

sold them the house. She circled the name and decided to call them tomorrow afternoon about putting the place up for sale.

With the excitement over, Roxanne wanted a cup of tea. She put the kettle on, but when she opened the cupboard to get the teabags, she knocked over something leaning against the box—the jar labeled Garlic Salt. Her breath caught in her throat. She was positive she'd thrown the stuff away yesterday. But, no, that had been yet another mistake. No longer in the mood for tea, she turned off the burner and took the bottle to the garbage can and, again, pushed it to the bottom of the trash bag. She put the top of the can on firmly before going back inside.

That afternoon, Roxanne went to see a movie. She couldn't bear being stuck in the house right then.

When she got home, the wall was still clean. She made tea and called a travel agent to set an appointment over the weekend to talk about Paris. Tea in hand, she took her brochures upstairs to bed with her and stayed there for the rest of the day.

THE MOLD was back in the morning, along with the taunting faces of her family. When Jameson arrived and saw the state of the wall he set down his tool box and made a grunting noise.

"I'm sorry, Mrs. Hill. I've never seen a mold patch like this before. I'm going to have to replace the drywall."

She stood behind him, hands clasped nervously. "The whole wall?"

"I won't know till I take down the worst of it over the sink."

"All right," she said. "But I'd like you to do the job yourself. I couldn't bear to have the house full of strangers and noise right now."

"That's okay. I'll pick up some drywall sheets and can start tomorrow morning."

"And it will take a couple of days, you said?"

He looked at the wall. "That depends on the damage."

"Of course."

Throughout their conversation, Roxanne's attention was pulled back to the edges of the mold. She could swear that it pulsed and changed shape, as did the large mounds of filth that were her family's bodies so that it looked as if they were writhing in pain.

Am I crazy or has it always been moving and it's something else I missed?

Then a dark thought hit her. If she could see the movement, could Jameson? Was he able to make out Sean and the kids contorting bodies and was keeping it a secret? She looked at him. He didn't seem any different, but she had to be sure.

She pointed to a patch on the side and said, "It's strange how the mold is like clouds. Full of shapes. Do you see the arm over there?"

Jameson looked where she pointed for a moment, then scratched his chin. "You're right. It's an arm. Isn't that funny?"

"And a leg over there."

"I see it."

Roxanne pointed to where the mold touched the ceiling. "And up there. It's almost like a face. A man's face, don't you think?"

"It's funny you mention that one," he said. "I actually noticed it earlier but didn't mention it on account of it being sort of strange."

"Strange how?"

Jameson tilted his head up and looked again. "Well, it looks a little—and I feel funny saying it—but it looks kind of like Sean. I swear those are his eyes."

Roxanne felt a cold weight in her stomach. She wasn't hallucinating. They were there. Her whole family looking down on her. Spying on her. And now Jameson had seen them too. Her mind raced, trying to figure out what it meant and what she might have to do about it. But her mind was a blank.

Jameson frowned. "I'm sorry. I shouldn't have said anything. It's just, I was surprised. It wasn't right, though, me bringing up bad memories like that."

"Don't worry," said Roxanne. "I was the one who brought it up."

"I guess," he said, still frowning. He picked up his tool box and headed back out of the house in a rush. Roxanne followed him to the truck.

A Trip to Paris

"I'll see you tomorrow?" she said.

"I'll be here. And, like I said, I'm sorry."

"Don't think anything of it."

As he drove away, Roxanne thought, *He knows what happened. If he doesn't go to the police now he will soon. I'm going to have to kill him.*

She went into the kitchen and looked around, hunting for just the right implement. Rummaging through the drawers she found the butcher knife, a large pair of shears, and a hammer. But none of those would do. She would be caught instantly. She needed something subtler.

Maybe the skillet? I could say that he attacked me. No. She recalled that Brainless Billy had always been a good boy. If he'd done anything inappropriate with anyone else in town she would have heard about it.

Roxanne put down the skillet and went into the living room and stood by the front window that looked over the row of houses she hated. Same lawns. Same mailboxes. Children's bikes on the lawns. It made her sick.

Later, she wondered if she might be overreacting to Jameson's words. Even if he suspected something, all he had for evidence was some strange mold. And he wouldn't have said anything about that if she hadn't prodded him. After going over it in her head a few more times she thought, *No. He's no threat.*

Later, she called the travel agent's office and bought a one-way ticket to Paris on a flight leaving at the end of the month. Her mood lifted instantly. When the wall was repaired, she could let the realtor handle everything else. She didn't need to be here. Taking a deep breath, she let it out slowly. It would be her first time on a plane.

I'm doing it. I'm really, finally doing it.

Though her mood was light when she went to bed, her dreams were troubled. One by one, each member of her dead family stepped from the wall and fed her the same poison she'd used on them. Jameson held her and let it happen.

Roxanne woke early and went into the bathroom. While washing up she found small patches of mold under her nails and on her fingertips. She scrubbed her hands clean with alcohol and hot water.

Knowing she wouldn't be in the mood to cook later, Roxanne took the stew from the freezer and left it out to defrost. Jameson arrived at nine, his truck weighed down with gray slabs of drywall. In the kitchen, he carefully measured the area over the sink, making notes on a pad he kept in the breast pocket of his overalls.

"Would you like some tea?" said Roxanne, watching his every move, waiting to see if he reacted to the figures protruding from the mold. Her family moved all the time now. Hands grasped at the air. Mouths gaped as if screaming. Yet Jameson didn't appear to notice any of it.

"No thanks," he told her. "I'm more of a coffee person."

"I have that too. It's instant, but I could put on some water."

As he spread out a tape measure across the wall he said, "Thank you. That'd be real nice."

She went to the cupboard for the Folgers. When she opened the door, it was there again. The little bottle of garlic salt. It felt like there was a frozen lump in her stomach. She put a hand on the counter to steady herself and took out the coffee. Roxanne smiled, but inside she was screaming.

Someone is doing this to me. I threw this away. Twice. I know it. Someone keeps putting it back.

She glanced at Jameson. He had his back to her.

Besides me, who else has been in here? Who else has seen the faces? No one but idiot Billy. What kind of game is he playing?

As she heated water on the stove for coffee, she glanced at the skillet. He still had his back to her.

I could do it. Right now. Scratch my face. Tear my dress. Tell everyone it was self-defense. I could do it.

Jameson turned then and, seeing his face, Roxanne's courage flagged. No. There had to be another way. Some way to be absolutely sure.

On the wall, her family writhed and shrieked.

Standing on the edge of the sink, Jameson picked at the mold that touched the ceiling. The lump in Roxanne's stomach tightened. He was

A Trip to Paris

practically face-to-face with Sean. Yet he didn't appear to notice anything. She relaxed at the thought that Jameson was simply too dumb to see the grotesque miracle right in front of his face.

When the water was ready, she poured some over the coffee crystals and offered Jameson the cup. She considered pouring herself one too when Jameson said, "Your family got sick. Isn't that right?"

Roxanne held herself very still. She turned to him and leaned on the counter trying to effect a relaxed air.

He knows. The bastard knows. He's playing with me.

"Yes," she said. "Why do you ask?"

He frowned with concern. "I'm sorry. I shouldn't have brought it up."

"It's fine. But I'm curious about what made you think about it."

He turned the tape measure nervously over and over in his hands. "My sister and the kids went apple picking and ate a bunch of them. Got real sick. Maybe the apples were bad or maybe it was pesticide. Anyway, they ended up in the hospital."

Roxanne raised her eyebrows in feigned concern. "I hope they're all right."

"They're fine. Though little Andy had to stay an extra day on account of he kept throwing up."

"But he's better now?"

"Yes, Mrs. Hill. He's just fine."

"That's wonderful."

Her mind raced. Was this part of his game, bringing up pesticide? She looked back at the garlic salt on the shelf thinking, *I have to know. I have to be sure. What if he really is just an idiot?*

Jameson said, "I hope you don't mind something."

"What's that?"

"Well, this job is so odd that I mentioned it to a couple of folks, including Jeff Delano. Do you know him? He was in school with us too. These days, he's a cop."

"No. I don't know him," said Roxanne quietly.

"He helps me out with jobs sometimes. You know, on the weekend for extra money. Jeff might come by in the afternoon. That is, if that's all right with you?"

Roxanne sat down at the kitchen table wondering what it would take to get her family's bodies exhumed. Not the word of an idiot certainly, but perhaps the testimony of a busybody cop.

"It's perfectly all right," she said.

"Did you hurt your hand?" said Jameson.

She looked down at her fingers. There was mold under her nails and smeared on her fingertips again. Using dish soap, she washed in the sink and said, "How funny. I must have touched the wall when I came in."

"You'll want to be careful. Mold like that is bad for you."

Yes. He is playing. Being coy until the police arrive. I should have seen it coming.

She wished she'd followed her instincts and simply abandoned the house, letting the realtor deal with repairs and the sale. She could have flown to Paris days ago instead of being trapped at home between a dim-witted monster and her screaming family. Still, she wasn't caught yet.

While Jameson made drywall calculations in his book, Roxanne put the stew on the stove over a low flame.

She said, "Do you like stew, Mr. Jameson?"

He glanced at the pot. "Call me Billy."

"Thank you, Billy. Call me Roxanne. So, do you like beef stew?"

"I do. A lot."

"Then you'll have to stay for lunch."

"Thank you, Roxanne. That'd be nice."

"What time did you say your policeman friend was coming by?"

"This afternoon sometime."

She glanced at the kitchen clock and said, "Maybe we should eat an early lunch so we'll be ready for him."

Jameson said, "I wouldn't mind that. I didn't get any breakfast."

"Then we'll feast as soon as possible."

He bustled around her in the kitchen while she stirred the stew on the stove, careful not to let it burn on the bottom. When it was warm

A Trip to Paris

and the comforting smell filled the kitchen, Roxanne took a bottle from the cupboard and poured the whole thing into the stew.

"What's that?" Jameson said.

She stirred the pot, relaxed and resigned. Jameson had won their little game. The police were on the way.

"Just something to add a little spice to our lunch," she said.

Roxanne ladled out two bowls and they sat together at the table. Jameson dug his spoon in eagerly and ate big mouthfuls of the stew. Roxanne left her spoon beside her bowl and stared up at the wall where her family screamed at her.

Jameson cleared his throat. "The other day, when I first got here, I saw a bunch of travel brochures in the living room. Are you going somewhere?"

"Yes, I am. Paris."

Jameson stopped eating and leaned back in his chair.

"Wow. I've never been farther than Galveston. Will you tell me about Paris?"

"I haven't been there yet."

"Yeah, but you know a lot more about it than I do."

"I suppose I do."

Roxanne sat quietly, a finger on her spoon, her mind racing for a way out, but she came up with nothing. The police were on the way. If she ran, Jameson would no doubt stop her. *Yes. That's exactly what he'd do,* she thought.

Jameson said, "Jeff would love this stew. Can we save him some?"

She didn't think about it for long. "What do you say we finish it ourselves and I'll give him the recipe."

"Sure. But you're not eating."

Roxanne looked at the mold on her fingers and up at her family. She picked up her spoon. "I wasn't sure I was going to, but I think I will after all."

With a half-full mouth Jameson said, "What's the first thing you're going to do when you get to Paris?"

She thought for a moment. "I'll check into my hotel and go out onto the balcony where I'll have a view of the Eiffel Tower. I'll breathe in the air and think, 'I'm free.'"

She took a bite of the stew. It was just as good as she remembered.

They ate and talked like old friends until the pot was empty.

A HINTERLANDS HAUNTING

Nick crossed the bridge on foot, moving from one world to another. Really, he was just leaving a bright and crowded district for one that was neither. But the one he was crossing to was older and being across the river, it felt like another country, with its own language and obscure customs. He made the crossing every year at the same time. Always 10 p.m. Always Columbus Day. He had to be careful because the date of the holiday changed from year to year and dates were something easy for a ghost to lose track of.

He thought it was unfair that every year on the pilgrimage he shivered at the frigid wind whipping up from the water. What good was it to sense heat and cold when you were dead? Still, Nick could do other things that most people didn't think ghosts could do, so he supposed it was part of the bargain. But still, the crossing was horrible and he ran the last few yards, leaving the living city behind and heading into what amounted to a vast necropolis.

This older part of the city had been condemned and was just waiting to be demolished—every apartment building, school, church, and bowling alley. Very few people lived here anymore so there were few lights on in the buildings. It was so quiet you could hear the wind through dead trees lining the main street. Tinny music echoed off the buildings. Someone's radio, maybe around the corner or maybe a mile away.

In school, Nick had read about pandemics. Spanish influenza. The Black Plague. They emptied whole towns. He imagined that it must have been like this. Still, the living had to keep their eyes open for groups of feral children and desperate old codgers with kitchen knives up their sleeves. Even a few gangs roamed the streets. Too small or too unlucky to cut it in the bright city, they'd retreated to the hinterlands. Then there were wild dog packs. What was terribly unfair was that some of these things were even dangerous to *him*. "What's the use of being dead if you're afraid all the time?" he would say to other ghosts, but few spoke to him and none had any answers.

Years before, he'd lived in this now desolate part of the city. On the corner ahead, a light was on in a bodega he would frequent with his wife. The owner, whose name was Robert or Roberto—something like that—was an aggressive, foul-mouthed man who, Nick used to joke, had a PhD in ethnic slurs. When he reached the corner, he went into the shop.

It was mostly as he remembered it: dusty cans of soup and meat, snack food, liquor, and cigarettes. Now, however, most of the merchandise was behind a screen of thick plastic that extended from the front counter to the ceiling. There was a crudely cut slot by the cash register where people would pass their money and get their change. A couple of feet down the counter was a small revolving door where customers would receive their goods. *It looks bulletproof,* he thought. *And tightly sealed.* The bodega owner sat by the register in a dense gray fog of cigarette smoke. Nick went and stood in front of him, casting a vague reflection on the plastic screen. It took a couple of minutes for the owner to notice him and when he did, he turned white and stumbled off his stool.

A circle of small holes had been drilled into the plastic at mouth level so that people could communicate with the owner. Nick leaned close to it and said, "Have you seen her?"

A Hinterlands Haunting

The bodega owner shook his head in short, nervous bursts.

"That's too bad," Nick said. "I was hoping. It's always so hard knowing where to begin looking."

The owner nodded stiffly and when Nick didn't move, he took a pint bottle of bourbon and passed it to him through the little revolving door. He took the bottle and put it in his coat pocket.

"Please," said the owner. "Go."

"Afraid of an old-fashioned haunting? I don't blame you. Take my word for it, the dead are mostly assholes."

The owner didn't laugh at the joke, which disappointed Nick. "Don't worry," he said. "I'm not here for you. I have places to be."

He walked a few aimless blocks trying to get his bearings. The city had taken down all the street signs to discourage people from living in the district. Nick used landmarks to navigate to the old apartment he'd shared with his wife.

Like the bodega, the neighborhood was mostly as it had been since the last time he'd lived there. It was the little changes that caught his eye. A burnt-out bar. A clothing store full of headless mannequins.

Down a block that used to house bakeries and antique shops for tourists was a sculpture of a snake that seemed to dip in and out of the pavement. Made of scrap metal and wood wired together, at its tallest, the snake was two stories high. He marveled at both the amount of work and madness necessary for someone to build such an enormous piece of art that no one but the lost and the dead would ever see. He recognized the corner where the snake stood and knew that he was close to home. Nick decided that the sculpture was a good omen. He would find his wife soon and be able to finish what he'd come for.

He turned right just past the snake and started up a gentle hill before the small apartment building where his wife would be waiting. He looked up at their window, but didn't see any lights on. Another good omen. Hauntings were always better when they began in darkness. He was almost at the front door of the building when he heard the dogs.

They came yipping and growling down the hill, at least a dozen of them. Living people could hurt him, but he had ways of dealing with them. Animals, on the other hand, weren't afraid of his fragile, spectral form and could easily tear it apart.

The glass front doors of the building had been shattered long ago. He ran inside and raced up the stairs to the old apartment. Unfortunately, it was on the third floor and, despite what was in stories and movies, ghosts like Nick couldn't fly. He had to go up a step at a time just like anybody else.

He was on the second floor, starting up the stairs to the third when he heard the dog pack burst into the lobby and thunder after him. He ran up to the third floor as quickly as he could, but the dogs were much faster and by the time he sprinted down the final hallway, the dogs were just a few yards behind him. He tripped and fell against the door of the old apartment and, to his shock, it swung open. This made no sense since Eleanor had always been a fiend when it came to security, installing extra locks on all the doors and windows. But he didn't have time to worry about it. Nick barely got inside and closed the door before the dog pack slammed into it. He threw all three locks and wedged a metal folding chair under the doorknob. Outside, the dogs snarled and scratched to get in, but Nick felt safe. While the building had never been elegant, it was sturdy, with thick, solid doors on each apartment. Still, he didn't like being so close to the pack. He backed away from the door and went into the living room.

When he saw the place, he stopped. It didn't make any sense. The whole apartment smelled of mildew and urine. Much of the furniture was damaged and what wasn't covered in dust was covered in mold. He sensed that no one had been here in a long time, but he went into the bedroom anyway. It was in the same condition as the living room. The carpet and bare mattress were black with mildew. He checked the dresser and looked in the closet. Both were empty. Nick went back into the living room and looked around for a clue as to where Eleanor might have gone. How could he haunt someone who wasn't there?

A Hinterlands Haunting

The few papers he found on the floor were either moldy or so damp that the ink had run, making them unreadable. A creak and a loud *pop* startled him. When he didn't see anything in the living room he went back to the apartment door. It moved back and forth slightly and it took him a moment to understand why.

Nick stepped on something metallic and picked it up. It was one of the door hinges. The dogs were still trying to batter their way in and while the door itself was thick and strong, all the damp and rot in the apartment had softened the frame around it. The screws in the second hinge were already working their way loose. He was certain that the chair he'd wedged under the doorknob was the only thing keeping the dogs outside. If they got in they'd rip him apart like an old sheet.

Nick knew the apartment and he knew the building and there were no other exits. He'd hated heights in life and the fear hadn't left him in death. Still, he knew the only way out was the fire escape.

He went back into the bedroom and headed for a broken window by the radiator. Moonlight and a damp mist streamed inside. When he stuck his head out the window to see the way down, he almost laughed. The fire escape was there, but on the ground in a twisted heap where it had collapsed. From the other room, he could hear the second hinge wrenching its way out of the wooden door frame. He looked up wondering if he could climb to the roof. However, the fire escape above him was gone too. Dark shapes streaked across the front of the apartment building. More dogs, attracted to the place by the howls of the pack in the hall. Whatever mad thoughts he had about making a run for it down the stairs vanished.

A piece of glass slid from the window frame and he watched it fall. It didn't hit the ground. Instead, it landed on a massive pile of garbage in front of the building. The city had cut off most services to the neighborhood long ago, beginning with garbage pickup. It looked as if the building's residents had simply thrown everything they didn't want from their windows until they'd created a small mountain. For a moment, Nick wondered what filth lay below him, but he cut off the thought when it became clear to him what he was going to have to do.

From what Nick could see, the trash pile was topped by several filthy mattresses. If what was below them was soft enough, they might absorb his weight enough to catch him. It wasn't like he was going to die again, but his spectral body healed slowly and the pain was just as acute as it had been in life.

A final *pop* echoed from the other room and the howling dogs shot into the apartment. Nick stood at the edge of the window and waited until he could feel the dogs right behind him. He needed the fear to let go of the sill and step out into empty air.

The sensation of falling seemed to last less than a second before it was replaced by a feeling that he'd been hit by a bus. Groaning, Nick slowly rolled into a sitting position at the edge of the mattress. He touched his legs and ribs. No pain there, and his limbs seemed to move the way they were supposed to. Nick's back was another matter. It felt as if he'd pulled and bruised every muscle from his neck down to his ankles. He tried to stand, but the pain made him gasp and he fell back onto the mattress. Above him, the dogs were still barking. When he tried to stand again, hands reached down and pulled him to his feet.

Three young men stood around him in a semi-circle.

"Thank you," Nick said.

"You can stand? You steady on your feet?" said the nearest young man. The one who'd helped him up.

"Yes. I think so."

Without warning, he punched Nick in the stomach. The pain shot all the way through to his back and he fell to his knees. From this lowered vantage point, he noticed that the young men were all wearing matching jackets. *A gang*, he thought.

The man who kicked him prodded him with the toe of his boot. "Give me your wallet," he said.

Nick shook his head. He said, "I don't have a wallet. Dead men don't carry money."

The young man smiled at his friends. When he turned back to Nick he said, "You're not dead."

A Hinterlands Haunting

"That's your opinion."

Nick reached into a coat pocket, pulled out a revolver, and shot at the young men. All three went down. He struggled to his feet and went to the one who'd punched him. "Still think I'm alive?" he said. When he didn't answer, Nick pulled back the hammer. The young man held up his shaking hands. Both were covered in blood.

"Still think I'm alive?" said Nick.

"Fuck you, you fucking freak," said the young man. "You're as alive as me."

"That's unlikely. But still, just to make sure." He opened the cylinder of the revolver and spun it. Slapped it closed, put the gun to his head, and pulled the trigger.

Click.

"That was disappointing," said Nick.

The man on the ground pointed at him. "Ghosts don't use guns."

"It's a ghost gun," explained Nick. Then he said, "You know a lot about spirits, do you?"

"More than you, I bet."

Nick spun the cylinder again and pointed the gun to his head.

Click.

"Maybe ghosts can't shoot themselves. What do you think?"

The young man said, "Suck my dick."

Nick held the gun out butt first. "Maybe you should try it."

The young man reached for the pistol with both hands, but they were slick with blood and he dropped it. He reached for it, but his hands were shaking so much he couldn't hold it.

Nick snatched the revolver off the ground and said, "You're useless. How am I supposed to be certain? You have me doubting myself. I need hard, empirical evidence of my spirit state."

One of the other gang members tried to get to his feet. Nick raised the gun and shot him. He collapsed onto his back.

"You're out of your fucking mind," said the young man he'd been talking to.

Nick looked down at him. "You know a ghost when you see one? How can you be so sure?"

"My grandma. She taught me how to look," he said. "Ghosts leave a trail in the air like fireflies. You don't leave nothing."

From his back pocket, Nick took out a photo. "Let's try another line of questioning," he said. "Maybe you've seen my wife. She's a little shorter than me. She's usually in a long yellow nightgown with pink flowers on the front."

The young man squinted at the photo and nodded. "Her I know. She haunts the white building right over there. We don't go near her."

"Why's that?"

"Spookshow baby don't talk much. She just kills you if you get too close. That's the other reason I know you're not a ghost. You talk too fucking much."

"I'm lost. I don't like talking, but I have no alternative."

The young man looked down at himself. "Oh shit. I think I'm dying."

"Point me to where you've seen her."

The young man pointed a shaking hand across the street.

"That can't be right," said Nick. "I don't recognize it. She should be in here," he said, looking at the building from which he'd just jumped. The dogs still barked from the window.

"I see her there all the time. She's a real ghost, not you."

"That's not possible, which makes you a liar." Nick pulled the trigger and the gun went off. The young man stopped moving.

He put the pistol back in his pocket and looked up. A woman in a yellow nightgown stood by the curb. "Eleanor?"

At the sound of the name, the woman ran to the building the young man pointed to earlier. Nick tried running after her, but he'd hurt his knee in the fall and had to limp.

"Eleanor!"

Nick's leg hurt terribly, but he went after her as fast as he could. He entered the white building. When he heard her above him he headed up the stairs. It was a funny thing, he thought. Out in the street and now in the building, above him he could see things like fireflies. Slowly and painfully, he followed them.

Nick couldn't hear or see the woman anymore, but a dwindling trail of floating lights led him to an apartment. He went inside—and recognized it immediately. He and Eleanor *had* lived there. After the other apartment. Everything had happened here, not there. How could he have forgotten that? He pushed the apartment door closed. "Eleanor!" he called. Before he could turn away, she rushed out of the small kitchen with a butcher knife and buried it in his chest. As he fell he marveled at the fireflies that surrounded her and how none surrounded him.

He lay against the wall, breathing hard. Eleanor went through his pockets. She took out the pistol and tossed it away. When she found the bourbon, she held the bottle out to him.

"Open it," she said. "I can't."

"You can stab me, but you can't open a bottle?"

Eleanor knelt down next to him. "Hate only gives me so much power and it's very narrow. Stabbing is easy. Bottles aren't. Open it for me."

Nick's left arm was numb, so he braced the bottle against him with his forearm and unscrewed the top with his right hand. He held it out to her.

She sniffed the bottle.

"Bottoms up," he said.

"Don't be an idiot," Eleanor said. "I can't drink. But I can smell. This is cheap stuff you brought me."

He shrugged, which was a mistake. The knife dug in deeper. His chest felt like it was on fire. "It was free."

"That's just like you. Cheap to the end."

Nick smiled at her. "You don't look so bad."

"Neither do you," Eleanor said.

"For a dead man."

She looked at the floor and shook her head wearily. "Christ, Nick. Every year. You're not the dead one. I am."

"But I feel dead," he said.

She took another whiff of the bourbon. "You need a shrink, not a mortician."

Nick looked down at the knife in his chest. "I might be dead soon."

"I aimed high. You'll be fine. You just need some stitches."

Nick felt weak all over. He dropped the bottle. "One of these years you're going to fuck up and kill me for real."

Eleanor shook a finger at him. "The day I kill you for real it won't be a mistake. Until then, enjoy bleeding."

He frowned and a wave of pain, physical and emotional, passed through him. "Did I ever apologize to you about the whole thing?"

"For murdering me? Count the scars on your chest. They'll tell you."

"Does it help?"

"What do you think?"

"But this does?" he said, looking down at the knife and his blood.

She sighed. "It breaks up the tedium."

He wanted to reach out to her, but his arm was too heavy. "I was hoping it would be different this year. Me dead for real. It's getting harder to tell the difference anymore."

"The difference is that you get to go home and watch TV and jerk off. That's how you can tell the difference."

"I think they have a TV at the bodega."

She made a face. "Bobby is too jumpy. It's no fun down there."

"Maybe I could bring you something," Nick said. "A TV. Maybe a satellite dish on the roof."

"Don't bother. They wouldn't last thirty minutes over here. You met some of the neighborhood beasts. They'll steal the gold from your teeth."

"Bet if I shoot a couple more they'll leave you alone."

She gave him a sour half-smile. "That's sweet, but no. I've made it this long. I can get by."

He looked around the apartment. "What happens when the bulldozers show up and they tear all this down to put up condos? What happens to you? Where will you go?"

A Hinterlands Haunting

Eleanor looked out the window. "I don't know. I think I might just vanish. All I am are memories. These places. You. This stupid nightgown you killed me in. Really, you could have waited until I was in something nice or at least had shoes on. Look at my feet."

They were black with filth. Glass and nails were embedded in her soles.

"Do they hurt?" said Nick.

"Of course not, but they're grotesque."

Nick's head slumped forward.

"Hey. You awake over there?"

He shook himself upright again. "Sorry. My head was kind of swimming."

"You're losing blood. Time for you to go."

He looked at her. "Go? Don't you want to finish tonight?"

Eleanor frowned at him. "Who would I be finishing for? Not me. Now get on your feet. I'll help you to the store. Bobby can call you an ambulance."

"What hospital should I go to? I can't get stabbed every year and go back to the same place. They've already started asking questions."

She thought for a moment. "Have you tried Saint Dymphna? She's the patron saint of idiots."

"Yeah. I haven't been there. I heard it's nice."

With Eleanor's help, Nick got to his feet. He leaned on her heavily as she walked him out of the building and back toward the bodega. At the corner, several young men blocked the street. A couple of them started forward, but when they caught sight of Eleanor they backed away and opened a hole big enough for them to pass through.

"That was impressive," said Nick.

"I told you. No one is killing you but me."

"Not even me?"

"Especially not you," Eleanor said. "And don't go back to that building next year. I won't be there."

Nick looked up at the stars. "You always were restless. You could hardly sit through a movie."

When they reached the bodega, Eleanor leaned him against the door. "Remember, don't let Bobby take the knife out. You'll bleed to death before the ambulance gets here."

Nick looked at her. "Same time next year?"

Eleanor nodded slightly. "Don't be late."

As she started away Nick said, "Happy anniversary, baby."

"Happy anniversary," said Eleanor, trailing fireflies into the dark.

SUSPECT ZERO

The rain that had pissed down all afternoon turned cold when the sun set, and it kept getting colder all night.

The boy waited on a corner among the nearly deserted warehouses. He waved at a passing eighteen-wheeler and it slowed to a halt, pulling over at the corner. The cab was taller than the boy expected. He had to climb up a couple of chrome steps to get inside. The drizzle made the metal slick and he slipped and almost fell, but the truck was warm and dry when he made it inside. The boy shivered and wrapped his arms around his old navy peacoat, trying to get warm, careful to keep his hand away from the pocket where he'd hidden the knife. For now, it was nice just to be out of the rain.

"What's your name, son?" asked the driver.

"Gabriel."

"Like the angel," said the driver as they pulled away.

"I guess. Supposed to be for an old relative. He was a general in the Civil War."

"I never heard of him."

"He didn't last long. I don't think he was much good."

The driver scanned the road ahead. Turned left, prowling the wet potholed streets. Water rolled down the gutters, miniature rapids.

The boy looked at the driver. He was wearing a heavy plaid hunting jacket. It made it hard to tell how big the guy was. His face was thin and covered with a couple of days' worth of gray stubble. His lank hair was pulled into a ponytail and held back with a grimy red Peterbilt baseball cap. A plastic eyeball tacked to the truck's dashboard swung back and forth like a pendulum ticking out the time.

"What do you do, Gabriel?"

"Mostly travel these days. I move around a lot."

The driver nodded.

"Some people are farmers and some are nomads. I'm a nomad. The Akkadians and Sumerians, they were nomads. They settled down, built up the first civilizations. The Mongols and Huns were nomads. They came along later and kicked those civilizations down." The driver laughed. "It's a good life for the right kind of people. Are you the right people, Gabriel?"

"I sure as hell am tonight. Anything that'll get me out of the rain," he said, hugging himself tighter, feeling the reassuring press of the knife against his leg.

The driver grinned.

"Don't sell yourself short, son. I have a feeling you're more than that."

"How can you tell?"

"I've been around for a while. You can't help but learn to read people."

"What's your name?" asked Gabriel.

The driver hunched his shoulders and peered out the windshield, straining to read street signs through the rain-streaked glass.

"Damn it. I know you're around here somewheres."

Gabriel didn't talk while the driver hunted for the destination. As he grew warmer, Gabriel relaxed.

The driver asked, "You know, I just realized I'm so wrapped up in these streets I never asked where you're headed."

"Far as you can take me, sir. Anywhere that's drier than here."

"Good answer. I could use a little company. I'm heading out of town tonight, but I've got part of a load left and work to do. Hope you don't mind a few stops along the way."

SUSPECT ZERO

"No, sir."

"And if you get bored or what you see looks interesting, jump on in. But no pressure. Good work is its own reward, but you being the right kind of people probably already know that."

"I suppose. Yeah." He didn't know what else to say. What was with the "right kind of people" thing? Had he let something slip? Did the old man know what he was there for? This time he let his hand brush the hilt of the knife, the one thing he still had from home.

"Grab me a pop out of that cooler by your feet, will you?" said the driver.

Gabriel leaned down to where a red-and-white plastic picnic cooler rested on the floor. It was the kind where the lid swiveled back on a hinge and the top opened like a trapdoor. When he popped open the top a plastic-wrapped .45 automatic fell out onto the floor.

"I was wondering where that'd got to. Thanks, son."

Keeping one hand on the wheel, the driver bent over, grabbed the gun, pulled the plastic off with his teeth and stuffed the gun into his jacket pocket.

A second later he looked to his left and said, "Thank you, Jesus and all the little baby Jesuses in Jesustown." He turned the wheel hard, swinging the big truck around and backing it against the loading dock of an old brick warehouse. It was too dark and wet for Gabriel to read the name of the place.

The driver climbed down from the cab the moment the truck stopped moving and disappeared around the side. Gabriel listened to the sound of the trailer door opening and boxes sliding out. The driver appeared by his window a moment later, pushing a dolly loaded with boxes and gesturing for Gabriel to follow him in.

"Come on. I'll introduce you."

He didn't want to get out of the truck and back into the rain, but Gabriel climbed out and followed the driver. After a few steps the old man stopped.

"Grab this for me, will you?" he said, nodding to the dolly piled with boxes. "I got to find the damn paperwork."

Gabriel tipped the dolly back, letting the load settle onto his body. It was surprisingly heavy. The old man was stronger than he looked. He'd have to remember that.

As they reached the door, the driver gave a loud "Aha!" and pulled a pink packing slip from his right rear pocket. He held the warehouse door open for Gabriel and followed him in.

A balding man with a beer gut and ballpoint pen behind his ear was counting boxes on a loading pallet and ticking off boxes on a piece of paper on a clipboard.

The driver called out, "What's the good word, Sonny?"

The balding man looked up and his face broke into an easy smile.

"How are you doing, ramblin' man? Haven't seen you in a coon's age."

Gabriel watched them shake hands and talk bullshit. Annoyed, he stood the dolly upright, tired of holding the weight.

"Who's the sprog?" asked Sonny, glancing at the boy.

The driver held out his hand in Gabriel's direction.

"This is Gabriel. He's helping me out tonight."

Sonny held out his hand and Gabriel shook it.

"Any friend of this road hog is welcome around here." He turned back to the driver. "What've you got for me tonight, good sir?"

The driver handed Sonny the paper he'd fished from his back pocket. Sonny attached it to his clipboard, glanced at the dolly and nodded. He pointed to an open area near the pallet he'd been counting earlier.

"You can drop those right over there, son."

I'm not a goddamn pack mule, thought Gabriel, but he kept quiet, not wanting to end up back in the rain. He leaned the dolly back, rolled it to where Sonny had indicated and began unloading boxes. It was late in the week, Gabriel knew. Friday night or maybe even Saturday. There was only a skeleton crew working. Just five other men spread out through the warehouse. As he unloaded the boxes, he listened to Sonny and the driver talking in low voices, laughing occasionally. He wondered if they were laughing at him. They wouldn't be laughing if he pulled the knife. He could have it out in less than a second if he wanted. He'd had plenty of practice and knew all the places you could pigstick a man without hitting bone.

He walked back to where Sonny was examining the paperwork. The bald man nodded to him.

"This feller's been telling me you might go out on the road with him. Looking for somewhere sunnier. I don't blame you. Me, I like the cold, but everyone's got to find their place in the world."

"Amen to that," said the driver.

Sonny ticked off a couple of boxes on the delivery slip, signed at the bottom and tore off a carbon. The driver folded it up and slid it into the same pocket from which he'd pulled the original.

He started to turn away, but stopped.

"I forgot the other thing, Sonny."

"What was that?"

The driver pulled the gun from his pocket so fast that Gabriel didn't know what was happening until he heard it go off. Sonny dropped the clipboard and fell to his knees, clutching his beer belly. He stayed kneeling and swaying until the driver lowered the .45 and shot him in the back of the head. Sonny went down hard. For a second, Gabriel couldn't breathe. He wanted to look up at the driver, but it felt like his eyes were stuck on Sonny's body by a powerful magnetic force. He didn't move until he heard the driver's voice.

"Hey. You just going to stand there? This is a work night. Come on."

The rest of the crew had scattered all over the warehouse at the sound of the first shot. It didn't seem to faze the driver. Gabriel watched in a kind of cold awe as he calmly walked the warehouse aisles shooting each man in turn. Like he knows exactly where they are, he thought.

The driver went into the enclosed dispatcher's office and Gabriel followed him. The driver had the gun pointed at something behind a battered wooden desk piled high with pink, yellow and green forms. When Gabriel got closer he saw the fifth warehouse worker in a fetal position on the floor. The man was in gray overalls and worn work boots. He shook like a child lost in a blizzard. When Gabriel was close enough to lean over the desk, the driver handed him the pistol.

"I saved this one for you. It's why you're here, ain't it? Why you got in my truck."

The driver kept the gun outstretched toward Gabriel. The boy stared at it, feeling his heart trying to beat its way out of his chest. He breathed and stared. He knew he was staring for a long time. It felt like years. The knife against his leg had gone cold, like it was strange and no longer a part of him. No, this wasn't exactly what he'd gotten into the truck for, but like before, he didn't want to end up back in the rain.

Gabriel reached out and took the gun. Pointed it at the man on the floor and pulled the trigger. He flinched at the deafening explosion. Gabriel looked at the driver, who had both hands clamped over his ears.

"Small rooms," the driver said and laughed. "Ain't they a bitch?"

The man on the floor moaned. They both looked at him.

"I think you missed, champ. Give her another go."

The man on the floor whimpered loudly.

"Shut up!" the driver shouted. "Can't you see the boy's trying to concentrate?"

Gabriel didn't hesitate this time. Bringing the gun up fast into firing position, he pulled the trigger. The man on the floor twitched, but there wasn't any blood. He'd missed again.

The driver came over and patted him on the shoulder.

"Don't feel bad. You're cold and tired. You'll get the next one."

The driver took the pistol and went to the warehouseman and kicked the sole of one of his shoes. He began to sing.

"When you're smiling, when you're smiling, the whole world smiles with you."

The man lowered his hands a little and looked up. The driver shot him through the right eye.

"We're done here, I think. You didn't spot anyone I missed, did you?"

Gabriel looked up from the body. It took him a second to register the driver's question. He shook his head.

SUSPECT ZERO

"No. He's the last."

"Let's do like that singer with the funny nose said and ease on down the road."

He took Gabriel's arm and led him out of the office, pausing only to steal a silver cigarette lighter off the dispatcher's desk. As they passed Sonny's body on the way out, the driver grabbed the dolly and took the signed delivery form off of the clipboard. He wadded it up and put it in the breast pocket of his shirt. Outside, he loaded the dolly back into the trailer while Gabriel got back into the truck cab.

A second later the driver climbed in and pulled the door shut. He reached behind Gabriel's seat and pulled out a green plastic trash bag. Slipping off his hunting jacket, he unbuttoned his shirt. Gabriel looked at him, at the man's calm, efficient movement. He took off the blood-splattered shirt, rolled it and the delivery form up and stuffed them into the plastic bag before tying the top and stuffing it back behind his own seat. Gabriel marveled at how the man had managed to shoot five men at close range without getting any blood on his coat. *It must be his favorite,* thought Gabriel, *and he doesn't want to have to bag it.*

The driver pointed to the glove compartment.

"Open it," he said.

Gabriel pushed the release and the door fell open. It was stuffed with purple nitrile gloves. The driver leaned back, reached behind Gabriel's seat and grabbed a clean T-shirt.

"Wear those next time," he said, pulling the shirt over his head.

Gabriel glanced at the driver's bare hands.

"You didn't wear gloves."

The driver held up his fingers in front of the boy's face.

"Don't need to. No prints," he said.

"How'd that happen?"

The driver shrugged, slipping on his hunting jacket. He fired up the eighteen-wheeler's big engine and they started to move.

"A gift of birth, I guess. I'm sort of special, but you already knew that, which is why you came looking for me."

121

The driver released the brake and eased the truck forward, back onto the rainy street.

Gabriel's voice was quiet, almost a whisper.

"Are you really him? I didn't really think you were real. I've been traveling for such a long time. I was starting to think you were just a story."

"I am a story, but not just a story."

"Suspect Zero," said Gabriel.

"I guess that's what they call me these days. Kind of funny-sounding if you ask me. Like a space satellite or some kind of oven cleaner."

Gabriel stared at the man, wondering, if he looked long and hard enough, would he be able to see through him?

"Are you a ghost?"

The driver shook his head, his eyes scanning the road ahead.

"Naw. I'm a man just like you, only different. Go ahead. Ask your questions, son. I know you have a million."

Gabriel couldn't talk right then. He looked out the windshield and then closed his eyes to the smeary wet light. He breathed in the scent of diesel fumes and pressed his back into his seat, letting the truck's vibrations rattle his bones, trying to lock into his memory all the sensations and feelings of the moment he met Suspect Zero. He'd waited for this moment for so long. It was like meeting the Headless Horseman or riding along with Godzilla. Had anyone in history single-handedly taken as many human souls as this ragged-looking man with the gray ponytail? And he never left any real clue as to who he was, where he came from or why he did what he did. He was the only name attached to hundreds of unsolved murders all across North America, not because any normal person believed in him, but because there was nothing else to call all those unsolved murders.

Gabriel's true-crime-book-reading friends said Suspect Zero's secret was that he was a man in constant motion, keeping to the road. That he never slept or ate. Gabriel didn't believe that shit before and he sure didn't believe it now that he was with him. The old man in the driver's seat was, no damn doubt about it, a man. But Gabriel knew he was something else, too.

"How did you know it was okay to take me with you back there? That I wouldn't freak out and call the cops?" he asked.

"First off, if you'd gone for the phone I'd have gutted you and hung you upside down from the rafters like a hog being cleaned for Sunday dinner. And second, I knew that wasn't going to happen. I recognized you the same way you recognized me. A killer knows a killer when he sees one. That's mostly why I picked you up. It's nice to have some company where I can kick back and just be my own self, you know?"

"Yeah."

Gabriel relaxed, knowing the man was right. It felt kind of good not to have to pretend anymore and hide what he really was.

"What kind of knife you got strapped to your leg? I noticed it when you first got in."

Gabriel was almost embarrassed. How stupid was he to try and hide a weapon from the Super Bowl champ killer of killers?

"It's a KA-BAR. It was my dad's in Nam. He was a Marine."

The driver held out his hand.

"Can I see it?"

Gabriel slid the knife from its sheath, but held on to it for a second, uncertain.

"Relax, kid. I told you. It's nice to act normal with someone. Our special kind of normal."

"The right kind of people normal."

"Exactly."

Gabriel handed Suspect Zero the knife. The killer hefted it in his hand, testing the weight of the thing. He twirled it between his fingers like a toy, like an extension of his body. Spun it like a top on the back of his hand. He flicked his wrist and the knife fell flat on his palm with a smack. He ran it once across his forearm and handed it back to Gabriel.

"Decent grip. Good weight and balance. Looks like it's seen some use, too. Yours or your old man's?"

"Mine, I guess. I don't think he used it much in the war. He gave it to me when I was ten and never asked about it again."

"You don't sharpen it with one of those cheap-ass grocery-store kitchen sharpeners, do you?"

"Never. Only by hand, slow and careful, with honing oil and a whetting stone."

"Good boy. A sloppy workman does sloppy work. You'd never catch a world-class chef using one of those plastic housewife sharpeners and they use their knives a lot more than we do. 'Course, I don't want to presume how you do your work. Maybe you're out hunting every day."

"No. I'm not looking to break any records."

The killer turned the wheel and they rounded a corner. He chuckled quietly.

"Liar," he said without malice. "You think about body counts all the time. You're a young man and young men are ambitious. You want to outdo your elders. That's good. Smart young men need goals."

"How many people have you killed?"

"Truly, I have no idea. I gave up counting long ago. It's like getting laid. You count the first few because it's new and exciting, but after a few lays you've proved you can do it. After that, counting is kind of crude. Body count's not the thing for me. It's the work itself."

"Want to know how many I've killed?"

"Sure. Tell me."

"Ten. And I only started last Christmas."

"Ten's not too shabby. Ten puts you up there with Charlie Starkweather, but way behind that Green River fella. He got upwards of sixty. Chikatilo, that crazy Russian kid killer, got fifty-some-odd. And ten's not half as many as some folks say Billy the Kid got, and he was dead before he was twenty-three. You look a bit older than that, so you're already way behind. See what I mean about body counts? Going for it's never going to make you happy."

They rode in silence for a minute, but Gabriel couldn't help himself.

"Just a guess though. Not an exact number. How many?"

"No idea. Seriously."

SUSPECT ZERO

Gabriel looked out at the buildings as the killer maneuvered the truck easily down unmarked service roads between the warehouses. He imagined he could hear the heartbeats of the workers beyond the wet walls. He was sure Suspect Zero could. He wondered if the man could read his thoughts. If he could, he was going to have to be quick, but now he wasn't sure if the KA-BAR was going to be enough.

"I like knives. You use a knife much?" Gabriel asked.

"I've used pretty much every weapon a man can use to kill another living thing. Knives. Guns. Garrotes. Spears. Arrows. A little strangulation here. A hammer to the back of the head there. Even poison a few times, though that's pretty unsatisfying since you want to be gone by the time they keel over, so you don't get to see the fruits of your labor. The important thing is to mix up your methods. Keeps Johnny Law on his toes."

"It's harder now than when you started, huh?"

The killer pulled a cigarette from an inside pocket of his jacket and lit it one-handed with the stolen silver lighter.

"Used to be, I could roll into a town, eat half the citizens and roll out again when I was done. Bury my clothes and boots and that was that. Now it's all DNA, chemical trace analysis and carpet-fiber databases. They can track you through credit cards. Toll booths. Cell-phone towers. There's cameras everywhere and they have biometric facial recognition software."

"Seems kind of unfair if you ask me," Gabriel said. "I thought about throwing Daddy's knife away after the first couple of times I used it, but I couldn't."

The killer nodded.

"Just keep moving. That's the best way nowadays. You do your work and get over the state line before anyone knows what's happened. The simplest methods are the best and moving'll do for now."

"Driving this truck must be a good job for you."

"The best. And I get paid well, too." He turned to Gabriel. "That thing back at the warehouse. Don't sweat it. Everyone misses from time to time. We'll get your body count up. You'll see."

The killer craned his neck at something ahead. Gabriel couldn't see anything until they were just a few yards away. *The old man must see in the dark like a goddamn bat,* Gabriel thought. The truck came to a stop on a street corner by an unlit bus stop. Three pretty girls in short dresses and high heels were huddled together holding damp newspapers over their heads so their hair wouldn't get wet. The tallest of the girls, a heavyset redhead, was still waving at them as they stopped. The killer nodded for Gabriel to open his door. He leaned across the boy.

"You ladies look like you're in need of a lift."

"Can you? We've been waiting a goddamn hour for the bus."

"You'll have to squeeze in the back. There's stuff there. It'll be a wee bit tight."

"That's okay," said the smallest and youngest of the three, a pretty blonde with hazel eyes and freckles. Gabriel thought she looked a lot like Penny Clark, a girl who'd lived down the street from him all through grade school, junior high and high school. He'd loved her the whole time and of the ten he'd done, hers was the only kill that hurt to remember. She was his first. It was on a balmy summer night parked at the old reservoir. He hadn't planned it and it wasn't fun at all. It was too quick and clumsy. And wet. He hadn't expected that much blood. In the end, after he weighed Penny down with rocks and dumped her in the reservoir, he had to burn everything, his bloody clothes and secondhand Camaro. He'd loved that car.

When the three girls had wedged themselves into the back behind their seats, the killer let off the air brake and the truck moved back into the street. He gave Gabriel a quick smile and nod. His eyes looked darker than before, like a wolf's.

"Thanks a lot, mister. We're just trying to get to Club Wasteland and this silly bitch's car broke down," said the blonde. Gabriel was relieved that her voice wasn't anything like Penny's. The brunette next to her crossed her arms and pretended to pout.

Suspect Zero asked, "Didn't your mamas tell you girls it's dangerous to hitchhike?"

SUSPECT ZERO

The redhead leaned forward between their seats.

"We're dangerous girls," she said.

"Uh-oh," said the killer, looking at Gabriel. "I think we might be in trouble."

The girls laughed.

The redhead said, "I'm Julia. Where are you men headed tonight?"

"It's a work night for my young friend and me. No rest for the wicked. Say hello to the nice girls, boy."

"Hi. I'm, uh, Gabriel," he said. He could see some of Julia's red hair out of his peripheral vision, but he didn't want to turn his head in case he saw Penny.

"You're cute, Gabe. You sure it's a work night for you, too?"

"Definitely for him. He about screwed the pooch on our last job, so he's going to make up for it on the next. Aren't you?" The old man turned his wolf eyes on Gabriel. He slipped a hand into his hunting jacket and slid out the .45, tucking it under his leg with the grip out just a little.

Julia leaned back and whispered something to her friends. They all laughed, high-pitched and a little sloppy. Gabriel wondered if it was about him. He realized they were drunk. He set his hand on the knife.

"No fair keeping secrets in the cab," said Suspect Zero. "First rule of trucking, ladies."

The blonde spoke. "Rachel thinks that maybe you're, you know. I mean this is like a rolling bedroom. Maybe you two are a little Brokeback Mountain?"

The killer glanced back over his shoulder at the drunken girls. All three of them started laughing. He elbowed Gabriel in the ribs and the boy smiled nervously.

"You hear that, boy? They think we're fruit salad. A couple of dandelions. Tell them."

Gabriel half turned in his seat.

"Uh no. It's not. We're not homosexuals."

The girls burst into laughter.

The brunette repeated "homosexuals" in a low voice, mimicking him.

Gabriel slid the KA-BAR out of its sheath.

Suspect Zero laughed along with the girls.

"Naw. It's not like that, girls. We're a couple of true-blue all-Americans and straight as apple pie." He hooked a thumb at Gabriel. "The quiet one here is my apprentice."

"Why does a truck driver need an apprentice?"

"'Cause the boy needs schooling. You think it's easy reading a map and pissing in a jar while doing sixty down the interstate?"

Together the girls made an *ewww* sound.

"I never tried," said the blonde.

"Give it a go sometime. Expand your horizons."

The brunette spoke up for the first time.

"You don't have any of those jars back here, do you?"

"No, little lady. They get chucked out the window over bridges and at parked highway patrol cars."

He grinned at the girls as they whispered to each other. Julia leaned forward between their seats.

"Too bad we didn't meet you two earlier. Maybe we could have walked on the wild side tonight." The blonde and brunette fell on each other trying to stifle giggles.

"Never say never, girls." The killer turned his nearly black eyes to Gabriel. "What do you think, son? Should we take these ripe young ladies on Mr. Toad's Wild Ride?"

"I... I don't know," he said, moving the knife from down his leg and up into his coat.

The killer shook his head in mock disdain.

"You see? It's not so much that I need an apprentice as the boy needs a teacher. He can't even recognize Heaven when it's breathing over his shoulder."

"You talk funny, mister. I like it," said Julia. She rested her hand on Gabriel's arm. His body stiffened and he sat up straighter.

"Why thank you, Julia. I like how you smell," said the killer.

SUSPECT ZERO

The brunette leaned forward between the seats and pointed.

"Can you turn left up here?"

"Sure."

The killer jerked the wheel right hard enough that Gabriel and the girls slid against in their seats and hit the wall. They were on a narrow pitch-black block where all the streetlights had burned out. Gabriel saw the killer slip the pistol out from under his leg a little and pull back the hammer.

"Sorry, girls. Guess I heard wrong. The boy and me'll get you sorted out in just a minute."

"What's with all the bags back here? They smell kind of funky," said the blonde.

"I apologize for that," the killer said. "Dirty laundry is part of the work and work has been messy lately. Leaks. Busted fan belts. A little blood, too. Everyone is skinning their knuckles and worse in this line of work. Isn't that so, Gabriel?"

The boy nodded in reply, feeling Julia's fingers flex on his shoulder.

"Why don't you dig under your seat, son? Put on some music for the ladies." He turned to Julia and flashed her a grin. "Something loud to cover up the sound of screams."

Julia smiled back and slapped his arm playfully.

"Dirty old man."

"When the wolf smells chicken he knows it's dinnertime."

The killer made two more sudden turns.

"Here," said the brunette.

"Here? Here seems downright impolite."

Julia pointed at dim lights ahead. "Club Wasteland's right up there by the corner."

The killer squinted.

"Really? Well I'll be damned. I've been driving these streets for days and never noticed. Looks like fun. Wish I'd known about it earlier."

"It's probably not your kind of place," said the blonde.

"Don't judge a book by its cover, girls. You never know who you're going to meet on a night like this." He let the hammer down on the gun and pushed it back under his leg.

"Open the door for the young ladies, Gabe."

Gabriel leaned forward as the three girls slid out from behind him and stepped down into the street. Julia gave his thigh a squeeze as she left.

"Thanks, mister," she called.

"My pleasure, girls. You have a nice time tonight. Take a walk on the wild side for me and the boy."

"We'll do our best," Julia said.

"Hey Gabe," called the blonde.

He looked at her. Penny stared back.

"Yeah?" he said.

She smiled at him. "Good luck with the pissing lessons."

The girl laughed and the killer joined in. Gabriel pulled the door closed.

They pulled away and when Gabriel looked out the window the girls waved to him and blew kisses. He gave them a small wave back.

He turned to the killer.

"You let them go."

Suspect Zero slid the gun from beneath his leg and put it back in his pocket.

"You noticed that, did you?"

"You had your gun out."

"And you had your knife. You waiting for an engraved invitation?"

Gabriel stared ahead not knowing what to say.

Suspect Zero backhanded him gently on the arm.

"I was just messing with you," said the killer. "I wasn't going to hurt 'em. Bunch of drunk girls? Too obvious. Too easy. We're the random factor made flesh. What we do transcends regular people's notions of reason, which means some get to live and others die and no one but us knows why. Tonight those girls'll run wild and tomorrow they'll hear about what happened at the warehouse back yonder. They'll tell their friends that they were stranded right by there. How they could have run into the killers if a couple of friendly fags hadn't picked them up. See what I'm saying? Knowing how close they came, each of those girls carries a little piece of us with them and when they tell their friends about tonight they'll pass it on to them. And then they'll pass it on. That's how legends start. That's the beginning of immortality."

Gabriel looked at the killer hard, like he'd never seen him before.

"Immortality? All these fucking rules? This isn't fun. When does it get to be fun?"

"Fun? You think this is Pac-Man? This is work. *The* work. We can take joy in it, try to make each kill as lively as possible, but fun and games aren't why we're here."

It's why I'm here, Gabriel thought. His stomach burned. This wasn't what he'd been looking for at all. Finding Suspect Zero, getting him at arm's length from his blade wasn't going to be like this. It was supposed to be perfect black madness. Racing engines, burning cars and the road boiling under their feet. Dice with devil heads and a landscape of pale skin with sticky red tracings like all the roads they would travel, crushing the weak, the stupid and the innocent under their wheels. And when he'd taken what he could from the man, there'd be the explosion of pleasure when he ripped Dad's KA-BAR across the older man's throat and took the truck as his prize. That's how it was supposed to be. *Instead, here I am with a scrawny, fucked-up old Ward Cleaver. I swear to God, one more piece of advice and the knife comes out.* He didn't need this "Killing for Dummies" bullshit.

Gabriel asked, "How do you choose them?"

"We can talk business later. You hungry? I could use a bite."

SUSPECT ZERO parked the truck on the street next to an all-night convenience store. The parking lot was littered with broken beer bottles and strewn garbage from where someone had kicked over one of the cans. So many rocks had been thrown through the lighted sign over the door all Gabriel could read was NITE MART.

Before the killer got out Gabriel said, "At least tell me something real. How long have you been doing this?"

"Drivin' this truck?"

"You know what I mean."

Suspect Zero looked thoughtful.

"I read somewhere that scientists reckon the first humans settled in North America somewhere between twenty and thirteen thousand years ago."

"So?"

The killer smiled. "I figure I was about fifteen minutes behind them. Come on. Let's get some grub."

"You sure you're not a ghost?"

"Cross my heart and hope to die. I'm just here like you, to take a walk on the wild side."

Inside the store a boy behind the counter thumbed through a motorcycle magazine. His acne was bad and he looked young. Gabriel wondered if it was legal for a kid his age to be selling liquor.

"Where do you keep the Bud?" asked Suspect Zero.

"Cooler in the back," said the boy without looking up from his magazine.

"Thanks."

The killer pulled the boy over the counter like he weighed nothing. He held him with one hand while he pulled a knife from behind his back and jammed the blade into the side of the boy's throat. When he removed it, blood fountained from his neck, out and onto the liquor bottles behind the counter.

The killer stepped back to the front door. It was the cheap aluminum kind with a lock on the inside. He turned the lock and tested the door. It held. Gabriel was surprised that no one in the store had noticed the attack, but it had been so fast and quiet.

Off to their right, a couple was going through bags of potato chips. A lone man with his back to them was loading cans of soup into a plastic basket. Three teenage boys were huddled by the beer cooler, trying to block the open door with their bodies. It was the lamest attempt at shoplifting Gabriel had ever seen. Either they had no clue about what they were doing or they knew the counter man was scared enough not to stop them.

Suspect Zero's voice came from right next to his ear.

"Good eye. I figured those boneheads by the beer would be good for you. Got your knife?"

Gabriel nodded.

"Here," said the killer and pressed a pistol into the boy's hand. "Always carry backup. I've got more. I think this is a garrote situation for me. Happy hunting," he said. He pulled two small pieces of wood wrapped in wire from his coat pocket and quietly went down the aisle, making his way to the man reading ingredients on soup labels.

The gun felt weird in Gabriel's hand. He'd gone shooting with his dad, but he'd never shot anyone. He put it in his pocket and unsheathed the knife, heading for the back of the store. After all the bullshit and chatter in the truck, it felt good to move his legs again. He looked at the boys as they whispered and argued about who should carry the beer under his jacket.

But he'd never gone for anyone he never knew before, much less three. He didn't even know if they were armed. He looked over his shoulder and caught the killer's eye. The older man gave him a smile and mimed slipping the garrote around the man's throat and pulling. A man in his element. Gabriel breathed evenly, trying to match the old man's ease.

He caught the first boy in the right kidney, jamming the knife hilt deep into his back. The boy screamed and fell forward onto his face, beer bottles exploding under him. Gabriel looked at him. Guess he wasn't the one who was going to carry. When he looked up, the other boys were frozen in place. He knew that look. The boys' minds were still trying to understand what they'd just seen. One at a time they searched Gabriel's face. *They want to know if they know me and I'm someone they have a beef with.* He stepped over the fallen boy's body and the nearest boy, tallest, reached under his jacket for something. He had the gun halfway out when Gabriel swung the blade across his body, hitting hard at the boy's wrist and cutting deep enough that the tendons and muscles stopped working. The boy dropped the gun. Gabriel lunged for him while he was still in shock, stuck his knife into the boy's belly, twisting the blade slightly as he pulled up so the wound wouldn't close.

He looked again. The third boy was running for the front door. Thinking he could push it open and escape, the boy bounced off the locked door. Screaming hysterically, he shook the door's aluminum handle and clawed at the glass. Gabriel didn't rush. He knew the boy's mind was too far gone to figure out that all he had to do was flip the lock right above his head.

It had taken Gabriel a long time to learn to throw the KA-BAR accurately. It was heavier than most throwing knives and the technique was a little different. He gripped it by the blade and threw it hard. He'd never thrown a knife at anyone's back before and for good reason. Just like he was afraid it would, the knife dug into the boy's shoulder blade a couple of inches, hung there and fell to the floor. There was too much bone in the back. You'd have to be William Tell to make a kill throwing it there. Still the blow to the shoulder blade had sent the kid facedown on his knees. He was crying and screaming something in Spanish, snot dripping from his nose. Gabriel rushed him, but at the last minute the boy spotted the knife, grabbed it and held it in front of him. Gabriel tried to stop, but he slipped on the boy's blood and fell forward, landing an inch from the blade.

There was an explosion from behind Gabriel's back and the boy's body slammed against the door and slid down, a gaping hole in its chest. Gabriel looked over his shoulder and saw Suspect Zero leaning over the shelves a couple of rows back, his gun smoking. He nodded to Gabriel. Gabriel nodded back and headed to him.

When he got to the killer's aisle, Gabriel found the soup man on the floor surrounded by dislodged cans. His head was almost severed from his body. The wire had cut cleanly all the way through skin, cartilage and muscle. All that held the head attached was the vertebrae at the back on the man's neck.

The killer had the couple cornered at the end of the aisle. He waited there for him.

When Gabriel reached him the killer said, "Good work with the boys. I know you would have finished the last one, but I had the shot, so what the hell."

"It's cool. Thanks," Gabriel said.

"Glad you don't mind some collaboration."

Suspect Zero turned his attention back to the couple. They were a couple of Goth kids, pale and skinny, dressed in shades of black and red.

The killer said, "What are you in the mood for tonight?" He pointed his pistol at the girl. "White meat?" He pointed the gun at the boy. "Or dark?"

Gabriel stood where he was, breathing hard. His throat had gone dry. He looked at his bloody hands.

He looked at Suspect Zero.

"I lost my knife."

"That's okay. I'll choose for you," he said, and shot the boy between the eyes.

Gabriel said, "I thought we were supposed to mix up how we kill. Guns twice tonight?"

Suspect Zero showed him his pistol.

"Different gun. Different caliber. Sometimes you have to improvise. I decided to do a quick one for you. Help you get your sea legs back."

The killer stepped aside, leaving Gabriel a clear view of the girl. He reached into his pocket for the gun the killer had given him. Gabriel took it out and leveled it at the girl's face. She held up her hands in front of her, not whimpering, just making little animal noises. *She might have peed herself,* he thought. For just a second he was back at the reservoir looking into Penny's shocked and staring eyes. She'd made noises like that when the first knife thrust hadn't killed her and he'd had to go in for a second and third. Gabriel's throat was dry. She didn't look anything like Penny, but he could feel the breeze on his face, the wind cooling as it passed over the water. He let the gun drop a few inches. He felt the killer move up beside him.

"Is that how it is, boy? You're a true disappointment. I thought you were the right kind of people," said Suspect Zero. "Guess I'll take it from here."

He moved past Gabriel with his knife out and grabbed a handful of the girl's hair. There was a click as Gabriel pulled back the hammer on the gun. The killer stopped and turned to him. Gabriel pointed the gun at Suspect Zero. A slow grin spread across the killer's face.

"You rascal you, playing possum this whole time. And here's me starting to wonder if your heart was in the work. You planned to kill me this whole time and waited until you found your moment. That's cold, son. Good for you."

The killer spread his arms like wings and took a step forward.

"You want to take my truck? Want to be an eighteen-wheel nomad? Roam the country like a king taking lives and giving them to those you leave alive? You want to be me? Do it, boy. Do it. We both know it's why you flagged me down and why I stopped."

Gabriel looked at the floor where all the blood on his clothes had mixed with the rainwater to form a pinkish pool at his feet.

"That was before. I don't know now," said Gabriel. He glanced at the cowering girl. She slid down the wall to the floor. Her boyfriend's blood had spread across the linoleum and she was half-lying in it.

The killer made a sour face.

"You don't know? Bullshit. People never mean it when they say that. What they really mean is they know exactly what they want, but they're afraid to take it. Don't be one of them. You got the drop on me. You beat me. Take the shot."

Gabriel looked at the killer and then the girl. Gabriel put the pistol to his temple and pulled the trigger. The gun clicked. Nothing happened. It was empty.

Suspect Zero gently took the gun from Gabriel's hand.

SUSPECT ZERO

"I told you a killer knows another killer when he sees one. You never hand a killer a loaded gun."

Without turning, keeping his eyes locked on Gabriel's, Suspect Zero shot the girl. Gabriel watched as the man walked down the aisle, then stood there waiting at the door. A few seconds later he followed.

The killer unlocked the door and said, "The kid behind the counter. Take his wallet and whatever's in the till. This'll just be a robbery gone sour."

"What about the security camera?"

"It isn't working. I can tell."

Gabriel did what he was told, stuffing the wallet and cash into the pockets of his peacoat. Suspect Zero pushed open the door and shoved Gabriel out. He'd left the truck idling. They got in and they started moving almost immediately, driving in silence for a few minutes. When Suspect Zero took the on-ramp to the freeway out of town, Gabriel finally spoke.

"If I'd've shot you back there, would I have become you?"

"You'd have become something. More than what you are, but no. You wouldn't become me."

Gabriel touched the sticky blood on his chest and legs.

"I don't think I want to do this anymore. I want it to be over. Can you help me out?"

"Kill you? I'm afraid it doesn't work that way. You want to sacrifice yourself, go feed the homeless for Jesus. I'm not interested in those who want to be taken. There's others for that kind of thing. There's no nourishment for me in suicides. For me eating suicides is like trying to eat the fog hanging in the empty spaces between the stones on a mountainside. There's nothing to sink your teeth into."

"If you're not a ghost, then what are you?"

They changed lanes several times. The killer turned the truck off the local freeway and onto the interstate.

"Please. I've got to know."

Suspect Zero reached up and pulled a cord, letting loose two long blasts from his air horn. He whooped with the sound.

"I'm a road shaker and a heartbreaker." They hit a straightaway and he looked at Gabriel. "But most of all, I'm the toll taker."

"What toll?"

"You asked me before if I was a ghost. I'm not. But I wasn't always such a grizzled bastard either. Hell, for the longest time I didn't have any form at all. You people called me all sort of nonsense back then. Devil. Old Wolf. Ogoun. Soo-oop-wa. Our Lord of the Flayed One. I grew two legs, two arms and two eyes. I walked on the ground because that was what I needed to do to be near you."

"Are you an angel?"

"Shut up and listen. Over ten thousand years you've been coming here. You walked here over ice bridges, marched up from the South and beached your ships on the coasts. You came to *me*. To the dirt. The mountains and the lightning. The rivers and the dust devils tearing up the Mojave. You wanted my blood and built your lives and homes on my flesh. Now I'm in your pavement and wires, your concrete, subways and sewers. I've always been here. I am this place. And you, every one of you, owes me a blood payment. Get it, boy? It's like this truck. It's my home. It's me and no one rides for free."

"You're God."

"Don't be stupid. But you're not the first who's thought that. I've been worshipped and exorcised. I've buried you people in blizzards and earthquakes. Cooked you in brush fires burning all the way from Mexico to the Yukon. I'm the price you pay for being here."

"You're all that and you still can't kill me?"

"I told you. I'm not an angel or your god. I'm not here to ease your pain. You're a nice kid. I wish I could help you out, but it's not my place."

Gabriel nodded thoughtfully, trying to absorb it all. His head was spinning. He only understood a little of what Suspect Zero said, but it was enough. Gabriel looked at the old man.

"You've been real nice to me tonight and I really appreciate it. I've been wandering around for so long. I'm glad I finally got to meet you. I hope you don't think I'm rude."

SUSPECT ZERO

"Rude how, kid?"

"I'm going to go now."

Gabriel pushed open the passenger door, stepped out and was gone.

The truck was doing sixty and the last thing the old man wanted to do was jackknife, so he eased on the air brakes and slowed enough that he could pull onto the shoulder and stop. He checked his mirrors, but didn't really expect to see the boy. He was probably a good half mile from where the kid had jumped. He got out of the truck and walked to the shoulder side. There was nothing to do now but wait. He lit a cigarette with the silver lighter. He finished one cigarette and was about to light a second when he saw Gabriel crest the nearby overpass. The boy had a slight limp where the bone stuck out of his left leg and his chest looked funny and puckered where the tires had run him over. His clothes were torn and he was covered in road rash. Other than that, the boy looked pretty presentable.

The killer put away the cigarette and lighter. When Gabriel reached him he helped the boy into the truck and got in on the other side.

"I'm proud of you, son," said Suspect Zero. "I couldn't help you, so you helped yourself. You doubted yourself tonight, but you came through in the end. You are the right kind of people."

"Can you help me now?"

"Absolutely. You smoke?"

"Yeah."

He handed the boy his cigarettes and the silver lighter.

"Keep them. You earned them."

They drove in silence. A few miles ahead, the old man took an exit Gabriel didn't remember as having been there before. Out the window, he watched as they pulled into an enormous truck stop. A bright sign stood over the parking lot. It read END OF THE LINE. He'd never noticed it before. How could he have missed something that big in all the times he'd hitched up and down this stretch of freeway? But he'd been alive back then. Maybe that made a difference.

His door opened and the old man helped him down. The night felt light and slightly unreal. The leg with the bone sticking out didn't hurt, but it wouldn't work right so he was slow getting across the lot to the diner.

Inside, the place was longer than a football field, lined with rows of booths and Formica tables. Gabriel couldn't even see the far end. The big parking lot hadn't been more than a quarter full of trucks and their drivers and passengers were spread out over so much space that even occupied, the diner looked empty.

The old man scanned their faces, spotted one fifty rows ahead and they headed to where a pretty, dark-haired young woman was sitting by herself, nursing a cup of coffee and a plate of corn fritters. The young woman looked up as she saw Suspect Zero and Gabriel.

She smiled an easy smile and said, "Hello, you old vagrant. Long time no see. Sit down and take a load off."

"Hello Crow, what do you know?" He and Gabriel sat down across from her in the booth. "I haven't hauled any special cargo for a while, so I haven't had a chance to stop in."

Crow, the young woman, glanced at Gabriel. She was beautiful. Her eyes were as dark as her hair, but not scary dark like Suspect Zero's eyes had been. Hers were soft. When he looked back at her, Gabriel felt something enter him. It was warm and curious, and as strange as the feeling was, he wasn't frightened. A moment later, it had passed.

"You must really be something for this bone picker to come out of his way like this," she said to Gabriel.

"He's been very nice to me."

She looked at Suspect Zero and cocked her head quizzically.

"Picking up strays? I never took you for sentimental."

"Call it old age. Call it helping out a colleague," he said.

"Those bones and crush marks don't look like your work."

"No. The boy did that himself. Straight up and out. Made the choice and did it like a man."

She took a sip of her coffee and drew in a breath.

SUSPECT ZERO

"Kid, if I give you a lift you know where I'm taking you, right? That old man next to you is special, but there's only one road for human killers. That includes suicides."

Gabriel nodded.

"It's okay. Everything is okay now."

Suspect Zero leaned over to Gabriel.

"Now's when you pay her."

Gabriel looked at him.

"She's a professional like me. Call her a psychopomp. And she doesn't haul freight for free."

Gabriel patted himself down, not sure what the old man expected of him. He still had the money from the convenience store in his pockets, but he was pretty sure money wasn't worth much here. Then he felt it in his pocket. He took out the silver lighter, set it down flat on the table and slid it to Crow. She picked it up eagerly.

"Shiny. Very pretty," she said.

"That enough to get the kid a ride?"

"First class. He can even ride up front with me like a big boy."

"Time for me to go," the old man said. He slid out of the booth and looked down at Crow. "Thanks for all your help, chickadee."

"Take care of yourself, road man."

"That's what I do."

The old man squeezed Gabriel's shoulder and said, "Try the peach pie before you go. It's the best you'll ever get." Then he turned and walked away.

Suspect Zero bought a cup of black coffee and a jelly donut, which he devoured on the way back to the truck. Inside the cab, he set the coffee in a holder on the dashboard. He took the pistol from his jacket pocket, reloaded it, wrapped it in plastic and stashed it back in the cooler.

He reached down and pulled a flat bog-iron box from under his seat. Inside were seven bone cups carved with runes. Inside each cup were slips of paper in a language only he could read. He pulled one slip of paper from each cup and set them on the dashboard. They read: MAN. 30S. BLOND. BANK. INSIDE. BUSINESS HOURS. HAMMER.

The killer sighed. This was going to take a little doing, but it would be a banquet when he pulled it off. Not fun, though. He wished the boy had stuck around long enough to understand that. Not fun. Just the work. The work and the blood that feeds the land.

BLACK NEUROLOGY— A LOVE STORY

Using my pull with an acquaintance at the city morgue, I convince the attending Medical Examiner to let me watch your autopsy.

He begins with a traditional Y incision, cutting two diagonals across your upper chest until they meet at your sternum, then a single long, straight slice down to your crotch. He opens you with a crack, snapping ribs and connective tissues, laying you open and bare, more exposed than you've ever been in a lifetime of extreme exposures. I stand quietly, a little behind the Examiner, clicking away, taking pictures with my phone.

This Examiner is a true professional, experienced and respected for both his precision and the speed of his work. But now that he's opened you, he's just standing there, looking down, his head craning slowly up and down the length of you. He reaches forward and pushes a finger into your abdomen, scooping out what he finds and pressing it quizzically between his fingertips. Your body appears to be packed with a pinkish-yellow modeling clay. The Examiner makes a face and scoops out more with his hands, trying to find his way through the muck to your organs. Without warning, he lets out a little yelp and pulls back his hands. He says that he felt something move inside you. Using forceps, he reaches tentatively into you and pulls something free—a hissing rattlesnake.

After disposing of the creature in the incinerator, he examines your insides further, this time using scissors and a metal probe. He soon hits a pocket of what looks like black tar. It oozes up through the clay, darkening it. The Examiner's probe drags new things from your gut. Rosaries. Straight razors. Old bottles of laudanum and arsenic. He finds your baby teeth. Leather wrist restraints. The hand-stitched belt your daddy used on you when you needed discipline

With his forceps, the Examiner digs into the thick clay and pulls out your heart. Instead of a fist of muscle, what he holds in the forceps is a glowing red coal, spouting a steady flame from the top and wrapped with barbed wire, like a miniature crown of thorns.

He turns and looks at me, holding up the glowing coal as if I might have an explanation. I shrug and snap a picture. "What's that?" I ask, nodding at your body. The Examiner turns to look and I reach around from behind, slicing his throat from the jugular to the carotid artery in one smooth motion, using the scalpel I stole from his instrument tray. He burbles once and I let him drop, bleeding into the cavity from which he'd extracted your burning heart. Snapping another quick photo, I run my hands down your throat, across the open halves of your chest, and along your legs, using my fingernails the way you always liked.

In the late 1990s, I read about new electronic scanning techniques that led to brain studies which revealed that our minds and bodies are all utterly unique. The neural pathways that mean pain and discomfort for some equal pleasure and contentment for others. The chemical compositions of our cerebral and spinal fluids can vary widely from person to person, perversion to perversion. Our desires are defined by our brains and our bodies are shaped by our desires. As William Blake once said, "Those who restrain desire, do so because theirs is weak enough to be restrained." The unrestrained, I wonder, watching the last of the

BLACK NEUROLOGY—A LOVE STORY

Medical Examiner drain into you, who knows everything the unrestrained are capable of?

There's a bubbling in the bloody clay. I touch you more insistently now. Your lips. Your thighs. I kiss your cold lips. Something rises from the muck. A hand. Then an arm. Another hand follows. I work my hand down your body and it begins to convulse in orgasm. In an instant, you pull free from the clay—up and out of your corpse. Covered in blood and muck like an infant, you're reborn from your own flesh, this stranger's blood, and our overwhelming desire. You rise up to your knees, breathe into your new lungs and open your mouth, searching for your voice. Finding it, you touch my cheek and say, "I told you I'd never leave you."

I wrap you in the Medical Examiner's lab coat and take you home.

FLAYED ED

In 1957, after the body of Bernice Worden was found strung up and gutted like a deer carcass in his barn, Ed Gein was arrested, declared insane and sent to Wisconsin's Central State Hospital, where he'd spend the rest of his life.

By 1959, the people of Plainfield, Wisconsin and the sheriff's department—who'd been first on the scene at Ed's farm—had done a pretty good job of putting Ed's grisly crimes out of their minds and getting the town back to where it had been two years earlier.

By 1960, no one at the sheriff's department ever spoke about the crimes and only the youngest and greenest recruits were dumb enough to ask about them. The weeks of counting scalps and putting human bones into evidence bags were long behind them and they'd returned to their more familiar duties, pulling drivers from ditches in the winter, investigating domestic disturbances and bringing in drunken brawlers on the weekends. There had never been many murders in Plainfield and since Ed had gone off to the loony bin, not a single cannibal psychopath.

By 1961, Ed's memory, his human skin furniture and the strange "skin suit" he'd sewn from the desiccated flesh of female corpses, had dulled to occasional Halloween water cooler jokes. But Ed's presence never disappeared entirely and he continued to haunt the area around Plainfield right through the millennium.

Then the flies came.

Then the rains of blood.

Then all of Plainfield's children went blind in a single night.

Deep in the eastern sky, the source of light, fertility and life, Xipe Totec—Aztec warrior, the God of suffering, the lord of Spring, the Ruler of the East, often called the Blood Red Mirror by his followers—stirred from his sleep. He became an eagle and rode the winds looking for his offerings and sacrifices, but found none. Starving and enraged, Xipe Totec frowned and blood and disease fell from the heavens.

Back in 1978 Ed was been relocated to the Mendota Mental Health Institute in Madison, Wisconsin. He died there in 1984 after serving as the hospital's barber for five years. No one in the hospital saw any problem with giving Ed access to razors and scissors. Ed had never killed or even hurt a man. Ed's interests were fixed exclusively on women. What no one in the hospital, especially the doctors, understood was why. What the doctors called "schizophrenia accompanied by psychosexual dementia," Ed called "God."

He knew the shape of the sacrifices that the old, forgotten deities found acceptable, the blood they demanded. The skin dances they craved were fed through the flesh of wise women, not foolish men. What tormented Ed more than being arrested, more than being locked up for so many decades, was that he hadn't finished his flayed offerings or properly done the offering dance. During his first years at the hospital Ed was afraid. Eventually he understood that he'd be long dead before the gods noticed the absence of their sustenance. In the spring of '84, when the cicadas chirped and mayflies appeared in swarms, Ed collapsed and was taken to the infirmary for the last time. It was thrilling. He knew that death was finally coming for him.

Xipe Totec, Our Lord of the Flayed One, is represented to mortals by a mask found in many Aztec archaeological digs. He's depicted as a man's face with blank eyes and what appears to be a mouth inside a larger,

FLAYED ED

toothless mouth. In reality the smaller mouth is that of the Aztec priest who wears the skin of a sacrifice, bloody side out. Blood and flesh are Xipe Totec's nourishment. The dance in the flayed skin is the platter on which Xipe Totec's meals are served. But being good, god-fearing Christians, none of the residents of Plainfield, Wisconsin knew any of this.

Around the millennium, when the blood rains first fell, Plainfield suffered terribly as they prayed fervently and sincerely to the wrong god. Their cattle convulsed and died in the fields. Ranchers and dairymen thought their herds had contracted mad cow disease. Hazmat-suited men from the Centers for Disease Control slaughtered and burned the cattle in the fields. Still, the CDC couldn't tell the farmers why their apples bled like gutted warriors when they picked them or why the kernels inside their corn crops were the rotten teeth of the dead.

News crews from around the world invaded Plainfield's sad, wet streets. The Army Corps of Engineers built levees to hold back the swollen, blood-colored rivers. The governor finally declared martial law and National Guard troops moved in to keep order. The soldiers were soon felled with boils and a new Ebola-like disease that left them bleeding through their skin. And the flies never left, but spread from Plainfield out across Wisconsin, bringing disease and the awful red rains with them.

In the eastern sky, Xipe Totec's appetite and anger grew. He couldn't understand why, after all his warnings and punishments, the mortals wouldn't simply make the sacrifices that would end their misery.

And from somewhere high above, Ed looked down on it all and laughed an old coot's laugh.

A SANDMAN SLIM
CHRISTMAS CAROL

I'm not saying that Christmas is for assholes, but a whole lot of assholes seem to love it. All the holly and mistletoe, the dying trees and jingle bells that give you a migraine. And don't get me started on the packs of drunk Santas wandering the streets like they invented bad behavior. One bumped into me a couple of years ago and wanted a light. When I said no, he took a swing at me, so I gave him a light after all. I set his beard on fire. Who's jolly now, motherfucker? I know I should get over it, but ever since I broke out of Downtown, the holidays get on my nerves.

Don't get me wrong. My friends are great and I like exchanging gifts with Candy, but I need a little down time too. Alone as in no goddamn anyone. That's why I came out here to Teddy Osterberg's estate in Malibu. It's fenced off now since the mansion burned, so it's empty except on Halloween when all the local Goth kids come here to frolic in Teddy's collection of cemeteries. It's the perfect place for a good brood on the night before the blessed event hallelujah.

I took the Hellion Hog out here just before sunset with my two best friends: a fresh pack of Maledictions and a full flask of Aqua Regia. After a couple of cigarettes and a couple of swigs of the good stuff, I sit back on Teddy's overgrown lawn, looking out at the ocean and thinking about absolutely nothing. I'm starting to relax and actually feel pretty good. Naturally, that's when everything goes to hell.

Out of the corner of my eye, I see a guy walking down the hill nearby. He's wearing nothing but a baggy bathing suit and carrying a coffin lid. Part of my brain goes, *What the holy fuck is that?* but the smarter part says, *Who cares?* So, I go back to smoking and drinking, letting Lloyd Bridges get on with whatever he has planned. But the glowing end of the Malediction gives me away. As he's about to pass me, he glances over and stops dead in his tracks. Just stares at me until, in the moonlight, I realize that he's a fucking vampire. He keeps staring because I don't say anything. Finally, he gets up the nerve to speak.

"Oh shit. You're him, aren't you?"

"I don't know what him you're talking about and I don't care."

"I mean the crazy one. The one who kills my kind on sight."

There goes my serene night out.

"First off, I'm not crazy. Not all the time. And I don't kill your kind on sight. You have to do something stupid first. And last, my name is Stark. Don't call me *the one*. It makes me sound like furniture. 'I've looked for this settee my whole life. It's the one.'"

"Uh. Okay," he says. "Are you going to kill me?"

I look him over. The vampire looks young. He was scrawny in life and he's scrawny in death. He's got long blond hair held back with a rubber band or something. Pukka shells around his neck. A real little beach bunny.

"Nah," I say. "It's Christmas. And I wouldn't kill the ghost of Frankie Avalon."

He frowns.

"Who?"

"Frankie Avalon. You know, *Beach Blanket Bingo* and *Bikini Beach*."

The vampire shakes his head.

"Never heard of him."

A Sandman Slim Christmas Carol

Now I shake my head.

"Christ. How old are you?"

"Twenty-four."

"You're just a little baby bloodsucker. When did you turn?"

He sets down the coffin lid. Even for a vampire, the thing looks heavy to hold.

"When I was twenty."

"What are you doing out here?"

"I come out here every Christmas. I surf, only I can't do it during that day so..."

I wave him off.

"Yeah. I get it. What's with the coffin lid?"

He wraps his arms around himself and looks around like he's thinking of running, only he knows he's not fast enough to outrun me or a bullet dipped in Spiritus Dei.

The shroud eater says, "Are you just fucking with me? Like a cat with a mouse before it kills it?"

I look at him hard.

"I don't know yet. What's with the coffin lid. And what's your name?"

"I'm Brayden. And the lid is my board."

I take a drag off the Malediction.

"Well shit. It's Christmas and I'm stuck with a vampire named Brayden."

For a second the fear leaves his eyes and he says, "Hey, I didn't choose the name. Blame my mom. She wanted to call me Bentley, but my dad said no. So, they compromised on Brayden."

"Family drama. I know something about that. Sit down, Brayden."

He hesitates. Looks around again.

"You're not going to kill me?"

I crush the Malediction under my boot.

"The night is young. Let's see where it takes us."

He sits holding the coffin lid against his chest like a kid clutching a teddy bear.

"Is that really your surfboard?" I say.

He nods and runs a hand over the mahogany.

"The crowd I hang out with since I turned, they don't understand the beach. They're all older than me and they grew up in the city. Not a surfer in the bunch."

"That still doesn't answer my question. With the coffin lid?"

He doesn't say anything for a minute, then, "I can't have a regular board these days. If they saw it, they'd never stop giving me shit. So, every Christmas I come out here, steal the top off a coffin in one of the cemeteries back there and catch some waves."

"You clever boots, you. Can you actually ride that thing?"

He nods.

"It takes some getting used to. The weight is off and there's no fin, but I can make it work."

I think for a minute.

"I guess whoever invented surfing must have started off on flat boards too."

"Sure," he says. "People have been surfing for hundreds of years. I'm just bringing it back to its roots again."

"Good for you, kid. Some people invent cures for cancer, you ride the waves on granddad's dirt box."

We don't talk for a minute and he looks nervous again.

"You're thinking about killing me, aren't you?"

"I'm just wondering if you might have bit anyone I know."

His shoulders slump.

"I'm sorry if I did."

"That makes everything fine."

"Can I ask you something else?"

"Shoot."

He scoots around on his butt a little so he's facing me.

"What are *you* doing out here?"

I think for a minute.

"Yeah. What *am* I doing here? Hiding from my friends, I guess."

A Sandman Slim Christmas Carol

"We have that in common, at least."

"I guess we do."

He looks out at the waves with a kid's kind of longing and says, "How old are you?"

I look at him.

"What do you care?"

"I'm just curious."

"I'm thirty-something. Maybe thirty-two. I stopped counting when I was Downtown."

"Wow," he says. "You're lucky."

I have the Aqua Regia flask halfway to my mouth and say, "Exactly how the fuck am I lucky?"

The kid looks out at the ocean again.

"It's just, you did so much. I mean, look at me. I was twenty when I changed. I've never even had a legal drink."

I gulp the Aqua Regia and say, "Don't kid a kidder. You were drinking when you were fourteen."

He shakes his head.

"Yeah, but it's not the same. I missed a lot of that, you know, regular people stuff. Don't get me wrong. Being a vampire has some cool things going for it, but I lost all my old friends. They're all in college. Look at me. Digging around in a graveyard waiting to see when you get bored and decide to kill me."

Oh hell. This little jerk is actually making me feel sorry for a vampire. I think about going to Hell when I was just nineteen and emerging eleven years later, completely out of my mind and looking to kill the whole world.

I say, "I guess we both missed a lot."

Brayden looks up and says, "The moon is nice tonight."

"Bright enough to see Santa and his reindeer."

"Did you believe in Santa when you were a kid?"

"Of course."

"I didn't. My dad, Dr. Delano—psychiatrist to the stars—didn't believe in filling his children's brains with commercial nonsense, so no Santa for us. No elves or even Christmas movies."

I frown at him.

"Not even when you were like little bitty little?"

"Nope. Never. The doctor wouldn't permit it."

"That's fucked up."

"My sister cried every year. I hate my old man."

I almost say join the club, but I still haven't decided what I'm going to do with Brayden the vampire, so I don't want to get too chummy.

Out of nowhere he says, "I miss my dog."

I put my head in my hands.

"Holy shit, Brayden. You are the most pathetic vampire I ever met. I mean, it's been four years. Time to move on, man."

"Is that what you did when you got back from, you know, Hell? You just forgot everything that happened before?"

"Some, I guess. Not all of it. Some things still hurt. Some tear you up inside so you can't breathe sometimes, but you learn to live with the wreckage and keep moving."

He gives me a sneer.

"Now you sound like my old man."

I raise a finger.

"Kid, if you want to die fast tell me again how I sound like a psychiatrist."

"Sorry."

I look out over the ocean. The moon is bright and the water shimmers in its glow. I pull out the Maledictions and light one—just as a star shoots across the horizon.

Goddammit.

I hang my head down for a minute, take a breath and say, "Get out of here, Brayden."

He's clutching the coffin lid to his chest again.

"What?" he says.

"Go. Get out of here. Go do your silly kid shit. Have fun or whatever vampires do when they're not killing people."

He slowly gets to his feet, not sure if I'm serious or not. "Really?"

A Sandman Slim Christmas Carol

I turn to him.

"But you never ever drink anyone in Hollywood, Brayden. Understand me? That's my turf. Go out to Beverly Hills and Brentwood. Those fucks deserve it. But you stay out of Hollywood."

"Sure, sure," he says and picks up the lid. "I'll go now."

"Scoot before I change my mind."

A big goofy smile spreads across his face as he runs toward the water. At the bottom of the hill, he turns and shouts, "Merry Christmas!" before running off again.

I sit there for a while. It's a long way down to the water, but in a few minutes, I see a straight line cut across the Malibu waves heading for shore. Go for it, kid.

After watching Brayden make a couple of more runs, I think about leaving when I hear a woman's voice say, "Well, that was adorable."

I look around and a few feet away a red fox is sitting in the grass. It stares right at me when I say, "Did you just talk?"

"Of course I talked," says the fox. "Who the hell else is out here?"

I shake my head, sure I've had a little too much Aqua Regia. The fox sighs.

"No, you're not drunk. It's really me talking."

"I've seen some weird shit, but never talking animals. What the hell are you really?"

The fox looks at me with its shiny eyes.

"I'm your Christmas miracle, dumbass. Didn't you know that animals can talk on Christmas Eve? A nice church boy like you should know these things."

"It's been a while since I paid the Pope a visit."

The fox lies down in the grass.

"That was a nice thing you did for the kid."

I look at Brayden cutting through the waves below.

"You think so? I mean, he's a vampire. I should have probably ripped his head off."

"But you didn't. That's why I'm here."

"Don't you dare tell me Mr. Muninn sent you as some kind of shitty consolation prize for not murdering Dobie Gillis."

The fox laughs.

"No. I'm here because you didn't just make a reasonable choice, you made a kind one."

"Fuck that. What are you trying to sell? Life insurance? A quick way into heaven? Tell me."

"I'm not selling anything."

I look hard at the fox in the grass.

"You some kind of shapeshifter or something? You're going to turn into Godzilla and try to eat me? Just remember that I've got my gun and six little friends with your name on them."

"Wow. You really are high strung."

"No, I'm not. I just don't like being messed with."

"Sure. You keep telling yourself that."

I turn away from the fox.

"Shouldn't you be off somewhere eating vermin? Isn't what foxes do?"

It sits up again and stares daggers at me.

"Hey! What you call vermin I call dinner. And without things like me around, you'd be up to your ass in mice and rats, so show a little respect."

I put up a hand.

"Sorry. You do a great service. The mayor should give you a medal."

It nods at my flask.

"You drink that and you criticize what anyone or anything eats?"

"I said I was sorry. You know, for a Christmas miracle, you're kind of an asshole."

The fox yawns and comes a little closer.

"Forget it. I'm in a mood. I've been stuck out here for days. I usually live in Griffith Park. With all the tourists, there's good pickings there."

"How did you end up all the way out here?"

"There was a dead bird in the back of a pickup truck. I jumped in to get it, but the driver floors the thing before I can get out. This is the first place he slowed down, so I bailed and have been here ever since."

A Sandman Slim Christmas Carol

"How long?"

The fox swivels its ears around like it's not sure it heard me right.

"I don't know. What, do I have a desk calendar with Arbor Day and the Fourth of July? I'm a fox."

"Okay. Now who's high strung?"

"Sorry."

"It's okay. It's been a weird night for everyone."

"That was a nice favor you did for the kid."

"You said that already."

The fox gets a little closer.

"I know, but I was wondering if, seeing as how this is a special night, you might do one more favor?"

I stare at it.

"Like what?"

"Could you give me a ride into town? I miss my friends. I haven't seen my husband and kids in days..."

"You can't just walk?"

The fox glares at me.

"Look at the size of my legs. It would take me a month to get back. That's if I don't get hit by a fucking Maserati on a blind curve."

"Yeah. They drive like assholes out here."

The fox nods.

"Fucking Malibu."

I put the flask away.

"I don't know though. It's late. I should be getting back before Candy worries."

The fox trots over the last few steps and puts its front paws on my leg. It says, *"Please please pleeease.* You gave the kid a break and I'm your Christmas miracle. Be my miracle, shithead, and take me home."

"I don't know."

The fox crawls onto my lap. It feels small, warm, and fragile.

"Come on. Don't be a putz. I know. As a reward, I'll sing you Christmas carols all the way into town."

"Then I'm definitely not giving you a ride."

"*Pleeeeease.*"

I get up and the fox hops around my feet.

"Fine. Okay," I say. "But no carols."

"Cool. I can do that. But you do realize that you're missing a once in a lifetime chance, right? I mean, how many other foxes are offering to serenade you? Zero. That's how many."

"I'll just have to live with that. Come on. The bike's over here."

I settle on the hog and the fox jumps up onto the gas tank and stretches out. As I button my coat it trembles for a moment.

"It's kind of cool tonight, huh?" it says.

"A little."

"It's going to be a cold ride."

"You have fur."

"But you have a coat."

"I'm not giving you my coat."

"No. But we can share."

I hadn't finished buttoning up, so the fox shoves its head in the bottom of the coat, crawls up inside, and pokes its head out. I have to open the top button so it doesn't breathe in my face.

"See?" it says. "Everyone is toasty warm."

"Right."

"Come on. Hit it, Sandman Slim. Let's see what this baby can do."

"You asked for it."

I kick the hog to life and we blast up to the 101 and head east.

While the goddamn fox sings *Joy to the World* the whole way home.

Fuck my life.

Oh, and Merry Christmas, assholes.

THE AIR IS CHALK

There were three million people in L.A. when the party started. Now there's a few hundred scattered around in shopping mall emergency shelters, office buildings, and the subway tunnels. It's okay where I am, but most of the others I talk to by radio are running out of food and water, so they'll have to go scavenging soon. We'll be down to less than a hundred people left by the end of the month. If the Rollers don't get them at night, Floaters and Stingers will get them during the day.

That's just how things are now.

It's hard to stay focused on anything besides life and death. Each minute is a choice: stay inside and live or go outside and die. It was easier when there were other people here with me. Now that I'm the only one it's harder to justify waking up, much less staying alive. The army is gone. The government vanished. Even the crazy militias and Jesus freak true believers who fought the freaks are gone. No white knights or cavalry riding to the rescue.

We're alone.

Actually, I should say *they're* alone. The other shelters. I'm never alone.

I wear noise-canceling headphones all the time now and when I forget to recharge them, I hear voices screaming my name day and night.

The truth is, I'd feel sorrier for myself if I wasn't a big part of what happened. Maybe I'm the main reason. Hell, there's no maybe.

It was my fault.

Now that there's no one around to blame me, I can go over it and put the pieces together.

I'M WHAT you call a celebrity bodyguard. *Was* a bodyguard, excuse me. I've taken care of starlets, studio heads, corporate assholes, and even a few foreign diplomats. I was good at my job. Could turn on the charm when I had to. People appreciate that in a big guy. Everybody loves a gentle giant. And even though the giant might get sick of it, not showing it is part of the charm. I took good care of people and got paid well for it. My wife, Macy, was a casting agent at one of the big talent agencies and she was good at her job too. We were doing all right.

Then Bill fucked everything up by talking me into doing a job with one of his clients.

He'd phoned me just after noon and said, "Darla's parents are going home tomorrow, which means they have to go on the Universal Studios tour tonight. Darla will never forgive me if I don't take them."

"Seriously? It's been ten days since I had a night off and you want me to make it eleven so you can see a plastic shark?"

"It's my in-laws who want to see the goddamn shark. I'm just a victim of circumstance. Come on, man. I've covered for you plenty of times."

"And I've covered for you too. But I'll do this extra special favor for you now because I'm that kind of guy."

I could hear the relief in Bill's voice. "Thanks, man. You're a life saver."

"All part of the service, man. Now, what kind of run is it?"

"It's easy. You're going to play chauffeur from Beverly Hills straight down to LAX, then you're a free man."

"Damn. I hate having to take care of people and drive their asses too."

The Air Is Chalk

"I know, but it's what the client wants," said Bill. "He's squirrely. Rich as fuck and afraid of everything. Don't touch him. That's rule number one. Don't shake his hand or anything. Just get him in the car."

"Sounds delightful. Just text me the particulars and I'll be there."

"Thanks. You're a life saver."

"That's what I keep telling everyone."

I PICKED up Bill's client at 2 p.m. sharp at the Beverly Wilshire Hotel. I've done the Beverly Hills to LAX run so many times I could do it napping in the back with the passengers. The client's name was McKee. I recognized him because he's the one standing all by himself, far away from the crowd. Yeah, claustrophobic as shit.

"Mr. McKee?" I said. "I'm Paul, your driver. Would you like me to take your luggage?"

"Yes. Thank you," he said. I didn't get too close to him or bother asking about his attaché case, which he was clutching to his chest with both arms like it was the Lindbergh baby. When I opened the backseat door for McKee, he looked around inside before getting in. That and the attaché case said a lot and made me a little nervous. I studied the crowd for a minute before getting back in the limo. If there was trouble coming, I wanted to know from which direction. But I didn't see anything funny, so I steered us out of the hotel and headed for the airport.

McKee didn't say a word on the drive down, just stared out the window and checked his watch. And he never once let go of the attaché case. I've driven around enough show biz low-lifes and business creeps to know that there's only a few things McKee could be so worried about. The case was full of either embezzled cash or drugs. I glanced at him in the rearview mirror and our eyes locked for a second. He gave me a tight little smile, gripped the case tighter, and went back to staring at the traffic on the 405.

I had to tell someone about this ridiculous situation, but my wife would be at a business meeting this time of day, so I got out my phone and texted Alexandra, my girlfriend. She was a singer with her first single on the charts and a lot more on the way. She was also beautiful and young enough that the fact I was married just made me more exotic and not a big fucking problem. And she loved hearing gossip about my clients.

I texted: *In the limo with a metric ton of coke. Want some?*

A second later, I got back: *YES!!!*

Where are you?

At home bring drugs and fuck me NOW

From the back, McKee said, "Are you texting? Could you please not do that?"

I looked at him in the rearview. "Sorry. Company business. I'll be done in a second."

I texted: *Be there soon. Don't bother with clothes.*

The accident happened in the second it took me to hit send. I didn't see a pickup truck cut across two lanes toward an exit until it was too late, and I realized what was happening just in time to rear end an Escalade that had hit its brakes to avoid the truck. A cab hit me from behind and nudged me over into the next lane where I got sideswiped by a moving truck. The limo slammed nose-first into the guardrail on the side of the freeway. We hit hard enough that McKee's door popped open. The asshole wasn't wearing a seatbelt and almost flew out of the car. His attaché case launched like a goddamn rocket out of his hands and smashed open on the freeway shoulder. When I got out and went around the car, he was on his hands and knees in a blizzard of hundred-dollar bills.

"My pills," he said over and over.

A million bucks was blowing down the freeway and McKee was worried about was his fucking *pills*? I reached out to help him up and he lurched back. Right. No touching. There was blood all over the money where he knelt. He touched his face. Blood trickled out of his nose. He sat back on his haunches and laughed. Took a handful of money and threw it in the air.

"What do you believe in?" said McKee.

"Are you all right, sir? Did you hit your head?" I crouched next to him, but he moved away.

The Air Is Chalk

"I mean it," he said. "When things go bad—really bad—what do you blame? Global warming? Chemtrails? Aliens? An angry God?"

"Please. Don't move around so much."

He waved a finger at me. "It's none of those things. It's just me. And I don't know why. It just happened one day."

Fuck this. He was bleeding and maybe something worse. I had to get him to settle down. "Calm down, sir. You'll be all right."

"Call it evolution. Call it *de*volution," he said. He smiled. "My wife evolved. I don't recognize her anymore. I hoped the pills would keep it from happening to me."

I'd seen this kind of thing before. People get a shot to the head and their brain goes sideways. They talked about their dreams, some movie they saw when they were six, all kinds of shit. He needed medical attention fast. I tried to get him to lie down, but he wriggled away.

"When my wife changed she tried to eat me."

Goddamnit. This was bad, but maybe if I went along with it it would calm him down. "What do you mean tried to eat you?"

He threw out his arms and looked around. "I don't know. I really don't. I'm sorry about all the blood. I was hoping to get far away before something like this happened."

"Just wait there, sir. I'm calling you an ambulance."

He stabbed a finger in my direction. "Some bodyguard you are. This is your fault. When the shit hits the fan, you're the one who threw it. I'm toxic, but I was going away. Now it's too late." He touched his nose and held out a bloody hand.

By now, there was a crowd around us. People were running wild, grabbing the cash. The situation was getting out of control. I gently put my hand on McKee's shoulder. "Please, sir. Stop moving."

He bit my hand until I let go. Then he jumped over the freeway guardrail and started down a small embankment toward the feeder road. "It's too late," he shouted. "It's out in the air. *I'm* out in the air. It's too late."

I followed him, but wasn't fast enough. McKee calmly stepped in front of a fuel truck headed for the airport. For someone who was worried about a few drops of blood a minute earlier, he sure left a lot around after that stunt.

Poor bastard.

Hell, poor *me*. I was about to be out of a job. Maybe worse.

I went back up the embankment and found my phone on the floor of the limo. Before calling work, I texted Alexandra.

Shits come up. Can't make it now. See you tonight?

And got back: 😘 *okay later gator*

I called the company and told them about the wreck and McKee offing himself. They were sending the cops, an ambulance, and a corporate rep. I was more scared of the rep than anything else that had happened that day.

I sat in the car, rubbed my shoulder and thought about what McKee had said. Something was out. What did that mean? And his wife tried to eat him? None of it made any sense, which I guess helps explain why he strolled out in front of that truck. He was nuts.

While I was waiting for the rep and others to arrive, the wind changed direction and my throat went dry. Nearby, someone said, "What's that smell?"

A few of us stood there for a minute with our noses in the air like a pack of dogs.

Finally, the cabbie who hit me said, "I think it's chalk. Like in school."

He was right. That was my first time smelling it on the wind. Later on, I realized that most of these grinning idiots with me on the side of the road were probably dead meat.

Me, on the other hand? If I didn't get arrested, I was going to a fucking party.

YOU LEARN your lessons the hard way these days. You learn or you're gone. It's not a rule. It's just reality.

The thing you need to know about Rollers is that while they look like one big beast, they're really made out of a lot of little ones. You see,

The Air Is Chalk

people who get infected change fast. You can hear their bones crack as they curl up into fetal balls, while spines like barbed wire sprout out of their backs. If more than one person is changing, they'll crawl together and spiral around each other into a spiked ball of bleeding meat.

Then they start rolling.

If those barbed wire spines get hold of you, you won't get away. You'll be pulled into the flesh mass and the only human part left of you will be your eyes. I've seen Rollers the size of two-story houses. A hundred blinking eyes staring down at you, the air smells like chalk, and there's nothing you can do but run.

Rollers might be meat and bone, but once they're moving, nothing can stop them. They'll crush cars and crash through buildings to get to you. I've seen them take down ten, twenty people in one mad run. So, you might wonder, why didn't a Roller ever get *me*?

It's like the old joke about how do you outrun a bear? I don't have to outrun the bear.

I just have to outrun *you*.

I HEADED home after the cops interviewed me and the company made me write a report on the accident. I mostly talked about the pickup truck that cut everyone off and didn't mention the texting because, really, who needed to know? My bosses were happy enough with my story, but not with me letting a client get killed. They fired me on the spot. But at least I wasn't going to jail.

The party that night was in San Teresa, a ritzy gated community for people who thought Bel-Air was for losers. The mansion was owned by Franklin Bradbury, one of those faceless secret masters of money who traded movie studios and record labels like kids used to trade Pokémon cards. Frank was made of cash and power—which can get you hated in L.A.—but he churned out enough good product and treated people well enough that he was everybody's favorite billionaire. He only had a few quirks I knew about. Like, when he found out I was a bodyguard, all he wanted to do was talk about guns. Frank had an impressive gun vault, and a safe full of ammo to go with all the toys.

"Don't worry, big guy," he always joked. "When you're in my house, *I'm* the one guarding *you*."

"I always appreciate it, Frank. We all do."

It wasn't a big party by Frank's standards, just a get-together of thirty or so people from his TV company. They were launching a new network that weekend so everyone was in a good mood and most of them were already lit by the time I got there. That included Macy, my wife. She'd come up with some other people from work and we hadn't spoken all day. I winced a little when she put her arms around my shoulders to kiss me.

She said, "What's wrong?"

"I'm just a little sore. There was an accident today at work."

Macy frowned. "*What?* Why didn't you call me?"

"It was no big deal," I lied, not wanting to get into it here. "Just a fender bender, but I got some nice bruises."

She pushed my hair back from my forehead, something she always did when she was concerned for me. "I'm glad you're okay, but call me next time."

"I promise."

She took my hand and led me into the botoxed masses. I was never comfortable with these people. They were all so pretty and tan that I couldn't tell them apart or remember half of their names. Still, it was drinks all around, so no one minded if you got their name wrong on the first try.

Frank had a television the size of Kansas and someone was flipping through the channels until they stopped on a late-night talk show. I watched just long enough to see Alexandra appear on screen and give the host a peck on the cheek. I looked over at the sofas. The real Alex was there with the remote in her hand. She looked at me and winked. I smiled back.

She was curled up next to Geoff somebody, a handsome up and coming actor. They had a good relationship. He got her into all of the big movie premieres and she was his beard, hanging on his arm whenever

The Air Is Chalk

he went out somewhere the studio wanted him to look macho. Macy was off talking business with Frank, so I went over and sat down with the happy couple.

Instead of hello Alex said, "So, did you bring any with you?"

"Bring what?"

"The coke! I told Geoff you'd have enough for all of us."

I shook my head solemnly. The one thing you never want to tell a twenty-something singer who's been waiting all day for a bucket of cocaine is that there isn't any. But there was nothing I could do. "I'm sorry, baby. The guy was a ringer. There was no coke."

Alex fell back against the sofa, bounced off and collapsed across Geoff's lap like a dying deer. She said, "You've ruined my life, you know."

"No, I didn't. I just slowed down your evening."

"I've got you covered," said Geoff. He took a small aspirin tin from his pocket. "My friend Sandra is seeing this Swedish DJ. She said he has a huge cock and great molly. Want one?"

Alex popped upright and opened her mouth like a baby bird waiting to get fed. Geoff took a pill from the case and tossed it onto her tongue. She swallowed and he held the tin out to me. "Paul?" he said.

I shook my head. "I had an accident today. The cops might call me in for a drug test."

"That's sad," he said, swallowing a pill. It broke my heart to not be able to join them. I started to say something when Alex shrieked.

"No! What the fuck is this shit?"

I looked and saw that the local news station had broken into her talk show with a special report. The sound was down on the TV, so all we saw were high helicopter shots looking down on the 405 near the airport. Cars were on fire. Trucks had flipped, spilling their contents all over the road. Stuck in an endless ribbon of burning traffic, people were abandoning their vehicles and running away. By now, the room had gone quiet as everyone stared at the screen.

"Does anyone know what's going on?" said Frank. He took the remote from Alex's hand and aimed it at the TV. But when he pushed the volume control, the TV remained muted. He banged the remote against his hand. "Goddamn fucking thing."

The whole room screamed as something massive crashed through the stalled traffic. The searchlight from the news chopper stayed on it as the thing smashed its way north. When the shot pulled back, it revealed that there were several massive *things* on the road, all heading toward the city, crushing and absorbing everybody in their path. It was our first glimpse of Rollers.

We watched for a while with the sound off. Frank switched from station to station, looking for different views of the carnage. A few more people screamed when Frank found a shot of Rollers moving down Hollywood Boulevard—all spikes, blood, and blinking eyes. He headed for the front door and I followed him.

His mansion is on a high hill with a view all the way across L.A. to the ocean. We stood on his circular driveway and looked down at Hollywood. The sky buzzed with helicopters, both media and LAPD. I counted six major fires across the city. Frank grabbed my arm.

"Paul, you're going to help me keep these people under control, right?"

"What does that mean?"

"We can't let them leave. Look at that shit down there."

There was a muffled boom in the distance as a gas station or something exploded.

I said, "I take your point, Frank, but you can't make people stay."

"But you will, right? You and Macy? I can lock this place down like nobody's business."

I looked back at the choppers and the fires. "Okay. We'll stay the night. I'll help you with crowd control, but you have to let anyone leave who wants to. Otherwise, it's technically kidnapping."

"Sure," he said. "Understood. Come on."

Frank made his pitch to the crowd and, goddammit, he was a good salesman, even saving the best bit for last. After he got through explaining about how disaster-prepped he was, he took what looked like a

The Air Is Chalk

garage door opener from his desk and pushed a button. Steel shutters slammed closed over all the outside doors and windows.

"Blast shields," he said. "You can hit those babies with an RPG and they won't budge."

It was a good speech. Still, half the crowd ran for their cars. Frank opened the gates at the end of the driveway just long enough for them to get through.

Then he locked us in.

Like a lot of heavy money types, the L.A. riots in '92 put the fear of god into Frank. That's when he started buying guns. But he turned his paranoia into art. Went full survivalist and with the kind of money he had, Frank made himself a bullet-proof Xanadu just thirty minutes from Hollywood. He had enough food, water, and medical gear to supply a small country. The mansion ran mostly on solar power, but he had a gas backup generator too. And because no one likes a boring siege, the mansion was stocked with movies and music, plus enough liquor and drugs to keep his guests high until the second coming.

After a couple of days, it was clear that whatever was happening wasn't going to end anytime soon. By then, the sky over L.A. was full of Floaters—sort of enormous jellyfish that hovered like hot air balloons and snatched up people with their long, dangling tendrils. It happened so fast you usually didn't see it, but you knew it was happening because Floaters bay like foghorns every time they snag a tasty morsel. The first Stingers had shown up in the city by then too, but we didn't know enough about them to be properly scared yet. We were preoccupied with something worse: what the freaks even *were*.

The first images were so strange it took a while to understand them. A news crew was out getting B-roll of Floaters near the Hollywood sign. One of the cameramen went into convulsions and a couple of his friends rushed over to help him.

That's when things stopped making sense.

The cameraman screamed as his chest and belly split open and what looked like tentacles coiled out. They latched onto his two friends as a translucent white *something* unfolded itself out of the guy's body and dragged his friends into the air.

That's when we knew we were fucked. The freaks weren't invaders from another planet. They were us. Maybe that's what McKee meant when he said his wife tried to eat him.

Anyway, that bit of good news was probably what inspired our first suicides: A record producer and his wife. Macy found them in one of the downstairs bathrooms, ODed on a bottle of Frank's Oxycontin. I didn't even know their names. I was just sorry Macy was the one to find them. She was hysterical when she came back upstairs and it took me a long time to calm her down. Frank opened the shields on the back doors long enough for the two of us to haul the couple outside and leave them by the pool.

That left ten people in the house. I knew Alex, Macy, Frank, and Geoff a little. They were my clients now. The rest, well, good luck.

When the world's burning, you have to make choices.

Over the next three days, I spent as much time with Alex as I could without Macy getting suspicious. By the end of the third day a few of us decided to make a run for it in one of Frank's armored limos. On TV, they were saying that the freaks were mainly over cities where the hunting was good. We wanted to see if there was a way out of L.A., maybe find somewhere with fewer freaks.

Besides, after a while, even a palace starts to feel like Alcatraz.

We left at high noon when we knew the Rollers would be asleep. That just left the Floaters to worry about, but if we kept moving we figured we could outrun them. In the limo was me, Frank, Mike (a reality TV director), and a kid who called himself Amped (one of the dead record producer's proteges—a buff Burbank white boy hip-hop kid. Really annoying).

We knew the freeways were clogged with dead cars and the main roads were the Rollers' and Floaters' favorite places to hunt, so we stuck

The Air Is Chalk

to back streets hoping we could weave our way around the danger and out of town.

I should never have let Frank drive.

He was so busy blasting down the empty streets, showing off his shiny armored toy, that he sideswiped a sleeping Roller. Lucky for us, it was big enough and we were small enough that it didn't seem to notice the hit. But its spikes ripped a nice chunk of the limo's side and shredded one of the rear tires.

After a short screaming freakout, I got Frank to pull into an empty gas station and park in the garage.

"I'm so sorry, guys," Frank said as we got out. "I fucked up."

I said, "Forget it. Let's change the tire and keep looking for a way out of town."

The limo was so heavy that it needed a special jack to raise it high enough to get the tire off. We finally got it working and wrestled the bad tire off and got the new one on, but it took us half an hour. Amped sat his skinny ass on a tall tool chest and smoked a spliff the whole time. We'd just gotten the wheel on and the jack stowed when my throat went dry and I smelled chalk. That's when Amped screamed and the rest of us got our first good look at a Stinger up close and personal.

The thing we didn't know at the time was that Stingers were the most dangerous freaks.

Shapeshifters.

The tool chest had unfolded around Amped and dug its barbed tentacles deep into his body. Then it began *absorbing* him. His body went soft, like a deflating balloon as the Stinger liquified him and sucked him down.

Frank, Mike, and me scrambled back into the limo. I had to elbow Frank in the gut to keep him from getting in the driver's seat, but he took it pretty well all things considered.

We needed to rethink the situation. I shot us out of the garage and back to Frank's place fast. The folks who stayed behind opened the blast shields on the front door when we got back.

Macy was the first one outside, a fist over her mouth as she stared at the torn-up car. When she saw me, she ran over and cried as she hugged me tight. I'll admit it: It was a tender moment, one of the nicest between us in a long time.

I let Frank explain what had happened to Amped. No one really knew the kid, so no one was too brokenhearted. They were a lot more interested in hearing about the Stinger.

It was another two hours before I could be alone with Alex. Once we found ourselves alone together, we crazy fucked in the room that had belonged to the ODed couple. They didn't need it anymore, and god knows we did.

Afterwards, we lay in bed and she said, "I thought I'd lost you today."

"No way, baby."

"How's Macy taking things?"

"She's fine. Let's not talk about her."

Alex got up and started putting on her clothes. "It's the end of the fucking world and we still have to sneak around."

"Don't talk like that. We'll figure a way out of this. Just you and me."

She didn't look at me as she left, just mumbled, "Sure."

Macy was at the bottom of the stairs when I came out of the room. She was looking the other way, so I don't think she saw Alex leave but we were going to have to be more careful in the future.

Everyone's phone was dropping calls so that night Frank got on a shortwave radio and started talking to people, trying to see if anyone knew a way out of town. I went into the kitchen for some food and when I got back, he'd drawn a route on a paper map from the limo's glovebox. We decided to go out again the next day.

Two more people died that night. A nice couple. Liz and Cassandra. A murder-suicide with one of Frank's guns. I checked the scene and didn't let people into their room. There was nothing anyone could do and no one else needed to see the mess. But it was clear that we

The Air Is Chalk

needed to get out of this fucking house before we all ended up the same way.

Frank tossed me the limo keys when we went out the next day. He knew I'd never let him drive again. Two other people came with us. A couple. I couldn't remember their names and didn't ask.

Why bother when they'd probably both be dead soon anyway?

We got a little over a mile from Frank's place, heading east when a shadow settled over us. I could hardly breathe, the air was so heavy with the chalk smell. And before we knew it, long serrated tendrils shot down from the sky and wrapped around the limo.

Then they lifted us into the air.

Everyone was yelling by then, even me. We knew Floaters sometimes went for cars, but none of them had ever encountered Frank's tank. We were about ten feet off the ground when a few of the tendrils snapped. It must have hurt because the Floater did its foghorn bellow and dropped us. We landed at a funny angle and ended up flipping over onto the roof. But the limo was tough enough that it held together and everybody was more or less fine and able to scramble out of the car.

The first to die was the woman whose name I didn't know.

The moment we were outside, a tendril dropped down and grabbed her in the bear trap grippers the fuckers had at the end of their appendages. A second later, she was gone. Her husband, boyfriend, or whatever he was, ran to the exact spot where she was pulled up. I tried to grab him, but another tendril hauled his dumb ass into the air a second later.

Me and Frank, we started to run.

Frank was a desk czar who paid other people to do his running for him. Between hiding and stopping to let Frank puke from exertion, it took us a couple of hours to make it back the mile or so to his house. When we got there, Alex ran out and grabbed me in a trembling hug.

"I shouldn't have let you go. I knew something bad would happen."

Macy was standing in the doorway. She just turned and went inside. I looked for her for maybe twenty minutes, but the damn mansion was the size of Houston. I couldn't find her anywhere.

I tried texting her, but it wouldn't go through. On the off chance she'd sent me a Dear John note, I checked my email, but I couldn't get into the site. I clicked some sites on Frank's computer and got the same results. The mansion's wifi was working, but it was like the whole goddamn net was down.

I went back to the living room and saw that the screen of the giant TV had gone black. Frank scrolled through the channels, but no one was broadcasting anymore. That with the net situation? Bad fucking signs. Still, we left the TV on in case something started up again.

About an hour later, I saw Macy. She opened the blast shields on the back door and went out. It was a stupid move after what had just happened with the Floater, so I went after her.

She was standing over the bodies of the ODed couple when I found her. We'd wrapped them in plastic garbage bags and duct tape, but by now in the L.A. heat they'd still gone pretty ripe.

"Are we going to end up like them?" she said.

More out of guilt than anything, I said, "No way. I'll take care of you."

She scowled at me. "How, when you're so busy taking care of Alexandra?"

I didn't want to have this argument now. I didn't want to have it ever. I guess I'm a little slow. I never really had a plan on how to deal with the situation. I just hoped that things would work themselves out. But even at the end of the world, here Macy and me were, having the same old arguments.

"Come inside," I said. "It's dangerous out here."

"What do you care?"

I took a couple of steps toward her. "I care."

"Liar."

The Air Is Chalk

"Not now."

Macy gave me a look that somehow wasn't all spite. She wanted to believe that we could work through this. "You mean it?" she said.

"I swear." And in that moment I did. But while I still cared about Macy, we were stuck in this endless goddamn cycle of hurt feelings and guilt. I just wanted it to be over.

I guess that's why, when one of the chaise longues by the pool began to move, I hesitated for a fraction of a second before I said anything.

She gave me a hopeful half-smile just before the Stinger grabbed her leg. I remember it was the left one. Macy didn't scream. There was just a gasping intake of breath. She reached out for me.

"Paul?"

On TV they'd said that Stingers secreted a liquid that numbed things so they wouldn't fight and would be easier to absorb. I remembered what happened to Amped. After the initial shock of being grabbed, he didn't yell much but just sort of let it happen.

I stepped back. By then the Stinger had both of Macy's legs and another tentacle was sliding around her head, muffling her voice when she yelled my name one last time.

Even though she was the one full of Stinger juice, I was numb too. In the end, half a fucking second's hesitation was all it took.

I went back inside and closed the shields. Frank was passed out on bourbon when I got back to the living room. I found a glass, filled it to the top, and drank it straight down. After a few minutes listening to Frank snort and snore, I went to look for Alex.

Geoff had his shirt off when I found them together on the bed in the ODed couple's room. I was more puzzled than mad when I saw them kissing. Alex opened her eyes and when she saw me, she pushed Geoff off. The gun Liz and Cassandra had used to kill themselves was still sitting on the nightstand by the bed. I grabbed it and put it in my back pocket before Geoff panicked and did something stupid.

"Would you excuse us for minute?" I said to him. He nodded and started to slink out of the room. Just before he reached the door I said,

"Don't forget your shirt, tiger." I'd stepped back into the doorway so the little creep had to squeeze past me to get out.

When he was gone I closed the door.

At first, I couldn't think of anything to say. I just stood there like a moron until I mumbled, "I thought you said Geoff was gay."

"Did I say that?" said Alex like a kid caught in a lie. "He's more like…bi."

"And you two have been doing this how long?"

"Don't ask stupid questions, Paul." She started buttoning her blouse. I reached out and took one of her arms.

"I thought you loved me."

She sighed. "I *do* love you, but the Macy thing…"

"That's over. She's gone."

Alex looked puzzled. "What's that mean?"

I pulled her close and whispered, "She's gone. Dead. There's nothing stopping us from being together. I did it for you."

Alex stared at me for a moment like she was trying to figure out what I'd just said. Then she shoved me away hard. "Fuck you, Paul. Don't try to put any crazy shit you did on me."

Before I could say anything, someone screamed from the main rooms. I ran down the stairs. Geoff was pointing at Frank, who was convulsing on the sofa. Blood was already seeping through his shirt.

"Help me get him outside," I yelled. Alex had followed me downstairs. She and Geoff grabbed Frank's arms and I got his legs. Geoff opened the blast shields over the front door. We just barely got outside as the Floater burst from his guts and started into the air. Alex stumbled back a couple of steps.

"Get over here!" I shouted. She started for me, but she was way scared and froze. One of Frank's tendrils grabbed her arm and pulled her up into the sky with him.

A second later, Geoff was by my side watching Alex float away. He got a funny look on his face, one I'd seen before.

"Don't do it," I said. "Be cool and we can survive this."

The Air Is Chalk

Geoff was not cool.

He made a clumsy grab for the pistol. The little prick was faster than I'd counted on. The gun went off, almost hitting me in the leg. I grabbed him and pulled him in closer, the pistol between us. I'm honestly still not sure which one of us pulled the trigger when the gun went off the second time. All I know is that it was Geoff who hit the concrete and not me. I actually felt bad for a minute, but when the Floater's shadow started to move, I knew what I had to do. I left Geoff's body on the driveway, went back inside and put up the shields.

When the world's burning, you have to make choices.

THAT NIGHT, I heard Macy outside the house shouting my name. I opened one of the shields over a second-floor window and saw her below. She was naked and smiling.

"Come outside," she said.

I yelled at her. "You'll have to try harder than that. You're not Macy." I closed the shield and haven't been outside since.

The damn TV had gone off the air before someone could tell us that Stingers could look like people. And that they absorbed whatever information was in their lunch's brain. I guess what it got from Macy and me was our anger. Stingers must also have some psychic ability to communicate with each other because the next day there were *two* Macys outside.

Soon there were a dozen.

Another day and it was a hundred.

Now the house is surrounded and my wife, naked and furious, stretches around me for as far as I can see.

WITH FRANK'S supplies and everyone else gone, I'm set for the rest of my life in Xanadu. I talk to people on the shortwave sometimes. I watch movies. Listen to music. At night I sometimes take off the headphones and listen to Macy. She doesn't always scream. Sometimes she whispers and coos, like a sly seduction. I put the headphones on right away on those nights.

The screams I can deal with, but not the sound of Macy in love.

Eventually a Stinger got into the house. I don't know how it did it. It looked like a butcher knife and when I reached for it, it grabbed me. Fortunately, it was just a small one. I hacked it off my arm with a real knife and shoved it down the garbage disposal.

Frank had laid in a good supply of antibiotics and I'm gobbling them like popcorn. Still, the infection where the Stinger touched me is getting worse. I can feel my arm going soft, dissolving from the inside. I wrapped it in a bandage and put it in a sling just so I don't have to look at it.

I wonder if, like Frank, I'll turn into a monster one day. By a lot of peoples' standards, I guess I already have.

There's not a lot to do around here anymore. It's harder and harder to find people to talk to on the shortwave. I've tried talking to Macy a couple of times on her cooing nights. But the sound of my voice soon gets her screaming again.

Here's the funny part, the part it took me a while to understand: There are so many Macys now that even with all the shielding over the doors and windows, if they rushed the place all at once, they'd be able to crash through. But that's not what the Stingers want. We're playing a game.

What they want is for me to open the doors and let them in.

When I dream now all I see is Macy's face disappearing under a tentacle. Alex being drawn into the sky. Frank splitting open. Geoff falling to the ground.

I know that one night when the dreams get too bad, my gamey arm starts dissolving the rest of me, or I can't stand watching *Die Hard* one more time, I'm going to call the Stingers' bluff. I'll open the doors and windows and invite them in for high tea. Will they absorb me right away?

The Air Is Chalk

I might be the last human in the world by then.

They might want to keep me for a while as a pet.

A memento of the early days when the world was full of people and the air wasn't always chalk.

Each minute is a choice: stay inside and live or let them inside and die.

THE TUNGUSKA EVENT

Old Anna began her story over tea. "Mikhail Vasilovich Boltrushko, the young master, had been smuggled to Canada just before the Great Patriotic War," she said. "Soon after the German surrender in 1945, he returned to the family's manor here in Irkutsk."

Tony Lansen looked at the old, weathered woman. He still wasn't sure how she'd found him at his hotel. He hardly ever came into Irkutsk, preferring the clean air of the Siberian taiga. But the old woman had insisted on speaking to him because he alone, an American scholar, might understand.

"I had been the head servant," Anna continued, "and the young master, he was kind enough to keep me on, though I was old, even then. I'd come east with the family when we left lovely Kiev for awful Siberia. When he returned, the young master had little interest in the family shipping business, so I mostly left him alone to his studies. He had arrived from Canada with crates of books and boxes of special inks, papers, and odd instruments I had never seen before. I was just happy to have someone to take care of again.

"Mikhail Vasilovich disappeared into his father's old study for weeks at a time. When I brought him his dinner—he soon stopped eating anything but a single evening meal—I found the floor littered with reams of parchment, papyrus, and rice paper covered in colored gibberish. What I saw disturbed me. Many of the letters looked like the writing on the old synagogue in Kiev that the people had burned. The master would never let me clean the room or remove any of the papers, but he would occasionally permit me to gather them from the floor and stack them on his worktable. One night, I boldly asked the young master what the papers were for. Was he writing a book in a foreign tongue? Had he converted to Judaism in Canada? If so, he must keep it a secret as the locals were backward and clung to old prejudices. I was talking above my station, but I was afraid, and it all spilled out.

"Mikhail Vasilovich laughed and drew a clean sheet of paper from a stack on the table where he worked. He took a fresh pen, dipped it into crimson ink, then wrote some of the strange letters. At once, a tiny flame appeared above the desk. I remember screaming at the sight, but he showed me that it was safe. He could control flame he had conjured. Then he licked his thumb and smudged one of the letters from the word he had written, and the flame flickered and disappeared. He said that he'd learned the True Name of fire and was trying to learn the true names of other things. Yes, some of the words he had been writing were Hebrew, but others were Tibetan. Still others were Mayan, who he said were a people of the southern Americas. I'd never heard of those languages, but when he assured me that he himself had not converted to Judaism, I felt better. The young master, always a prankster as a boy, even offered to show me that he wasn't circumcised. That made us both laugh and I went to bed happy.

"That night, I dreamed of the whole sky on fire, and of angels.

"One day," said Anna grimly, "a German came to the manor. Nothing was the same after that. I hated him on sight, with his greasy hair and long, filthy nails. He left the same day he arrived, but the young master became more elusive than ever. He even stopped eating his single

The Tunguska Event

daily meal and would only munch some toast every day or two. This was too much. I wouldn't have the head of the family starving himself while I was running the household. After finding another cold, uneaten dinner outside the study, I opened the door to demand an explanation.

"Above his worktable, the moon circled slowly.

"'I learned to write its name,' he explained, beaming at me like a happy child.

"There was a machine on the table and he brought me over to see the thing. It was like the typing machines I'd seen Communist Party clerks and secretaries using in government offices. But this machine had dials and wheels and little lights that shone when you touched a letter.

"'It's called an Enigma Machine,' he said. The German had brought it. One of the few that hadn't been captured by the Allies after the war, he said. It had cost the young master a small fortune.

"'The Nazis were madmen and despots,' he said to me, 'but they were also powerful occultists.' The Enigma had written unbreakable codes for the Germans during the war. He said, 'What are codes, but a kind of secret language which reveals mysteries to those with eyes to see?' He had conjured the moon by writing thousands of variations of its name on the machine. There was much more work to do, he said. More names to learn. After promising to eat more, he shooed me from the room.

"I was concerned for the young master, but I didn't want to enter the study after that. I know I should have been more courageous, for his sake. Sometimes I peeked at him through the keyhole. Soon a star hovered near the ceiling, and the moon circled it. Then there were planets. Light poured from the keyhole night and day. Then suddenly it was gone. I stooped and peered into the room. It was empty. No floor, no walls, no ceiling. The young master still sat typing at the worktable as a galaxy spun slowly over his head. That night, the good people of Irkutsk saw strange things in the sky. Swarms of fireflies filled the streets. Ball lightning spooked the cattle. The stained glass in the old church collapsed on itself.

"Perhaps a week later, imps invaded the house. I heard them at night, tittering as they crept past my bedroom door. In the morning, my kitchen would be a mess. All the sugar and lard would have been eaten, often along with the crockery in which they had been stored. This was too much. I marched straight to the study. When I opened the door and saw the burning sulfur lakes of Hell, I, strangely, wasn't surprised. I stood my ground and explained that I simply could not run a proper household with beasts roaming the halls all night. Instead of being angry with me, Mikhail Vasilovich—he was such a kind boy—came and embraced me. He agreed with me, and, over my protests, left for the country the next day. He took only his Enigma machine, some of his books, and the family Victrola on which he ceaselessly played American jazz records. As much as I hated to see the young master go, I was relieved that, the very night he left, the study reverted to its former appearance, and there were no more demons in the kitchen.

"But things weren't right. My dreams kept me awake at night. I got down on my knees and prayed for peace, but it didn't help. When I read my bible for comfort, I finally understood the fear that haunted me. If the young master had gone so far as to conjure up the stars and Hell, the only thing left for him to manifest was heaven itself. This was inconceivable. The monstrous blasphemy of it. There would be no forgiveness for such bloated pride. In the middle of the night, I dressed and went to the train station to catch the early morning coach to Tayshet. Using the remaining household money, I hired a boat to take me to the Angara and thence to Keshma. It took another three days overland to reach Vanavara, a stinking trading town, full of Cossacks and filthy nomads smelling of sweat and the seal fat they gobbled to keep warm. The boatman would go no further into the wild country where the young master had his izba—not much more than a hut, really—and I had to hire a horse-drawn wagon with the last few rubles I dug from my pockets.

"Later, I dearly wished that I hadn't found the money and had simply returned to the manor in Irkutsk.

The Tunguska Event

"Mikhail Vasilovich's izba wasn't far from the village. When the wagon made it through the woods and onto open land, I could see the small house on a rise above us. It was glowing with the pure white light of stars and angels. When we reached the bottom of the hill, the driver stopped, refusing to get any closer. Celestial voices drifted down to us. Stars spilled from the chimney, sailed into the sky, and tumbled back to earth with the light snow that had begun to fall. Meteors streaked across the heavens. More and more, until they were a storm. Overhead, a star glowed, brighter than all the others combined. The star seemed to hover over the little house. I thought of the star of Bethlehem and wondered if the young master had conjured it so that he could proclaim himself some mad, new messiah. I didn't understand what was happening, until the driver pulled me back to his wagon. The star wasn't hovering. It wasn't a star, at all. It was something bright and enormous and it was falling straight at us.

"The star, the size of a mountain at least, seemed to fall forever. I prayed as the wagon driver cursed his horse to go faster. When the star hit the young master's house, I closed my eyes and waited to die.

"But the wagon trundled on and I looked back at the mountain. The light was gone and so was gone the izba. A few last stars shot across the night sky. Snow fell and thunder echoed from far away across the taiga.

"Farther than that, even," Anna whispered, leaning across the table and taking Tony Lansen's hand. "The thunder was from forty years in the past.

"You see, during one of his infrequent meals, the young master had told me that time and space were the same thing, that one could affect and pervert the other. So, when God reached down to slap Mikhail Vasilovich Boltrushko from existence—for that could only have been God's hand in the sky—the weight of the creator's wrath had warped time and space. The man God obliterated with a falling star in 1946 had been blown through time to be felt in 1908, near the Little Tunguska River. I remember hearing about the event as a girl. Whole forests had been laid low. Lakes had been burned dry in a split second by the blast of the falling star."

The old woman finished her story and looked at Tony, as if expecting an answer of some sort. The American didn't say a word but got up from the table and went to one of crates stacked along the wall. He pushed aside his field notes and collections of local plants, until he found what he was looking for. Then he fumbled in the dim light for a few minutes, assembling the contraption. When he came back to the table and sat with Anna a tinny music filled the room. From the crate, Benny Goodman and his band jumped through a rendition of "It's Only a Paper Moon." Anna moved one of her wrinkled hands to her mouth and began to weep quietly.

Tony knew how to fudge data in his geology reports to keep the grant money flowing in, but until that night, he had no idea what to say about the stack of old jazz 78s or the scorched Victrola he'd dug up in the same layer of geological strata as the Tunguska explosion. He certainly had no idea what he was going to say when he got back to the university.

Pouring them shots of good local vodka, Tony silently toasted Boltrushko. Then he took Anna's hand, and in the little room, they began to dance.

HORSE LATITUDES

Fame is just schizophrenia with money.

I died on a Sunday, when the new century was no more than four or five hours old. Midnight would have been a more elegant moment (and a genuine headline grabber), but we were still on stage and I believed at the time that suicide, like masturbation, might lose something when experienced with more than 60,000 close, personal friends.

I don't recall exactly when I accepted the New Year's Eve gig. The band had never played one before, but it became inextricably tied in with my decision to kill myself. Somehow, I couldn't bear the idea of a twenty-first century. Whenever I thought of it, I was overwhelmed by a memory: flying in a chartered plane over the Antarctic ice fields on my twenty-ninth birthday. A brilliant whiteness tinged with freezing blue swept away in all directions. It was an unfillable emptiness. It was death. It could never be fed or satisfied—neither the ice sheet nor the new century. At least, not by me.

No one suspected, of course. Throughout this crisis of faith, I always remained true to fame. I acted out the excesses that were expected of me. I denied rumors that I had invented. I spat at photographers and doubled my press coverage.

The suicide itself was a simple, dull, anticlimactic affair. The police had closed the show quickly when the audience piled up their seats and started a bonfire during our extended "Auld Lang Syne." Back in my room at the Pierre Hotel I swallowed a bottle of pills and half a bottle of vodka. I felt stupid and disembodied, like some character who had been written out of a Tennessee Williams play—Blanche Dubois' spoiled little brother. I found out later that it was Kumiko, my manager, who found me swimming in my own vomit, and got me to the hospital. When I awoke, I was in Oregon, tucked away in the Point Mariposa Recovery Center, where movie stars come to dry out. There wasn't even a fence, just an endless expanse of lizard green lawn. Picture a cemetery or a country club with Thorazine.

I'd become bored with the doctors and their endless questions and insistence that I was hallucinating. They called me an "unreliable narrator of my own life." So, I left the sanitarium three weeks later without telling anyone.

Going out for my evening walk, I just kept on walking. The Center was housed in a converted mansion built on a bluff over a contaminated beach near Oceanside. I had, until recently, been an avid rock climber. Inching your way across a sheer rock face suspended by nothing but your own chalky fingers is the only high comparable to being on stage (death, spiritual or physical, being the only possible outcome of a wrong or false move in either place). It took me nearly an hour to work my way down the granite wall to a dead beach dotted with Health Department warning signs and washed-up medical waste. I checked to see that my lithium hadn't fallen out on the climb down. Then, squatting among the plastic bags emblazoned with biohazard stickers and scrawny gulls holding empty syringes in their beaks, I found a rusty scalpel with which to slit the cuffs of my robe. Twenty thousand dollars in hundreds and fifties spilled out onto the gray sand.

I left my robe on the sand, following the freeway shoulder in sweat pants and a T-shirt. In Cannon Beach I bought a coat and a ticket on a boat going down the coast to Los Angeles. However, my ticket only took me as far as San Francisco. We reached the city two days later, in the dark hours of the early morning. As we sailed in under the Golden Gate Bridge, San Francisco was aglow like some art nouveau foundry, anesthetized beneath dense layers of sea fog. Far across the bay, on the Oakland side, I could just make out the tangle of mangrove swamp fronting the wall of impenetrable green that was the northernmost tip of the rainforest.

Six weeks later, I left my little apartment in the Sunset District and headed for a south of Market Street bar called Cafe Juju. A jumble of mossy surface roots, like cords from God's own patch bay, had tangled themselves in the undercarriages of abandoned cars on the broad avenue that ran along Golden Gate Park. Here and there hundred-foot palms and kapoks jutted up from the soil, spreading their branches, stealing light and moisture from the smaller native trees. The Parks Department had given up trying to weed out the invading plant species and concentrated instead on keeping the museums open and the playgrounds clear for tourists who never came any more.

Downtown, the corners buzzed with street musicians beating out jittery sambas on stolen guitars, and improvised sidewalk markets catering to the diverse tastes of refugees from Rio, Mexico City, and Los Angeles. Trappers from Oakland hawked marmosets and brightly plumed jungle birds that screamed like scalded children. In the side streets, where the lights were mostly dead, golden-eyed jaguars hunted stray dogs.

Overhead, you could look up and watch the new constellation: Fer-De-Lance, made up of a cluster of geosynchronous satellites. Most belonged to NASA and the UN, but the Army and the DEA were up there too, watching the progress of the jungle and refugees northward.

Inside Cafe Juju, a few heads turned in my direction. There was some tentative whispering around the bar, but not enough to be alarming. I was thinner than when I'd left the band. I'd grown a beard, and since I had stopped bleaching my hair, it had darkened to its natural and unremarkable brown. As I threaded my way through the crowd, a crew-cut blonde pretended to bump into me. I ignored her when she said my name, and settled at a table in the back, far away from the band. "Mister Ryder," said the man sitting across from me. "Glad you could make it."

I shook the gloved hand he offered. "Since you called me that name so gleefully, I assume you got it?" I said.

He smiled. "How about a drink?"

"I like to drink at home. Preferably alone."

"Got to have a drink," he said. "It's a bar. You don't drink, you attract attention."

"Fine. I'll have a Screwdriver."

"A health nut, right? Getting into that California lifestyle? Got to have your Vitamin C." He waved over a waitress and ordered us drinks. The waitress was tall, with close-cropped black hair and an elegantly hooked nose sporting a single gold ring. In my too-large T-shirt and baggy jeans, she barely noticed me.

"So, did you get it?" I asked.

Virilio rummaged through the inner recesses of his battered Army trench coat. He wore it with the sleeves rolled up; his forearms, where I could see them, were a solid mass of snakeskin tattoos. I couldn't be sure where the tattoos ended because his hands were covered in skin-tight black kid gloves. He looked younger than he probably was, had the eager and restless countenance of a bird of prey. He pulled a creased white envelope from an inside pocket and handed it to me. Inside was a birth certificate and a passport.

"They look real," I said.

"They are real," Virilio said. "If you don't believe me, take those down to any DMV and apply for a driver's license. I guarantee they'll check out as legit."

"It makes me nervous. It seems too easy."

"Don't be a schmuck. The moment you told me your bank accounts were set up with names from the *Times* obituaries, I knew we were in business. I checked out all the names you gave me. In terms of age and looks, this guy is the closest match to you."

HORSE LATITUDES

From the small stage nearby, the guitarist cut loose with a wailing solo, like alley cats and razor blades at a million decibels over a dense batucada backbeat. I closed my eyes as turquoise fireballs went off in my head.

"You never told me why you needed this," said Virilio.

"I had a scrape with the law a few years ago," I lied. "Bringing in rare birds and snakes from south of the border. Department of Fish and Game seized my passport."

Virilio's smile split the lower part of his face into a big, toothy crescent moon. "That's funny. That's fucking hysterical. I guess these weird walking forests put your ass out of business."

"Guess so," I said.

The waitress brought our drinks and Virilio said, "Can you catch this round?" As I counted out the bills, Virilio slid his arm around the waitress's hips. Either she knew him or took him for just another wasted local jackass because she didn't react at all. "Frida here plays music," said Virilio. "You ought to hear her stuff, she's real good. You ever play in a band, Ryder?"

"No," I said. "Always wanted to, but never found the time to learn an instrument." I looked at Frida the waitress and handed her the money. From this new angle I saw that along with her nose ring, Frida's left earlobe glittered with a half-dozen or so tiny jeweled studs. There were more gold rings just above her left eyebrow, which was in the process of arching. Her not unattractive lips held a suppressed smirk that could only mean that she had noticed me noticing her.

"That's interesting," Virilio said. "I thought everybody your age had a little high school dance combo or something."

"Sorry."

Frida folded the bills and dropped them into a pocket of her apron. "They're playing some of my stuff before the Yanomamo Boys set on Wednesday. Come by if you're downtown," she said. I nodded and said "Thanks." As she moved back to the bar, I saw Virilio shaking his head. "Freaking Frida," he said.

"What does that mean?"

"Frida was okay. Used to sing in some bands; picked up session work. Now she's into this new shit." Virilio rolled his eyes. "She sort of wigged out a few months ago. Started hauling her recorder over to Marin and down south into the rainforest. Wants to digitize it or something. Says she looking for the Music of Jungles. Says it just like that, with capital letters." He shrugged and sipped his drink. "I've heard some of this stuff. Sounds like a movie soundtrack, *Attack from the Planet Whacko,* if you know what I mean."

"You ever been into the deep rainforest?" I asked.

"Sure. I've been all up and down the coast. They keep 101 between here and L.A. pretty clear."

"L.A.'s as far south as you can get?"

"No, but after that, you start running into government defoliant stations, rubber tappers, and these monster dope farms cut right into the jungle. Those places are scary. Mostly white guys running them, with refugees pulling the labor. And they are hardcore. Bloody you up and throw your ass to the crocodiles just for laughs."

"I may need you to do your name trick again. I have some money in Chicago—"

"Not anymore you don't. Not for two or three months. Nothing but monkeys, snakes and malaria out that way, from Galveston to Detroit. If you have any swamp land in Florida, congratulations. It's really a swamp." Virilio took a sip of his beer. "Of course, I could do a data search, see where the Feds reassigned the assets of your bank."

"Never mind," I said, deciding I didn't particularly want this kid bird-dogging me through every database he could get to. "It's not that important."

Virilio shrugged. "Suit yourself," he said, and shook his head wearily at the bare-breasted young woman who bumped drunkenly into our table. "Run, honey," he told her. "The fashion police are hot on your trail," as she staggered over to her friends at the bar. The local scene-makers had taken the heat as their cue to go frantically native. The majority of them were dressed in Chinese knockoffs of Brazilian Indian gear. It was like some grotesque acid trip combining the worst of Dante with a Club Med brochure for Rio: young white kids, the girls wearing nothing but body paints or simple Lacandon hipils they had seen on Wikipedia; the boys in loin cloths, showing off their bowl-style haircuts, mimicking those worn by many Amazonian tribesmen.

As Virilio watched the revelers he said, "You know, the Santeros say that this shit, the jungle, the animals, all the craziness, it's all revenge. Amazonia getting back at the greedy bastards who've been raping it for all these years."

"That's a pretty harsh judgment," I said. "Are you always so Old Testament?"

"You've got me all wrong. I'm thrilled. L.A.'s gone. They finally got something besides TV executives and mass murderers to grow in that goddamned desert." Virilio smiled. "Of course, I don't really buy all that mystical shit. The FBI are covering up for the people who are really responsible."

"The FBI?"

"It's true," Virilio said. "They hushed it up—same branch that iced Kennedy and ran the Warren Commission.

"A couple of geneticists who'd been cut loose from Stanford were working for the Brazilian government, cooking up a kind of extra fast-grow plants to re-seed all the burned-up land in the Amazon. Supposedly, these plants were locked on fast forward—they'd grow quick and die quick, stabilizing the soil so natural plants could come in. Only the leafy bastards wouldn't die. They kept on multiplying and choked out everything else. Three months after they planted the first batch, Rio was gone. It's all true. I know somebody that has copies of the FBI reports."

"I believe you," I said, not impressed by either story.

The band finished their set and left the stage to distracted applause. I stood and dropped a jiffy bag on Virilio's side of the table. "I've got to go now. Thanks for the I.D.," I said. Virilio slipped some of the bills from the end of the bag and riffled through them. "Non-sequential fifties," I said, "just like you wanted."

He smiled and put the bag in his pocket. "Just to prevent any problems, just to short-circuit any second thoughts you might be having about why you should give a person like me all this money for some paper you could have maybe gotten cheaper somewhere else, I want to make sure you understand that the nature of my work is facilitation. I'm a facilitator. I'm not a dealer, or muscle, or a thief, but I can do all those things if required. What I got you wasn't a birth certificate; any asshole could have gotten you a birth certificate. What I got you was *the* birth certificate. One that matches you, close enough so that getting you a passport, letting you move around, will be no problem. I had to check over two years of obituaries, contact the right agencies, grease the right palms. It's knowing which palms to grease and when that you're paying me for. Not that piece of paper."

I slid my new identity into my jacket and nodded. "Thanks."

Outside Cafe Juju, the warm, still air had taken on the quality of some immense thing at rest—a mountain or phantom whale, pressing down on the city, squeezing its Sargasso dreams from the cracks in the walls out onto the streets. I pulled out my emergency hip flask and took a drink. I was reminded of the region of windless ocean known as the Horse Latitudes, called that in remembrance of the Spanish galleons that would sometimes find themselves adrift in those dead waters. The crews would strip the ship down to the bare wood in hopes of lightening themselves enough to move in the feeble breeze. When everything else of value had been thrown overboard, the last thing to go were the horses. Sometimes the Horse Latitudes were carpeted for miles with a floating rictus of dead palominos and Arab stallions, buoyed up by the immense floating kelp beds and their own churning internal gases. The Horse Latitudes were not a place you visited, but where you found yourself if you allowed your gaze to be swallowed up by the horizon, or to wander on the map to places you might go, rather than where you were supposed to be.

I'd walked a couple of blocks up Ninth Street when I realized I was being followed. It was my habit to stop often in front of stores, apparently to window shop or admire the beauty of my own face. In fact, I was checking the reflections caught in the plate glass, scanning the street for faces that had been there too long. This time I couldn't find a face, but just beyond a wire pen where a group of *campasenos* and local construction workers were betting on cock fights, I did catch sight of a jacket. It was bulky and black, of some military cut, and one side was decked with the outline of a bird skull done in clusters of purple and white rhinestones. The jacket's owner hung back where vehicles and pedestrians blocked most of the streetlight. It was only the fireworks in the rhinestones that had caught my eye.

Just to make sure it wasn't simple paranoia, I went another block up Ninth and stopped by the back window of a VW van full of caged snakes. When I checked again, the jacket had moved closer. I cut to my right, down a side street, then left, back toward the market. The jacket hung behind me, the skull a patch of hard light against the dark buildings.

I ran down an alley between a couple of closed shops and kept going, taking corners at random. The crumbling masonry of the ancient industrial buildings was damp where humidity had condensed on the walls. I found myself on a dark street where the warehouses were lost behind the blooms of pink and purple orchids, like frozen fire along the walls. Behind me, someone kicked a bottle and I sprinted around another corner. I was lost in the maze of alleys and drive-thrus that surrounded the rotting machine shops and abandoned wrecking yards. Sweating and out of breath, I ran toward a light. When I found it, I stopped.

It was a courtyard where a building had once stood. Fires were going in a few battered oil drums, fed by children with slabs of dismantled billboards, packing crates, and broken furniture. Toward the back of the courtyard, men had something cooking on a spit rigged over one of the drums. Their city-issued mobile shelters, something like hospital gurneys with heavy-gauge wire coffins mounted on top, were lined in neat rows against one wall. I had heard about the tribal homeless encampments, but had never seen one before. Some of the homeless were the same junkies and losers that belonged to every big city, but most of this group were displaced tribal people—spillover from refugee centers and church basements. Whole villages would sometimes find themselves abandoned in a strange city after being forcibly evacuated from their farms in Mexico or Belize. They roamed the streets with their belongings crammed into government-issue snail shells, fading into a dull wandering death.

But it wasn't always that dismal. Some of the tribes were evolving quickly in their new environment, embracing the icons of the new world that had been forced upon them. Many of the men still wore lip plugs, but their traditional skin stains had been replaced with metal-flake auto body paint and dime store makeup. The women and children wore necklaces of auto glass, strips of mylar, and iridescent watch faces. Chinese silks and burned-out fuses were twined in their hair.

Whatever mutual curiosity held us for the few seconds that I stood there passed when some of the men stepped forward, gesturing and speaking to me in a language I didn't understand. I started moving down the alley. Their voices crowded around me; their hands touched my back and tugged at my arms. They weren't threatening, but I still had to suppress an urge to run. I looked back for the jacket that had followed me from Cafe Juju, but it wasn't back there.

I kept walking, trying to stay calm. I ran through some breathing exercises a yoga guru I'd known for a week in Berlin had taught me. After a few minutes, though, some of the tribesmen fell away. And when I turned a corner, unexpectedly finding myself back on Ninth, I discovered I was alone.

On Market, I was too shaky to bargain well and ended up paying a pedicab almost double the usual rate for a ride to the Sunset. At home, I took a couple of Percocets and washed them down with vodka from the flask. Then I lay down with all my clothes on, reaching into my pocket to hold the new identity documents. Around dawn, when the howler monkeys started up in Golden Gate Park, I fell asleep.

I tried to write some new songs, but I'd become overcome with inertia, and little by little lost track of myself. Sometimes, on the nights when the music was especially bad or I couldn't stand the random animal racket

HORSE LATITUDES

from the park, I'd have a drink and just walk. The squadrons of refugees and the damp heat of the rainforest that surrounded the city made these nights miserable much of the time, but I decided it was better to be out in the misery of the streets than to hide with the rotten music in my room.

I was near Chinatown, looking for the building where I'd shared a squat early in my career, when I ran into a crowd of sleepwalkers. At first, I didn't recognize them, so complete was their impression of wakefulness. Groups of men and women in business suits waited silently for buses they had taken the previous morning, while merchants sold phantom goods to customers who were home in bed. Smiling children played in the streets, dodging ghost cars. Occasionally someone from the same neighborhood as a sleepwalking grocer (because these night strolls seemed to be a localized phenomenon, affecting a single neighborhood at a time) would reenact a purchase they'd made earlier that day, entering into a kind of slow-motion waltz with the merchant, examining vegetables that weren't there or weighing invisible oranges in their hand. No one had an explanation for the sleepwalking phenomenon. Or rather, there were so many explanations that they tended to cancel each other out. The one fact that seemed to be generally accepted was that the night strolls had become more common as the rainforest crept northward toward San Francisco, as if the boundary of Amazonia was surrounded by a region compounded of the collective dreams of all the cities it had swallowed.

I followed the sleepwalkers, entering Chinatown through the big ornamental gate on Grant Street, weaving in, out, and through the oddly beautiful group pantomime. The city was almost silent there, except for the muted sounds of unhurried feet and rustling clothes. None of the sleepwalkers ever spoke, although they mouthed things to each other. They frowned, laughed, got angry, reacting to something they had heard or said when they had first lived that particular moment.

It was near Stockton Street that I heard the looters. Then I saw them, moving quickly and surely through the narrow alleys, loaded down with merchandise from the sleepwalkers' stores. The looters took great pains not to touch any of the somnambulists. Perhaps they were nervous about being caught, but more likely they were afraid of being infected with the sleepwalking sickness.

Watching them, cop paranoia got a hold of me, and I started back out of Chinatown. I was almost to the gate, dodging blank-eyed children and ragged teenagers with armloads of bok choy and DVDs when I saw something else: Coming out of a darkened dim sum place—a jeweled bird skull on a black jacket. The jacket must have spotted me too, because it darted back inside. This time, I followed it.

A dozen or so people, mostly elderly Chinese couples, sat miming silent meals inside the unlit restaurant. Cats, like the homeless, had apparently figured out the pattern the sleepwalking sickness took through the city. Dozens of the mewing animals moved around the tables, rubbing against sleepers' legs, and licking grease off the stacked dim sum trays. I went back to the kitchen, moving through the middle of the restaurant, trying to keep the sleepers around me as a demilitarized zone between me and the jacket. I wasn't as certain of myself inside the restaurant as I had been on the street. Too many sudden shadows. Too many edges hiding between the bodies of the dreaming patrons.

There were a couple of aproned men in the kitchen, kneading the air into dim sum. Cats perched on the cutting tables and freezer like they owned the place. Whenever one of the sleepwalking cooks opened the refrigerator doors, the cats went berserk, crowding around his legs, clawing at leftover dumplings and chunks of raw meat. There was, however, no jacket back there. Or in the restroom. The rear exit was locked. I went back out through the restaurant, figuring I'd blown it. I hadn't had any medication in a couple of weeks, and decided I'd either been hallucinating again, or had somehow missed the jacket while checking out the back. Then from the dark she said my name, the name she knew me by. I turned in the direction of her voice, and the jeweled skull winked at me from the corner.

I had walked within three feet of her. She was slumped at a table with an old woman, only revealing herself when she shifted her gaze from the tablecloth to me, doing a good imitation of the narcotized pose of a sleeper. She motioned for me to come over and I sat down. Then she pushed a greasy bag of cold dim sum at me. "Have one," she said, like we were old friends.

"Frida?" I said.

She smiled. "Welcome to the land of the dead."

"Why were you following me?"

"I was raiding the fridge." She reached into the bag and pulled out a spring roll, which she wrapped in a paper napkin and handed to me. As she moved, I caught a faint glimmer off the gold rings above her eyebrow. "You, I believe, were the one who only seconds ago was pinballing through here like Blind Pew."

"I'll have my radar checked. Do you always steal your dinner?"

"Whenever I can. I'm only at the cafe a couple of nights a week. And tips aren't what they used to be. Even the dead are peckish around here."

The old woman with whom we shared the table leaned from side to side in her chair, laughing the fake, wheezing laugh of sleepers, her hands describing arcs in the air. "So maybe you weren't following me tonight," I said. "Why did you follow me the other night from Cafe Juju?"

"You remind me of somebody."

"Who?"

"I don't know. Your face doesn't belong here. But I don't know where it should be, either. I know I've seen you before. Maybe you're a cop and you busted me. Maybe that's why you look familiar. Maybe we went steady in high school. Maybe we had the same shrink. Ever since I saw you at the cafe, I've got all these maybes running through my head."

"Maybe you've got me mixed up with someone."

"Not a chance," said Frida. She smiled and in the half-light of the restaurant I couldn't tell if she knew who I was or not. She didn't look crazy, but she still scared me. I'd gone to the funeral of more than one friend who, walking home, had turned a corner and stumbled into his or her own Mark David Chapman. Frida's sad smile made her look almost as tired as the sleepers, which surprised me because her eyes were anything but that. Her face had too many lines for someone her age, but there was a kind of grace in the high bones of her cheeks and forehead.

"You're not a cop or a reporter, are you?" I asked.

Her eyes widened in an expression that was somewhere between shock and amusement. "No. Unlike you, I'm pretty much what I appear to be."

"You're a waitress who tails people on her breaks."

She shrugged and bit into her spring roll, singing, "Get your kicks on Route 66."

"Now you're just being ridiculous," I said. "Virilio didn't tell me that part. He just said you were crazy."

"Did he say that?" She looked away and her face fell into shadow. I leaned back, thinking that if she was crazy, I might have just said the thing that would set her off. But a moment later she turned back, wearing the silly smile. "Virilio's one to talk, playing Little Caesar in a malaria colony." She picked up a paper napkin from the table and, with great concentration, began wiping her hands, a finger at a time. Then she said: "I'm looking for something."

"The Music of Jungles?"

"Jesus, did he tell you my favorite color too?"

"He just said it was something you'd told him."

"Right," she said and shrugged. "I *am* looking for something. But it's kind of difficult to describe."

"California is on its last legs. If you want to play music, why don't you go to New York?"

She reached down and picked up a wandering cat. It was a young Abyssinian, and it immediately curled up in her lap, purring. "What I'm looking for isn't in New York," she said. "I thought from your face you might be looking for something, too. That's why I followed you."

"What is the Music of Jungles?" I asked.

She shook her head. "No, I'm sorry. I think I made a mistake."

HORSE LATITUDES

I slid the hip flask from my pocket and took a drink. "Tell you the truth, I am looking for something, too."

"I knew it," she said. "What?"

"Something new. Something I've only seen in flashes. A color and quality of sound that I've never been able to get out of my head. I started out looking for it, but got distracted along the way. I figure this is my last chance to see if it's really there, or just another delusion."

"You're a musician?" she asked.

"Yes."

She picked up the flask, sniffed, and took a drink, smiling and coughing a little as the vodka went down. "What's your name?" she asked.

"You already know my name."

"I know *a* name," she said, setting down the flask. "Probably something store bought from Virilio."

I shrugged and took the flask from her. "Your turn. What's the Music of Jungles?"

She looked down and leaned back in her chair, stroking the cat.

"First off," she said, "it's not the Music of Jungles. Jungles are in Tarzan movies. What you're trying to describe is a tropical forest or a rainforest. I don't use rainforest sounds in my music because I think they're beautiful, although I do think they're beautiful," she said. "I use them because they're the keys to finding the Songtracks of a place."

Frida set the cat on the floor and leaned forward, elbows resting on the table. "Here's what it is," she said. "Some tribes in Amazonia believe that the way the world came into existence was through different songs sung by different gods, a different song for each place. The land, they believe, is a map of a particular melody. The contours of the hills, the vegetation, the animals—they're notes, rests and rhythms in the song that calls a place into being, and also describes it. Over thousands of years the tribes have mapped all the songs of Amazonia, walked everywhere and taught the songs to their children.

"Where we are now, though, is special," Frida said, and she drew her hands up in a gesture that took in all of our surroundings. "The forest that surrounds San Francisco, it's Amazonia, but it's also new. And it has its own unique Songtrack. That's what my music is about. That's what I'm about. No one has found the song of this part of the rainforest yet, so I'm going to do it."

"When you find it, what will the song tell you?"

She looked away, pressing her hands deep into the pockets of her jacket. "I don't exactly know. Maybe the story of the place. What went on here in the past; what'll happen in the future. It's enough for me just to do it."

I put the flask in my pocket. "Listen, Frida," I said. "The atmosphere in here is definitely not growing on me. Would you like to go someplace?"

"I don't live too far away." She paused. "Maybe I could play you some of my music..." she said, trailing away softly, embarrassed.

"I'd like that," I said. As she stood she said, "You know, you managed to still not tell me your name."

I looked at her for a moment. An old man shuffled between us, nodding and waving to sleeping friends. I thought about the Music of Jungles. Was this woman insane? I wondered. I'd been dreaming so long myself, it hardly seemed to matter. I told her my real name. She hardly reacted at all, which, to tell you the truth, bothered me more than it should have. She picked up a bulky purse-sized object from the floor and slung it over her shoulder, looped her arm in mine, and led me into the street.

"This is a digital recorder," she said, indicating the purse-thing. "I go to Marin and Oakland whenever I can; fewer people means I get cleaner recordings. I prefer binaural to stereo for the kind of work I do. It has a more natural feel."

"Teach me to use it?" I asked.

"Sure. I think you can handle it."

"Why do I feel like I just passed an audition?"

"Maybe because you just did."

In the quivering light of the mercury vapor lamps, the activity of the Chinatown looters was almost indistinguishable from the sleeping ballet of children and merchants.

SNUFF IN SIX SCENES

Scene 1

FADE IN

We see a basement or a room in a warehouse. The walls are old, scarred metal. The floor is concrete. Fluorescent lights illuminate the space in a greenish glow. There are two chairs and a metal meat hook hanging by a chain from the ceiling. The walls, floor, and edges of the room are covered in transparent plastic held neatly in place by identical segments of gray duct tape. A rolling table stands nearby. It's piled high with tools: hammers, carpet knives, saws of various kinds.

A man in white Tyvek coveralls, a hood, gloves, and booties is in the foreground, making adjustments to the white balance on the camera. We look straight into his face through the lens. He is middle-aged, with fine crow's-feet around his eyes. In the background is a young-looking woman. She has a blond Mohawk and is dressed in boots, shorts, and a torn EAT THE RICH T-shirt.

The young woman rubs her arms as if she's cold.

Finally, the white-suited man nods and steps away from the camera. He turns to the young woman. "Say something so I can see if the audio levels are right."

"What should I say?"

"Why don't you start by saying why you're here today?"

She nods and looks down at her boots. "I'm Jenny..."

"Careful. No last names."

"Right. Hi. I'm Jenny. I'm here today to get murdered by Ward over there." She holds her hands out to the side, like a model on a game show indicating a prize. "Is that all right?"

The man looks at something off-screen. "It's perfect. The levels all look good."

"Now you introduce yourself?"

"Indeed I do." Ward beams into the camera. "I'm Ward. No last names, like I said earlier. And I'm here today to murder Jenny. It's important you know that what we're doing is entirely consensual. Isn't that right?"

Jenny purses her lips, uncomfortable. "It's true. I volunteered to let him kill me."

Ward looks at her. "Should we talk about how we met?"

Jenny shrugs. "It's your movie."

"That's true. Okay. Jenny and I met through an online app called—"

"Maybe you shouldn't say the name. You might lose your membership."

"Good idea." Ward stands next to Jenny with a hand on her shoulder. She rubs her arms again, trying to warm them. "Let me just say that I recently became aware of a certain phone app—not unlike Tinder—on which people with exotic needs and desires can meet. In my case, I wanted to kill someone. In Jenny's case, she wanted to die."

She holds up a finger and says, "For a price. I'm not dumb."

"And a pretty price, too. Fifty thousand dollars. Who's that money going to, by the way?"

"My mom. She's kind of an asshole, but she's sick and Dad left. Fifty grand will help a lot."

"That's sweet of you."

"Thanks."

Ward thinks for a moment. "Is there anything else we should say?"

"Um," Jenny says as she ponders this. "I know. I was wondering why we're doing this today and not, say, last week or next? You were very specific about the time."

"Right. I almost forgot," says Ward. He walks to the tool table and picks up a long steel cylinder with two prongs on the end. When he presses a button, there's an electric buzzing sound. "I kill people every ten years. It's kind of my thing. But this year is special. I just turned fifty. It's why I'm recording this session. I figured that I needed to get in one more big kill before I'm too old for this stuff anymore."

Smiling, Jenny says, "I'm your midlife crisis."

Ward laughs. "Exactly. It was get a Corvette or kill you."

Jenny laughs, too, and says, "That's funny. You're funny."

"Thank you. Anyway, I think it's about time to wrap up this first chat. I'll be getting to know Jenny more throughout the session. We're going to talk about all kinds of things before I let her die."

"I have one more question," Jenny says.

"Hold it for later."

Ward jabs the metal cylinder—a cattle prod—into Jenny's side. She screams and writhes in pain.

CUT TO BLACK

Scene 2

FADE IN

Jenny is blindfolded and bound to the chair with duct tape on her wrists and ankles. She's sweating and breathing hard. Ward slaps her and she jumps in surprise. When he walks around behind her she cranes her head back and forth trying to figure out where he is.

Ward has something in his hand. When he turns we see that it's a circular saw. He puts it close to Jenny's ear and turns it on for a second. She jumps in her seat, frightened by the sound.

"Fuck!" she yells.

"Are you scared?" says Ward.

"Of course I'm scared, you bastard."

He sets the saw on the tool table and rolls the whole thing in front of Jenny so that when he takes off her blindfold, she can see what he has in store for her.

Quietly Jenny begins to cry.

Ward says, "It's a bit more than you bargained for, isn't it?"

"Yeah," she says and looks up at him. "Tell me about yourself, Ward. Please? It will help."

"Why should I help you?"

Jenny tries to wipe the tears from her eyes with her shoulder, but can't reach. "My life sucks. I bet yours is great. Tell me about it. Please?"

He picks up a curved carpet knife, drops it. "I know your life sucks, you fucking idiot." When he finds a hacksaw, Ward weighs it in his hand. "Who else would volunteer for this?"

"Don't be mean," whispers Jenny.

Ward takes a breath and lets it out. "Unlike you, I come from a good family and I've gotten pretty much everything I ever wanted. I'm a partner at work. I have a great wife and a smart, lovely daughter. A nice home, too. Even a motor boat where Carla and I go fishing on weekends at the lake. Carla is my daughter."

Jenny opens her mouth, then closes it.

"Go ahead. Say what you want," says Ward.

"It's going to sound weird."

"That's okay. You'll be dead soon, so it won't matter."

She bites her lip and in a rush of words says, "I wish I had a dad like you when I was growing up. Mine didn't give a shit about any of us. You know, he tried to fuck me once. He only stopped because Mom came home."

SNUFF IN SIX SCENES

Ward frowns. "That's awful."

"Yeah. It was."

"Well, thank you for your kind thoughts about me as a father. I tell you what. Seeing how much your life stinks and how fulfilling mine is, when I kill you, I'll do it fast."

Jenny sits up. "You promise?"

"I promise."

"You know," she says. "Your ad didn't really specify that you were going to torture me. You just wanted to kill someone."

He comes over and sets the blade of the hacksaw on Jenny's arm. "I guess I lied."

She turns and says, "Did you ever consider that maybe I lied, too? Maybe I'm a pain freak. Maybe I'm getting off on this. Would that ruin things for you?"

Ward chuckles. "I saw your face. You were scared shitless."

"That's what I mean. Maybe I get off on being scared."

"Oh yeah?" Ward moves in front of her, blocking Jenny. He tosses the saw away and grabs something else from the tool table, but we can't see what. "You get off on being scared? Well, try this."

All we can see is Ward's back. Jenny screams.

CUT TO BLACK

Scene 3

FADE IN

Ward's frowning face fills the screen. The camera tilts back and forth as he shakes it. "Damn thing. I should never buy used equipment. You missed some great stuff."

He steps back. Jenny is slumped in the chair. Blood trickles from her mouth and nose. Her arms and legs are bruised. "Say it," he says. "Say how a lot of great stuff just happened. Tell the me in the future just how goddamn magnificent I am."

"You're the worst," Jenny screams. "You're a monster!"

Standing beside her, he tousles her short hair. Jenny lurches for his hand, trying to bite him. Ward stays just out of her range. Finally, he takes the circular saw off the table and walks behind Jenny, turning the saw on and off. She cringes but can't move away. Leaning over her, he whispers in her ear, "What should I cut off first, I wonder? Should we start with a leg?"

Jenny sniffs and says, "Wait! What kind of medical supplies do you have?"

A puzzled expression spreads across his face. "For you?"

"Of course," she says. "Cut off my leg and I'm going to go into shock and bleed out. Trust me. My sister-in-law is a nurse. It's not like in the movies. You hack off too much too soon, there's no more fun for you."

Ward walks around her and lowers the saw. "I hadn't thought of that."

Jenny cocks her head at him. "I thought you'd done this before."

"It was always quick. Not like this."

She leans back in the chair, a faint smile on her lips. "Holy shit. You're a virgin. You've never killed anyone."

"Yes I have," he shouts.

"Then you should have thought this through better," says Jenny. "I bet you hear that a lot at home."

Ward slaps her hard across the face. "Don't talk to me like that."

"My mom had me young and she said it screwed up her whole life. She had to settle down. Take any shitty job. No more fun for her. Did you have a kid young?"

"Well, aren't you little miss know-it-all?" Ward says. "You're not as dumb as I thought you'd be. After I've had some more fun, I'm going to cut off the top of your head and scoop out your brains."

"I love that idea," says Jenny happily. "But don't get excited and finish too quick. Do you have that problem with your wife? Finishing too quick?"

SNUFF IN SIX SCENES

Ward balls up his fist and swings at her.

CUT TO BLACK

Scene 4

FADE IN

Jenny hangs from the overhead hook by her bound wrists. She's stripped down to her panties. Ward hits her repeatedly with a heavy flogger. Jenny screams and squirms with every blow.

Finally, Ward lowers his arm to his side. He slumps into one of the chairs, breathing hard. He flexes and rubs his flogging arm.

From the hook, the bruised and sweating Jenny says, "You okay?"

"Shut up," says Ward.

"Look, if it's any consolation, if you die down there, I don't think I can get down. I'll probably starve or freeze. Isn't that comforting? Even if you stroke out, I'll die."

Ward flexes his arm. "A little, I suppose."

"You should exercise more."

He nods, sweat on his brow. "I know. Like I said, that's why you're going to die. I'll be too old and used up before long."

Jenny wipes blood off her face onto her arm. "Don't feel bad. Lots of older people do great things. Henry Miller didn't publish *Tropic of Cancer* until he was forty-five. Ray Kroc didn't start McDonald's until he was fifty-two. Grandma Moses was seventy-six before she started painting."

"I'm going to gag you," says Ward.

"Don't you want to hear me scream? Here. Listen." Jenny shrieks at the top of her lungs. Over and over again.

Ward clamps his hands over his ears. "Stop that!"

CUT TO BLACK

Scene 5

FADE IN

Jenny is back in the chair, but this time she isn't bound. Ward holds her in place, weakly, slapping and punching her. She laughs the whole time.

CUT TO BLACK

Scene 6

FADE IN

Ward is sitting on the chair next to Jenny. He's sweating heavily and softly crying. She has an arm around him. Gently, Jenny says, "Can I tell you a secret?"

"Sure. I guess."

"I was fibbing earlier. Remember when I said I was a pain freak?"

Ward drops his head into his hands. "Oh shit. You really were getting off the whole time?"

Jenny shakes her head. "It's worse than that."

"How could it be worse?"

"Have you ever heard of CIP?"

Ward lurches away from her. "Oh god. Is that like AIDS? Did you infect me?"

Jenny laughs. "No, stupid. CIP is congenital insensitivity to pain, aka congenital analgesia. I don't feel pain. All your so-called torture was a joke. I know it's sad, but you're a failure, Ward. A complete and total failure."

He shakes his head. "Don't say that." Ward reaches for her, but Jenny shoves him away. Exhausted, he falls back in his chair and weeps quietly.

"Remember how you were afraid of being old and useless one day?" says Jenny. "I'm afraid today is that day."

SNUFF IN SIX SCENES

"This is so humiliating."

Jenny puts an arm around him again. "Don't take it so hard. There's still someone you can kill."

He pulls away and looks at her through narrowed eyes. "Who? Not you. The moment's over. I blew it. All the money. All the planning. Worse, it's all on video. Shit. I have to destroy it."

Ward starts to get up, but Jenny grabs his hand and pulls him to the tool table. "You don't have to go out a failure. Think about it. There's still time to go out a winner."

Jenny puts a box cutter in Ward's hand. He wraps his fingers around it and sighs. "Thank you," he says wistfully.

Slowly, his eyes on the box cutter the whole time, he walks to the camera and kneels so that his upper body fills the frame.

"My name is Edward Thomas Jensen," he says. "And I'm a winner." He puts the box cutter to his throat and slashes himself deeply from ear to ear. His body shakes as blood pours onto his white Tyvek coveralls. He gurgles and his hands claw at his throat as he chokes. Soon, Ward's eyes roll back in his head. A few seconds later, he collapses onto the concrete floor.

For a minute, all that's in the frame is the plastic-covered room. One of the chairs has fallen over. Then Jenny's face fills the screen. Her EAT THE RICH T-shirt is back on. She lowers her head, then looks up. "I have one more confession." She looks around, as if making sure no one is there to hear. Then, beaming at the camera, she says, "Hi. My real name is Samantha. And I always wanted to kill someone."

She moves out of frame. All we see is Ward on the floor, then Samantha's hand as she turns off the recorder.

CUT TO BLACK

WHAT IS LOVE BUT THE QUIET MOMENTS AFTER DINNER?

Caleb was beginning to think that dinner might have been a mistake. He'd been on the dating app for months and, while he'd made connections with some other women, Patti was the first he'd actually agreed to meet, as his loneliness finally won out over the wariness that defined almost every aspect of his life. So far, though, the evening had been painful. He'd mumbled all the way through the appetizer and wasn't doing much better when their dinners arrived. Still, Patti chatted on as if he wasn't the stammering fool he felt like.

Picking at her honey smoked salmon, she said, "It must be so interesting being a journalist."

Caleb hesitated before answering, but fed up with his fear of human contact he said, "It's fun, but I shouldn't have said journalist. I'm just someone who freelances to a few magazines and papers. Mostly music, film, and book reviews."

Patti raised her eyebrows. "Ah. You're a 'film' person."

"Because I said film instead of movies?"

"Yeah."

He felt a little flutter of panic in his stomach and said, "I hope it doesn't make me sound hopelessly pretentious. It's just a leftover from all the film…movie magazines I read growing up."

Patti smiled brightly. "It's okay. I say film too."

"If I understood your ad right, it's your job. Digital film restoration?"

"That's right. Though I don't work with the film itself. I get digitized files and clean them up, frame by frame."

"That must be fun."

"Sometimes. A few months back, I got to restore some new footage for Fritz Lang's *Metropolis*."

"Okay. You can't deny that was fun." To Caleb's surprise, he began to relax as they talked about their jobs. He'd originally been interested in Patti because she worked with movies. He was sure if he kept the subject on that, he'd be all right.

But she wasn't so easily pinned down. She said, "I suppose it was entertaining. But enough about work. What do you do for fun?"

Caleb froze again. What *did* he do for fun? The things he wrote about used to be fun, but now they were just how he passed his nights.

"I can see I stumped you," said Patti. "That's okay. I'll go first. I like hunting."

Caleb looked at her. "You mean animals?"

Patti set down her fork, frowning slightly. "Was that the wrong thing to say? I'm sorry I brought it up."

Before Caleb could reply, the waiter appeared and asked if they wanted dessert. Neither did, so he left to get their check.

Knowing he had to say something to try and salvage the evening, Caleb said, "I'm sorry. I just never met a hunter before. Well, one, but I didn't like him."

"I upset you," said Patti. She reached across the table and put her hand over his. "Come back to my place and let me make it up to you."

That's a surprise, he thought. With his clumsiness earlier and his reaction to her hobby, he was sure he'd ruined the whole evening. Still, part

WHAT IS LOVE BUT THE QUIET MOMENTS AFTER DINNER?

of him wanted to bolt and head home, but Patti was genuinely interesting. He wondered if maybe things would be easier somewhere less public. "Okay. Yes. I'd like that."

Patti wiped her mouth and said, "Great. How did you get here?"

"A cab."

"Perfect. I drove. We can take my car without worrying about yours."

Since he'd invited her out, Caleb insisted on paying for dinner. Patti led him outside to a sporty-looking Mercedes GT and opened the door for him. Once she got behind the wheel, she steered the car at breakneck speed all the way across town, blowing through red lights and letting the tires squeal around corners. Caleb wanted to look relaxed when she glanced at him. Smiling tightly, he tried to think of small talk. "How long have you been restoring films?"

Patti wagged a finger in the air. "No more work talk."

"Then what should we talk about?"

"You'll see."

She lived in a condo complex out by Ocean Beach. The neighborhood looked expensive and Caleb wondered briefly how well film restoration paid if she could afford a Mercedes and a bungalow out here. He theorized that she might have inherited the place from a relative or maybe she made good stock investments. He could ask her for some tips. It wasn't much in the way of conversation, but it was something.

However, once they were inside the apartment, Patti didn't leave any room for small talk. She pushed Caleb down on the sofa and climbed on top, straddling him. Shy as he was, when she kissed him fervently, he kissed her back just as hard. The feeling was both glorious and achingly sad as his loneliness clashed with the joy he felt being with someone—anyone—after so long alone.

They'd been kissing and touching for several minutes when he felt Patti shift position. Still on his lap, she leaned away from him, pinning him in place with one hand. Caleb didn't see the other hand until it was too late.

She drove the butcher knife into his chest up to the hilt, pulled it out and did it again. Over and over, she drove the knife into him, a wolfish grin on her face the whole time. Caleb started to double over in pain, but gathered his strength and shoved her off hard enough that she rolled across the coffee table and onto the floor. Before she could get up, he pulled the knife from his chest, jammed it into the wall, and broke off the handle. He tossed it to her mockingly as she got to her feet and said, "I guess this is what you meant by hunting."

"Bright boy," said Patti. She ran to an easy chair across the room and pulled out an axe hidden behind it.

Caleb said, "How many people have you done this to?"

"That would be telling." He waited for her to rush him, but she stood where she was, looking at him and his clean shirt. Finally, she said, "Why aren't you bleeding?"

Now *he* smiled. "It's not in my nature."

"Everybody bleeds."

"Not me."

Patti frowned. "You have some kind of disease?"

He laughed. "People like me, we don't get diseases. We don't bleed and we don't die."

Even though she was holding the axe at shoulder height, Patti looked less certain of herself. "What are you saying? You're some kind of vampire or something?"

"You've never heard of anyone like me. And that axe isn't going to help you."

Patti took a nervous step back. "Are you going to try and kill me?"

"I'm not a killer. A killer is a wretched thing."

"Then what are you?"

"I'm leaving now."

"You can't. The door is locked and I've hidden the key. What are you?"

Caleb tried the door and, indeed it was locked. He turned back to Patti. "Fine. You want to know? I eat the dead."

WHAT IS LOVE BUT THE QUIET MOMENTS AFTER DINNER?

She made a face. "You're a cannibal?"

"You wouldn't understand."

"Try me."

"I told you what I am, and you know you can't kill me. Open the door so I can go."

Patti lowered the axe to the floor and gave Caleb an odd look. "Are you sure you want to leave?"

He laughed. "Now I'm suddenly interesting enough for you not to murder?"

She shrugged. "I'm a funny girl."

"Please open the door."

Patti left the axe against the easy chair and took the keys from her pocket. As he left, she grabbed Caleb's arm. He whirled, but before he could hit her, Patti said, "I'm sorry about your shirt."

"Good night."

AT HOME, Caleb poured himself a tall glass of scotch and drained it all at once. He set the glass on the kitchen counter, removed his ruined shirt, and threw it in the trash.

What the hell was I thinking?

He went over the evening in his head for the tenth time.

There are so few like me, and most of us are loathsome. What kind of relationship could I ever have with a regular person? No. I'm just a bug scuttling around at night, bribing morgue and funeral home lackeys for food. It's worse when they smile or try to make small talk. I can smell their terror, even as they take the money. No. No more fuck-ups like tonight. No friends. Never love.

TWO NIGHTS later, Caleb received an email telling him that he had a message from Patti on the dating app. At first he ignored it, but the more he thought about it the more unsettled he became. In his anger, he'd said more than he'd intended. What if she told someone? Or worse, what if Thacker had gotten to her? He logged onto the app and before he could check his email, a new text came through from Patti. It read, "I've been thinking about you. The things you told me about yourself."

He texted back, "Trust me. I've thought about you too."

"I want to see you again."

"That sounds like a bad idea."

"I promise it will be different this time."

"Why should I believe you?"

"Because of what I know now. To do what happened last time would be pointless and just spoil the evening."

Caleb typed, "Then why?"

"I told you. I can't get you out of my head."

"Maybe it would be better for everyone if you tried harder."

"See me. Tonight. No funny business. I promise."

"Why would I do that?"

"You said you'd been thinking about me. See me tonight. If the evening displeases you, I promise to leave you alone."

As much as he wanted to keep his distance from her, Patti was the first person he'd felt any interest in for so long. As it had on the night he met her, the loneliness welled up inside him. She was beautiful, and she was interesting.

She knowns she can't hurt me, and if she tries I could be ready.

He typed, "I can't say I'm not tempted."

"Come at ten. Not my place. At a hotel. Here's the address and room number."

"I'll have to think about it."

"See you at ten."

TENSE AND fairly certain that he was making a mistake, Caleb arrived at the room number Patti had given him at ten minutes after ten. He hesitated a moment before knocking and slipped a hand into his jacket,

WHAT IS LOVE BUT THE QUIET MOMENTS AFTER DINNER?

taking hold of the snub-nose .38 he had hidden there. *I might be foolish enough to show up,* he thought, *but I'm not dumb enough to get stabbed twice.* And there was the Thacker question in the back of his mind.

Finally, he knocked. A shadow passed over the door's peephole and he heard locks opening. A moment later, Patti was standing before him. She was nude except for nitrile gloves and a pair of disposable hospital booties. She was covered in blood.

"What the hell...?" said Caleb.

She put a finger to her lips and said, "No questions yet. Here. Put these on."

Patti handed him disposable booties like hers. When he hesitated, she dropped to her knees and put them on over his shoes, then pulled him inside.

It was an ordinary businessman's room, functional and forgettable—except for the body lying on a plastic tarp spread out over the floor. Caleb lifted the edge of the blanket covering it and the smell of blood filled his nostrils and made his stomach growl.

He looked at Patti and said, "My god. Did you do this because of me?"

"Maybe," she said coyly. "Partly. Show me. I kept him warm for you under the blanket. You must like them fresh, right?"

Caleb shook his head. "This is insane."

"Show me," said Patti as she pulled away the blanket to fully reveal the body. He too was nude and his clothes were folded neatly on a corner of the tarp. The smell of the fresh meat was overwhelming. Caleb hadn't eaten properly in a week. There was just the old woman from the morgue where he had an understanding with one of the attendants. There had been so little of the woman that she was mostly bones. Hardly a meal at all. Except for the slit across his throat, the body on the floor of the hotel room was in the prime of life.

He tried to stop himself, but the hunger was overwhelming. Caleb took off his jacket and shirt and tossed them on the bed. Then, as Patti watched, he slid his fingers into the flesh above his sternum and pulled himself apart. His torso parted easily, becoming a gaping maw lined with a row of sharp, ragged teeth.

From close behind him he heard Patti say, "Yes. Yes."

Caleb turned around to check that she wasn't armed. When he saw she wasn't, he knelt over the body and fed it into his jaws quickly, starting with the man's head.

He'd been so hungry that the feeding only took a few minutes, and when he finished he fell onto his back panting as strength returned to him. He hadn't realized how drained he'd become. Caleb looked up at Patti standing over him. Her expression wasn't fear or disgust, but one of pure wonder. Before he closed his chest, Patti reached down and ran her fingers lightly over his torso's lips and teeth. Caleb looked down at himself. He was almost as bloody as Patti now. When he tried to get up, she pushed him back onto the tarp and pulled off his pants, sliding down onto his cock. They thrust against each other for what to Caleb felt like a delightful forever until Patti groaned and dug her fingers into him. Falling on top of him, she kissed him hard.

PATTI TURNED on the shower for him because he wasn't wearing gloves and she didn't want him leaving fingerprints. As he washed, she folded up the tarp and blanket, put them into the dead man's suitcase, and set it by the door. Then she joined Caleb in the shower and they scrubbed each other clean.

Lying together in bed, Patti said, "The other night, you said that killing people was a wretched thing. But you're wrong. It's easy and it means nothing."

Rolling onto his side so he could get a better look at her, Caleb said, "Do you really believe that?"

She nodded and held out her hands, making a rectangle with her fingers. "Killing is easy because people don't exist. They're like frames of film. I can see right through them. Their death is just editing out frames here and there."

WHAT IS LOVE BUT THE QUIET MOMENTS AFTER DINNER?

"Can you see through yourself?"

"Oh yes. I'm not here either. But here's the thing. Why I asked you here tonight."

"So you could watch me feed."

"That too, but mostly it's because I can't see through you. You're real. You exist. I've never met anyone like you before."

Caleb laughed once. "No. I bet you haven't."

Patti crawled on top of him and kissed him again. "I want... I want to know you. I've never felt anything for anyone."

"Because they didn't exist?"

She touched his face. "Yes. But you. I actually feel something," she said. "Stay with me. I'm not afraid of you or anything I saw tonight. I know you're lonely or you wouldn't have come here. Please. Take a chance and see what wonderful things we can do together."

Caleb stared up at her. She was so beautiful. Her skin was warm, unlike the dead, who were the only other bodies he'd known in years. A part of him wanted to run from the room, but another, stronger part of him held him where he was. He pulled Patti down onto his chest and said, "I suppose we can try."

She sat up and smiled at him. "Yes? That makes me so happy."

He looked up at the ceiling. "I was wondering something. These men you kill, do you steal from them too?"

Patti smiled. "You mean how can I afford my Mercedes? Of course I take their money. Killing them means nothing, why should going home with some trinkets?"

"I thought so. That brings me to the other thing I need to say."

"What? Tell me."

"If we're together, you can't kill people anymore. You'd have to be content helping me gather bodies. It's not always easy. Maybe that would be adventure enough for you?"

Patti looked down, her brow creased and mouth drawn down. "I thought you might say something like that, so I thought it over before I got here. And, yes, I promise to try."

"If the urge hits you could always, I suppose, do things to the bodies before I feed."

Patti brightened. "Yes. I think I'd like that."

"And don't worry about money. The kind of work I do doesn't pay much, but I have an inheritance."

She wiggled her body against his. "I guess we're an item then."

Caleb chuckled. "I guess we are."

They kissed for a few minutes and got dressed. Patti put their booties in the suitcase with the tarp and as they were leaving, she looked serious for a moment. "Is this what love feels like?"

Caleb kissed her. "It's the beginning, at least. We'll know if it's love soon enough."

Smiling, Patti said, "Take me to your place. I want to see it."

"All right."

She drove them out to the ocean first, where they walked along a rocky cliff out of sight of the road. In the darkness, she threw the dead man's suitcase into the churning water below. They waited until it sank beneath the waves, then drove to Caleb's apartment where they made love the rest of the night.

AFTER A month without a kill, Patti grew restless and began going to martial arts classes. For all its power, aikido turned out to be too passive for her, while judo was too much ground work and didn't possess the aggression of kicking and punching that she craved. She soon moved on to Taekwondo and Krav Maga where pummeling and being pummeled gave her something like the excitement of the hunt. She soon declared herself Caleb's bodyguard and accompanied him on all his runs to the morgue and funeral homes, looming quietly in the background in shades and a long coat, wishing she had a knife in her pocket, but satisfied with knowing how much damage she could do to any rogue attendant who attempted to deny Caleb his meal or tried to shake him down. Back at his apartment, she never tired of watching him feed.

What Is Love but the Quiet Moments After Dinner?

One evening, after dinner he said, "I never asked you this because I didn't want to pry, but how long have you been killing?"

Patti thought for a moment and said, "My whole life, I suppose. I can't remember a time when the urge wasn't there."

"How often did you feel compelled to do it?"

"With people? Never more than once a month, and always on different days, using different weapons. I wanted to avoid having too much of a pattern for the police to follow."

"Do you miss it?"

Again, Patti took a moment. "I thought I would, but between the martial arts and sneaking in and out of morgues with bodies, I don't really."

Caleb smiled. "That's wonderful to hear. Still, I feel guilty for asking you to stop doing something so fundamental to you."

"But that's what I mean. Things are different now. I can't see through you and I can see myself more and more."

"I never wanted to try and tame you."

"Trust me, you're not. You should come to class and watch me toss people around. I love feeling them hit the ground."

"I'd love to see you in action."

Sitting on the sofa, Patti put an arm around him. "Can I ask you something?"

"Of course."

"You don't get sick. You don't get hurt. You don't die. So, how old are you?"

"That's a hard question to answer because I don't know," said Caleb. "There weren't really countries back then. Just snow and tribes of people who kept on the move looking for game. I'd drift from group to group, trying to settle down. With the cold and lack of game, death was much more common back then, so if the tribe couldn't feed, I still could. Sooner or later, though, when enough bodies disappeared, they'd realize what I was. Some tribes wanted to kill me. Some wanted to worship me. I didn't like either, so I stayed mostly to myself."

Patti kissed him tenderly and said, "You don't have to be alone anymore."

WHEN SHE went back home the next day to pick up some clothes and her mail, there was a bald man waiting for her on the sofa. He kept a hand in his pocket like he might be hiding a pistol, but Patti had dealt with enough prey that she prided herself on picking up on facial and bodily cues enough to be fairly certain that it was a bluff. Before she said a word, she went to the easy chair and took out the axe hidden there. The stranger immediately shrank back and his hand came out of his pocket. She'd been right. It was all an act. But he wasn't too frightened to speak.

He said, "Don't do anything stupid, lady."

"Like breaking into my apartment?" she said, advancing on him.

"Thacker put me on to you two. You and your freak show boyfriend."

Patti frowned. "What the fuck are you talking about?"

The bald man sat up a little straighter. "But I don't want him. He's Thacker's problem."

"Who the fuck is Thacker?"

The man ignored her. "Worry about me. Brubaker. I know who you are and I know what you've done. I have photos. Dates. Names. All of it." When he finished, he reached into the pocket she thought might have held a gun, took out a pile of photos, and tossed them on the coffee table.

Patti kept the axe as she looked over the shots. Brubaker wasn't bluffing now. There were photos of her with the last three kills she'd made the month before she and Caleb had become lovers and she'd sworn off murder. "Did you take these?"

"Does it matter?"

"What do you want?"

"A hundred thousand dollars."

She held up the axe a little higher. "You think I have that kind of money lying around?"

What Is Love But the Quiet Moments After Dinner?

"Sell that pretty car of yours. Take out a second mortgage on this place. I don't care."

Patti kicked the coffee table out of the way and swung the axe down so that it embedded itself in the sofa frame between Brubaker's legs. He scrambled back a bit and shouted, "Don't even dream about killing me. Thacker has copies of all the files. If I disappear, he goes straight to the cops."

She knew she needed time to think, so she said, "When do you want the money?"

"Tomorrow night at eleven. Meet me at the Blue Cuckoo." Patti remembered the place. It was a shabby little tavern she'd shown some of her wealthier victims who wanted to see a real live dive bar.

Pulling the axe out of the sofa, Patti said, "I don't know if I can put it all together by then."

"Ask your boyfriend. He has money stashed away."

Patti spun the axe in her hands a couple of times while thinking. Brubaker said, "Don't do anything suicidal. All I want is the money."

"Who's this Thacker? I want to talk to him."

"No," said Brubaker flatly. He got up slowly and inched across the apartment to the door, never taking his eyes off Patti. "Tomorrow night at the Blue Cuckoo or the cops get everything."

Brubaker backed out into the hall. Patti hated letting him go but looking at the photos that had fallen to the floor, she knew the man was serious. She put the axe behind the easy chair and called Caleb.

"Can you come over?"

"What's wrong? You don't sound good."

"Please, just get over here as soon as you can. I'm in trouble."

A HALF hour later, Patti let Caleb inside.

"What's wrong?" he said.

She handed him the photos. "A man named Brubaker was waiting for me when I got home."

"Do you know him?"

"I've never seen him before. He wants a hundred thousand dollars or he'll send these and a lot more to the police. I have to kill him before he can do that."

Caleb took her hand and led her to the sofa. "I think killing him would be a bad idea. If he got in here without you knowing, I'd guess he's resourceful enough to be ready for an attack."

Patti looked concerned. "Have you heard of someone named Thacker?"

Caleb shook his head. "That idiot. He's mixed up in this?"

"Brubaker said he's working with him. Who is he?"

"Some mad vigilante character. He's been after me for a long time."

"Is he dangerous?"

"Potentially. But I've been dodging him for years, so I'm not too concerned."

"Should I pay Brubaker?"

"We. You're not on your own in this. And no, we can't pay him. He'll just come back for more. Why don't you let me handle this?"

"What are you going to do?" Patti said. She grinned. "Are you going to eat him?"

"No. I don't eat the living. But he doesn't know that. I'm just going to inform him that he's not just dealing with you, but with the two of us."

Patti put her arms around him. "I love you, baby."

"I love you too."

Patti frowned. "Be careful."

"I promise."

"I'm coming with you."

"All right. But once you point Brubaker out, let me handle things."

"Deal."

It was a long night and day waiting for eleven p.m.

WHAT IS LOVE BUT THE QUIET MOMENTS AFTER DINNER?

They arrived at the Blue Cuckoo at ten and found a table in a dim back corner of the bar. Caleb bought them drinks and when he returned to the table, Patti's hand was resting on top. She had a stiletto in her hand.

Caleb sat and put a hand over hers. "You should put that away before someone sees."

"I can still kill him," she said. "It would be so fast and easy. No one would ever know."

"You agreed to let me handle things."

"I know, but…"

He put an arm around her. "It's going to be all right. I promise."

She slipped the knife back in her coat pocket and sipped her drink.

At eleven on the dot, she sat up straighter. "He's here."

"Which one?"

"The bald guy at the end of the bar."

"I see him. Wait here."

"Be careful."

Caleb came up behind Brubaker and put the .38 in his pocket against the man's back. "You should come with me," he said.

Brubaker stiffened. "This is a dumb move."

"Walk over there. To the men's room."

"Whatever you say, Dirty Harry."

Once they were inside, Caleb jammed a metal trash can under the doorknob so no one could come in.

Brubaker leaned against the wall, seemingly unconcerned. "Let me guess," he said. "You're the boyfriend."

"Leave Patti alone."

"Did she send you here to scare me? This is so cute. But she must have told you where the information goes if anything happens to me."

"She told me. And I'm telling you again to leave her alone."

Brubaker jabbed a finger at him. "Fuck you. You aren't going to shoot me. I can tell you're not the type. Besides, the whole bar will hear and the cops will be here before you finish wetting your pants."

Caleb let go of the pistol and took his hand out of his pocket. "You're right. The gun was just to get your attention."

"If you're not going to kill me, then get out of my way."

Brubaker tried to push past, but Caleb shoved him back so that he fell against the wall. He said, "I'm not going to shoot you. But I might eat you."

The bald man made a face. "Fuck off."

Caleb unbuttoned his shirt, dug his fingers into his flesh and pulled himself open. The ragged teeth around his maw shone grayish green in the men's room flickering fluorescent lights. Brubaker pushed himself against the far wall. "Oh shit. Oh god. What is that?"

"Leave Patti alone or I'll swallow you down a piece at a time. I can make it last hours."

Holding up a hand Brubaker said, "Get the fuck away from me, you freak."

Caleb grabbed the man's hand and shoved it between his torso teeth. "How does that feel? Want me to snap it off?"

Brubaker froze. "Oh fuck. Please stop."

"Leave Patti alone."

The man nodded. "Okay. Fuck. Just get away from me."

"If you're lying, I'm not going to give you a second chance."

"I'm not. Just please leave me alone."

Caleb went to the door and shoved the trash can out of the way. "Get out. I never want to see you again."

"You won't," said Brubaker rushing out of the room.

After buttoning his shirt, Caleb returned to where Patti was sitting. "How did it go?" she said anxiously.

"He won't bother you again."

She laid her head on his shoulder. "Thank you. Thank you so much."

"Don't thank me. We're in this together."

"Let's go home."

They walked out of the Blue Cuckoo hand in hand. As they turned the corner to go to Patti's car, a man stepped out from behind a light

WHAT IS LOVE BUT THE QUIET MOMENTS AFTER DINNER?

pole. Thin to the point of being gaunt, he wore a long black silk coat and round wire rim glasses. He said, "Hello, Caleb."

"Thacker?"

The gaunt man slid a hand from his pocket and shot three times. Caleb stumbled back, bounced off a fire hydrant, and fell to the ground. Thacker took a couple of steps toward him when Patti charged, her knife out. She stabbed him once in his shooting hand and again in the arm. He dropped his pistol and fell back against a car, setting off the alarm. Patti kicked the gun into the street and pulled Caleb to his feet, shoving him into her car and speeding away.

WHEN THEY reached her place, he was weak enough that she had to put an arm around Caleb's shoulders to walk him inside. He finally collapsed on the bed, pale and sweating. Patti put a hand on his forehead and felt him cold and trembling. She sat down next to him and took his hand. She said, "I don't understand. Why are you hurt? Nothing can hurt you."

Caleb opened his eyes and said, "It's Thacker. He knows how to kill people like me. He put something on the bullets. Some kind of poison."

Patti squeezed his hand. "How can I help?"

He shook his head. "You can't. I need to feed, but it has to be fresh. Nothing from the morgue. Normally, if something like this happened, I'd scour the alleys looking for a recent death, but I'm too weak now."

"This has happened before?"

Nodding, Caleb said, "Thacker isn't the first who wanted me dead. There have been a few others."

Patti stood. "I'm going to get you something."

He reached for her as she got up. "No. Please stay with me."

She pulled out a box from under the bed. It was lined with purple velvet and full of blades. Selecting a Bowie knife and an old bone-handle dirk, she pushed the box back and put on her coat. "I won't be long."

Caleb tried to call to her, but his voice was hoarse and weak, so she didn't hear.

Patti was opening her car when something hard smashed into her back. The pain was sharp and deep, numbing her whole body so that she fell to the ground. Stunned, she felt hands roll her onto her back. Long legs stood astride her, and when she looked up, she recognized Brubaker. He was leaning casually on a baseball bat like it was a cane.

"You put that maniac onto me?" he said. "Fuck both of you. Thacker's got the freak, but I've got you."

The feeling came back to Patti's arms as he stood and held the bat over his head. She slipped the Bowie knife from her coat and shoved it through Brubaker's left calf, giving the blade a twist before yanking it out. He groaned and collapsed onto one knee, so she stabbed him in the right calf before he could push himself up. Falling flat on his back, Brubaker swung the baseball bat wildly at her, knocking the knife from her hand. While she stumbled to her feet, her knife hand aching, Patti kneed Brubaker's bloody leg. This time he didn't groan. He screamed at the top of his lungs and swung the bat again, but she dodged it and kicked him in the groin. He rolled on to his belly and started crawling away, shouting for help at the top of his lungs. Up and down the street, lights came on in homes and apartments. Before Brubaker could make it to the corner, Patti dropped her knees onto his back, pulled the bone dirk from her coat with her uninjured hand, and jammed it through the back of his skull until she heard a satisfying crunch. Brubaker made a gasping sound and kicked a couple of times, his hands grasping at the air. However, a few seconds later he was still. Patti pushed herself to her feet and grabbed Brubaker's collar, hauling him to her bungalow, ignoring the trail of blood his body left on the pavement.

A few minutes later, she went into the bedroom and helped Caleb to his feet, walking him into the living room. When he saw Brubaker's body he stopped and Patti had to hold him to keep him from falling over.

WHAT IS LOVE BUT THE QUIET MOMENTS AFTER DINNER?

"Baby, what have you done?"

"It's okay," she said, gently lowering Caleb onto his knees. "He attacked me this time. It was self-defense."

Caleb reached down and pulled the dirk from Brubaker's neck. "I'm not sure that's what the police will say."

"Worry about them later. Now shut up and eat."

He kissed her. "Thank you."

Taking off his shirt, Caleb pulled himself open and leaned over Brubaker's corpse. He fed the man's head into his chest first, then tilted the body to swallow the left shoulder, then the right. Feeling heat and his strength returning, Caleb tore into the rest of the body, swallowing it all in under a minute. He remained there on his knees breathing, feeling Brubaker's raw meat absorbing the poison in his system. As he stood, he saw the blood trail leading from the door. Patti helped him to the sofa. She put her hands on his cheeks and looked into his eyes. He put his hands over hers and said, "It's okay now. I'm feeling a lot better. You saved me."

Patti put her arms around him. "What else would I do?"

Eyeing the blood trail seeping into the carpet, Caleb said, "Did a lot of people see you?"

She sighed. "Probably everybody on the block. The cops will be on their way. We have to get out of here."

In the time it took Patti to get to the bedroom, tires squealed, and bright red and blue lights pulsed through the curtains. "Turn out the lights," Caleb said. When the room was dark, he went to a front window and peeked outside. "Fuck. Thacker is with the cops. God knows what he's told them about us."

Patti shook her head. "I'm not going to jail and leaving you."

"No one is going to jail."

She went to the kitchen and looked out the back door. Blue and red lights flared off the walls. Back in the living room she said, "We're surrounded."

"They'll want us outside soon. That's if they want us to come out at all."

"What do you mean?"

Caleb pulled Patti away from the window. "I mean that Thacker will have told him a story. That we're maniacs or terrorists. Someone beyond negotiating."

"You think they'll listen?"

"They're cops. What do you think?"

Patti went to the bedroom and came out with a Marine KA-BAR in each hand. "Fine. Let's take them on together."

Caleb said, "Maybe we can..." and glass flew into the room as all the windows exploded. Metal cannisters landed on the sofa and easy chair, while a couple rolled under the curtains. A choking mist filled the room and Patti began to cough violently.

"Tear gas!" shouted Caleb as he grabbed her, pulling her into the windowless bedroom. While she sat on the edge of the mattress, still coughing, he stuffed her bathrobe under the bottom of the door to keep out the fumes.

They could hear the cops, shouting something at them through megaphones.

Catching her breath, Patti said, "What happens now?"

"I don't know. I have a feeling if we went out now, they'd just gun us down."

"That's okay. You could save yourself."

"But it's not okay for you, so no one is giving themselves up."

Something in the air changed. A second scent mixed with the caustic tear gas fumes. Caleb touched the door and snatched his hand away.

"What's wrong?" Patti said.

Caleb opened the door a crack. The paint bubbled on the outside as heat and smoke poured into the room. "The cannisters," he said. "They've set the whole place on fire."

Patti put a terrycloth robe over her nose so that she could breathe.

"Cover your eyes too and give me your hand. Get ready to run."

"The smoke doesn't bother you?"

"I'll be all right. Just follow me."

WHAT IS LOVE BUT THE QUIET MOMENTS AFTER DINNER?

She put out her hand and Caleb led them in a dead run down the hall and into the bathroom. Inside, Patti coughed and wiped her eyes as Caleb pressed towels at the bottom of the door. "Why are we in here?" said Patti. "Could we stand in the shower, so the flames don't get us."

Caleb shook his head. "If the cops haven't turned off the water, the pipes will burst soon enough. The shower won't save us."

"You've been through this before."

"Something like it."

"With someone else?"

"Yes."

"Did they survive?"

Caleb didn't reply. Stronger than the smell of tear gas now, smoke snaked and swirled from under the bathroom door. The paint began to blister.

"Do you still have your gun?" Patti said. "I'm not going to the cops, but I'm not burning either."

"We could go out that window," Caleb whispered, thinking.

"But they'll shoot us if you do. That's what you said." Patti coughed as the room grew hotter and the choking smoke began to fill the place.

"There's still something," Caleb said.

"Tell me!"

He took Patti's hands and looked at her hard. "Do you trust me?"

"Yes."

"Do you want to live forever?"

"With you?"

"Yes."

"Then I do."

Caleb took a breath. "I told you once that I don't eat the living."

"I remember."

"There's a reason for that. The dead are just food. My body absorbs them and that's that. But for my kind, to eat the living is to have them inside you forever. Fused to you, body and soul."

"We'd be one person? Forever?"

"Forever."

Patti took off her clothes as the bathroom door turned black with heat. "Do it," she said.

When she was nude, Caleb held her to him and began to feed.

WHEN THE house was fully engulfed, the police pulled their men and cars back from the conflagration. Covered in flames, Caleb kicked out the bathroom window and ran westward toward the sea. A sniper on a roof nearby spotted him and shot a volley of bullets into his back. At the end of the block, Caleb found a deep puddle and rolled in it until the flames were out. By the time the police had their searchlights on, he'd rounded a corner and dashed for the beach, where he dove under the waves. The police soon found his footprints and followed him there. They searched the shoreline and sent divers down into the cold, churning water. They brought in helicopters and search dogs. They called in forensic experts and the FBI, but found nothing in the apartment except for a charred box of knives. No bodies. Nothing. One police officer fell off a cliff during the search and landed on a cluster of boulders below. By the time his companions scrambled down after him, the body was gone. When the police searched Caleb's apartment, they found his clothes closet empty and an unsigned Valentine's card on the living room table.

No one ever saw Caleb or Patti again.

DEVIL IN THE DOLLHOUSE

The Unimog bounces down a shattered freeway that looks like a set from *Crackhead Godzilla Goes on a Bender and Fucks up Everything*. Exit signs and overhead lights are melted to slag. Buildings along the edges of the road look more like the stone skeletons of giant fish than settlements. We have to inch our way down and then back up collapsed overpasses like arthritic grasshoppers.

And it gets worse. This thousand-mile-long ribbon of shit? Technically, I own all of it. All of Hell is falling apart and one of my jobs is to put it back together. But not today.

Let's back up and get a look at the big picture.

There are just as many assholes in Heaven as there are in Hell. The only difference is the ones in Hell aren't slick enough to hide it. Therefore Hell is a kingdom of assholes, and thus the Devil is the king of the assholes.

Hi. I'm the Devil. No, seriously. I used to be James Stark or sometimes Sandman Slim, but then the Lucifer 1.0 pissed off back to Heaven and stuck me running Hell. I thought that was the worst thing that could ever happen to me. That was three days ago. Today things got worse. Today I'm in a truck convoy heading somewhere I never heard of to find some place that scares even these evil fallen-angel pricks. Plus, I can't eat the lunch they packed for me. I never could stand unicorn salad.

Here's how it all started: I was hanging out in Lucifer's library—my library now—when a bookcase opened and two Hellions came in, looking at me like I was a two-headed rattler in the reptile booth at a Texarkana side show.

"So, this is him," said the smaller Hellion.

"I guess so," said the big one.

"He doesn't look like much of a monster."

"He's the monster who kills monsters, so naturally he's a lesser monster."

"He still looks like any other mortal to me."

"You know I'm standing right here, right?" I said.

The smaller Hellion raised his voice, like maybe I was hard of hearing.

"I was saying that you don't look like much of a monster."

"I look better covered in blood. You never saw me fight in the arena?"

Big Boy shook his head.

"Merihim there is a priest. He can't go. Me, I don't like to go. Fighting for fun doesn't make sense to me."

"Trust me. It wasn't fun."

The smaller Hellion was in sleeveless black robes. Every inch of visible skin was tattooed in sacred Hellion script, like he'd been mugged by the tiniest graffiti crew in the universe. Big Boy looked like the Hulk's runt cousin in rubber overalls. Dangling from his thick leather belt were enough vicious-looking tools to give Torquemada the vapors.

"I'm Ipos," said Big Boy. He hooked a thumb at the tattooed squirt. "He's Merihim."

I recognized the names. Samael, aka Lucifer 1.0, left me a note with their names. They're a couple of his spies and sometime advisors.

"Hi," I said. "I'm the Devil."

Merihim nodded. Pursed his lips.

"Yes. That's what we're here to talk about. You're not, entirely, quite Lucifer."

"Then you better tell whoever is Lucifer, because I'm living in his palace, wearing his clothes, and peeing in his shower."

"Yes," said Ipos. "You have all the trappings of Lord Lucifer. And you certainly have the title."

"What you lack is the belief," said Merihim.

"I seem to remember killing Mason Faim and stopping a war with Heaven."

"And those facts are what earned you the title. But the title is a thing of the mind. Belief is a thing of the heart. And that you don't have."

"Not yet," said Ipos.

"In a conversation like this when someone says 'not yet' it makes my balls ache. You know why? Because that's where the knee is going. Because 'not yet' means I have to do something and it's going to hurt. Am I right?"

"Your balls are very wise indeed," said Merihim. "But you need to see our problem."

"You need to see mine. I don't care."

Ipos held up one of his big hands.

"We're here to help you become what destiny has led you to."

"To become the Lord of the Underworld."

"Don't call me 'Lord.' I don't like it. So how are you going to do it?"

Ipos said, "There's something Samael was going to do before he left us. A kind of quest."

Perfect. Not only does Samael stick me with Hell, he leaves me to clean up his last job. And I know him well enough to know that this is one he didn't want to do.

"Fuck you both. I never wanted this gig. One of you can play Lucifer. How about you, preacher?"

"I'm a simple priest, unsuited for a life in politics."

"What do you say, Mighty Joe Young?"

"I'm head of maintenance. Your palace would fall apart without me."

"Well, I'm not Sir fucking Galahad out looking for adventure. I'm a schmuck who wants to go home."

"You have to be alive to do that," Ipos said.

"Not all of Hell is willing to accept a mortal as Lucifer. Considering that you are going to be with us for quite some time…"

"Forever maybe."

"You might want to consider ways to minimize your chances of being murdered."

"Not being killed is pretty high on my agenda. What kind of quest are we talking about?"

Merihim idly picked up a book from a nearby table.

"It's really more of an exorcism. Not much more than clearing out a haunted house."

"Maybe a bit more like a fortress," Ipos said.

"With a coterie of unpleasant residents doing mischief with travelers."

"What's a coterie?"

"A somewhat large group."

"How large?"

"Some say an army," said Ipos. "But a minor one."

"Why didn't you say so? It sounds completely reasonable."

"Good."

"No, it doesn't. I was being sarcastic."

Merihim frowned.

"You don't do it as well as Samael."

"My wise balls are telling me to pass on the offer."

"But they know you can't."

He was right. If I'm going to survive I need some juice, and the fastest way to get that down here is to kill something.

So now here I am, bouncing along in a truck with concrete shocks surrounded by a Hellion legion that smells like a fish-market Dumpster. I'm not usually the dragged-along-for-the-ride type. Usually, I'm the one doing the dragging, but I'm a little out of my depth here. Like

Devil in the Dollhouse

Marianas Trench out of my depth. I fought in the arena long enough to know that sometimes the best strategy is to shut up, go along with the game, and make sure that someone is standing in front of me when the tentacles hit the fan. So far though, all my Cool Hand Luke plan has gotten me is a numb ass from sitting and a ringing in my ears from the engine noise. Worst of all, the unicorn is starting to smell good.

Up ahead, the whole world is on fire. Our three-truck convoy is off the freeway and in open desert plains following a narrow winding road to fuck all.

"Ah. The first ring of suffering," says Geryon, the scholar. "Henoch created three before we reach the Breach. They're designed to break the spirit of anyone approaching."

"I thought we made the suffering. We don't do the suffering."

"If you think Hell isn't Hell for every creature in it then you're blind, False Lucifer."

"That's getting annoying."

"No more so than being ruled by a usurper."

"A usurper has to want the job. I want to be home, drunk and breaking hotel beds with a girl named Candy."

"Of course, False One. You merely fell into the lordship of Hell. It's happened to all of us."

"Then you admit I'm head of the pit crew down here."

He looks away. Geryon loves me. The conversation has been like this all the way out from Pandemonium.

"If you're unhappy you can walk back to Pandemonium. It shouldn't take more than a week."

"Merihim should be doing this," says Geryon.

"Merihim and Ipos are too chicken to leave the capital, so they gave me you, sweetheart. Start talking or we're going to see if you can dog-paddle through fire. I wonder if fried Hellion tastes like spicy or original recipe?"

Geryon looks at me like I'm a moldy ham sandwich someone forgot in the back of the fridge at work.

"What is it you want of me?"

"The rest of the story. You were telling me about Henoch Breach."

Lucifer got me into this Hell mess and deserted me. Then Merihim and Ipos got me into this haunted house bullshit and they deserted me too. If you can't trust a fallen angel, who can you trust? Geryon is supposed to have the lowdown on where we're going but he hates me more than Aelita and Marshall Wells combined. Maybe Merihim and Ipos are smarter than I thought. Maybe they stuck me with Tiny Tears here to show me how much some of the townies despise me. Maybe I can even learn something from this guy if I don't get bored and make his guts into a new fan belt for the truck.

"Before the Breach there were the beasts. They were here when God threw us from Heaven's walls. Few remember them and those who do think of them as nightmares. Nightmares from the terror of landing in this place. Some of us though, we still remember the truth. Great, fat obsidian snakes like blind worms and rats with fur like steel spikes."

I look out the front window. The air shimmers over the heat like waves on a lake. Molten rock flows in thick streams around burning boulders. Blackened bones of hellbeasts stick up from black patches of cooled lava like slaughterhouse stalagmites.

"How in fuck's sake are we supposed to get through that?"

Geryon glances at the window and looks away. He's scared but he doesn't want to look bad in front of the mortal. Cry me a river.

He says, "The rings are cruel. They are designed not to kill, but to break our spirits. We turn back now or we go through them, stopping for absolutely nothing. The choice is yours, thief."

The Unimog driver slows down and stops, waiting for me. He looks almost human, if the human summered in a trash compactor. His head is twice the size it should be and roughly the shape of a rotten pumpkin. His back is hunched and one of his arms looks like it was chiseled out of concrete. I nod to him.

DEVIL IN THE DOLLHOUSE

"Pour on the horses, Elephant Man, and don't stop for anything."

The heat hits hard and fast, like one minute we're fine and the next some bastard has dumped a ton of burning compost on our heads. Hellions might be fallen angels but they're still angels, and seeing angels sweat like rotten meat is the kind of thing that can make a person tense.

The ribbons of heat turn the air to Jell-O. It's hard to breathe and I can barely see anything out the window. The driver inches us along the road at a crawl. The engine whines like it's about ten seconds from melting down. I swear I can hear the tires sizzling underneath the truck. The troops in the back of the truck are getting restless, and by getting restless I mean pressing their ugly Hellion noses to the window, trying to see who's going to panic first and do something incredibly stupid.

Geryon sticks his head in the back and speaks to them.

"We can make it. Others have and in lesser vehicles than this. We just have to be strong."

Geryon might be smart but he doesn't have the best timing. Just as he finishes, both rear windows crack in the heat. One begins to fall apart but the other holds. Some of the troops grab their guns like they can shoot the heat away.

The truck lists to the right and then lists more as we hit a patch of melting road. For a minute it feels like we're going to roll over. Elephant Man shifts hard. Gears grind and scream like they're about to pop out through the hood. Slowly the truck rights itself and just like that we're clear of the flames. Like closing a window, we're out of the smoker and onto a nice cool plate with cornbread and potato salad. The other two trucks are moving slow. I go to the back and look out the broken window.

Truck Two is where we just were, leaning to the side on the soft road. The driver inches forward and the truck starts to right itself. Then with a *crack* like God's own cannon going off it's gone. All that's left is a molten rock void in the road over a river of streaming lava. I press myself against the ceiling, and through the window I can just see the edge of the truck's front bumper sinking into the thick orange flow. Then that's gone too. The driver of the third truck takes a big chance and drives off the road onto the rocky shoulder, taking the long way around the hole. It's a smart move. They take it slow and in a few minutes pull up behind us, the truck's body steaming, the undercarriage glowing bloody red. There's nothing to do about the other truck. I tap Elephant Man on the shoulder and we drive on.

"You were talking about monsters."

"Yes. I was."

I fish a pack of Maledictions from my pocket, take one and offer him one. He shakes his head. I hold one out to Elephant Man and he takes it. I light it and then mine.

"Monsters."

Geryon nods.

"The story isn't about monsters. It's about Henoch. He, like you, was a traitor to Lord Lucifer and was exiled in the outlands with other traitors in a wretched town made of tunnels carved from the barren landscape. Traders from Pandemonium traveled from there along this very road to bring back their goods. Most never made it home."

"The beasts?"

He nods.

"But not the old ones. These were new beasts. Henoch mated with the creatures and created an army of unnatural horrors. If he couldn't return to Pandemonium, he was determined that no one and nothing would ever get there. His monsters attacked even the smallest groups of travelers."

"And you want me to go up to a demonic freak show that no one even believes in but scares you all shitless."

"I'm afraid so, King of Liars."

"No wonder Lucifer took a powder."

"Lord Lucifer isn't a coward," Geryon shouts. The soldiers in the back of the truck look up at Mom and Dad fighting.

"I didn't say he was a coward. I said he was smart."

Geryon turns away, staring out the back window.

"What's that up ahead?"

DEVIL IN THE DOLLHOUSE

The terrain is changing again. A lush forest along the banks of a river. Trees dripping with fungus and moisture. Then the smell hits. I'm glad I skipped the unicorn. Geryon doesn't turn around.

"The second ring. The Alpheus Swamp. The very bowels of Hell."

He's not kidding. I'm one bad pothole away from telling Elephant Man to turn around and head us back into the fire. The river ahead is a thick, crawling torrent of swirling blood and shit. Downtown's sewers have to empty out somewhere. Why not in the middle of no-goddamn-where? And why not put a road through it to keep Lucifer's traitors in and curious morons out? Like the fire, we have no choice of where to go. We head straight into Puke Swamp. I'm on the edge of vomiting up everything I ever ate since childhood, strained peas to chicken and waffles. Damn. Wrong memories. My stomach starts doing a hillbilly two-step. I think of Candy but she makes me think of sex and rolling, moving, and tumbling over furniture. My gut tells me to move along. I look ahead and concentrate on the trees. Dark branches dripping with emerald green parasites. My insides cool off and settle back about where they're supposed to be.

Elephant Man slows, losing sight of the road in the brown bog.

"Off to the left," I tell him. "Follow the roots of the big tree up ahead and in between the two little ones."

He nods, picking up the outlines.

Geryon looks like I feel. He's slumped in his seat, his head between his knees. Even the fish-store-stinking soldiers are having a bad time of it.

I didn't sign up for any of this, but at worst I always thought being the Devil would be at least a little fun. Shooting BBs at Hitler as he tightrope walks over a lake of boiling lemon juice and broken glass. Playing Pin the Tail on the Stalin. After lunch, maybe a few rounds of Ted Bundy Whac-A-Mole. Instead I get a literal river of shit. What's the old saying, "The road to Hell is paved with good intentions?" This one is paved, carpeted, and wallpapered with skin off my sore ass.

We're halfway across the river when Elephant Man pulls to a stop.

I say, "What is it?"

He stretches up and looks over the Unimog's hood.

Geryon stands too and says the words I was hoping I'd never hear.

"We're stuck."

Lucifer, you motherfucker, you must be looking down at us from Heaven and laughing your holy ass off. I swear someday I'll make you surf this river from end to end.

I pull up the handle and open the door. Geryon grabs my arm.

"What are you doing?"

"We need to get out and push."

His forehead creases as he stares at me. "Pushing is what the soldiers in the back are for. Not the Lord of the Underworld."

"You said I'm not the Lord."

"For the moment you represent him."

"Good. Until you come up with another Lucifer, it's my kingdom and my rules. Let's go."

He gives me a shocked smile. Spreads his hands.

"I'm a scholar, not a slave."

"You can get out and help or I'll throw you out and you can swim to Mordor, Frodo."

I lean into the rear compartment where the soldiers are.

"Come on, kids. Time to pat your feet on the Mississippi mud."

Grumbling, they hustle out the back.

"Go find some big branches to put under the wheels."

How do you describe standing knee-deep in the evil shit of an evil bunch of bastards? It's unique. Warm and with unexpected bits of floating things that I don't want to think about. The drowned carcasses of little winged lizards that pass for Hellion pigeons. My biggest fear is tripping on a hidden root. I don't want to go facedown in this muck. There isn't enough penicillin in the world to save me from the badass microbes living in this chocolate oatmeal outhouse.

Geryon is doing even worse than I am. He's frozen by the side of the truck, turning around and around in horrified circles like he's trying to stomp shit into wine. He only moves when soldiers arrive with

DEVIL IN THE DOLLHOUSE

tree limbs and push him out of the way so they can wedge them under the back tires.

"How are you doing, Geryon?"

He doesn't answer. Just stands with his arms crossed in front of him, watching the soldiers try to pry the wheels from the sludge.

"Why don't you tell me more about Henoch?"

He can't answer. Geryon is gone. I might have broken him.

Something moves past my leg.

"Hey. Didn't you say one of the monsters out here was a kind of snake?"

He looks at me blankly, and then nods.

"Why do you ask?" he says. Then disappears, yanked below the surface by something underneath.

A dozen nearby soldiers drop the branches they've been maneuvering and pull their sidearms, firing blind into the river.

"Stop!"

It takes a few seconds but they do.

"Feel with your feet. Use your hands. Find him."

They're not happy but the only Lucifer they know just gave them an order. Instead of rebelling and stringing me up like Il Duce's corpse, they do what I say, reaching under the muck and feeling for Geryon.

Elephant Man, still above us in the truck, points and grunts.

A round hump breaks the surface of the river. Six soldiers reach down to grab it. They pull out one end of what looks more like a fat ten-foot earthworm than a snake. The snake is blind but its jaws are wide and round, like a lion-toothed lamprey. A few feet down from the head, the snake's body is wrapped around Geryon's waist.

"Grab him. That's an order."

This time no one gives a good goddamn what Lucifer has to say. They're too busy firing their pistols at the snake's head. They're hitting it too, with what should be kill shots. Maybe the thing really is more like a worm than a snake, because for all the hits it's not going down. This thing must have the nervous system of a chicken burrito.

I grab the na'at from inside my coat, extend it into a spear, and shove it into the snake's body a couple of feet above Geryon. The snake whips around in my directions and takes a couple of blind nips at the air like it's not sure where the wound came from.

I twist the na'at's grip and it goes slack. I flick it out like a whip and it goes around the snake's body twice. Twist the grip again and the na'at is as rigid as plate steel. The whip loops dig deep into the snake's flesh, drawing a dirty white ribbon of pus-like blood. It screams and lunges for the soldiers. They keep firing and I keep pulling. Its neck twists to the side as I cut through its thick jelly-like flesh. Geryon is holding onto the snake's body, trying to keep his head above the filthy river. I dig in my feet and give one last, hard pull. The snake stiffens and lets out a piercing scream that's like getting an ice pick through my ears. And its head slides off the body, trailing luminous insides into the muck. I reach down and pull Geryon to his feet.

"Nice job, St. Francis. Were you trying to romance that thing?"

Back at the truck I help him up and Elephant Man pulls him inside.

The troops are all looking at me. I don't know if it's because they're impressed or because they've never seen their boss covered in enough shit to fertilize all the weed fields in Humboldt County. I put the na'at back in my coat and say, "Get those branches and your asses in gear so we can get out of here."

Fifteen minutes later we're moving again. A couple of minutes after that we crest a hill and it starts to rain. Shit streams off the windshield. I roll my window and stick my head outside, letting the water wash my face clean.

Geryon pulls his hands from his filthy face and quietly says, "Oh no."

"What?"

"It's the last ring. Regret."

Yes, I was stupid enough to think being Lucifer would be just a little fun.

The troops have the rear door open. Some lean out and others jump, running along behind the truck and letting the rain wash them clean. Other soldiers pull them back in, then jump out to take their place.

It doesn't look like regret to me.

There's a choked sound.

I look over at Elephant Man. I've never seen a Hellion cry before. It's disturbing. The mood in the back is changing. A second ago everyone was whooping like their team won the Super Bowl on the same day they hit the lottery. Now nothing.

A wave of memories.

Crawling out of Hell to save Alice, only Alice was dead and there was nothing and no one there to save. Then there's Candy. I told her I'd be gone for three days. It's been a week now and I don't know when I'll figure a way out of here, if ever. I see the arena. The early days Downtown: Most Hellions had never seen a live mortal. The months of flat-out torture, games, and fun fair experiments on me for a paying audience. Then the arena and learning to kill. What's worse: Committing murder or learning you're good at it? Mason killed me and he's kept on killing me every day for years. I'm going to be here forever. I'm never going to leave.

Geryon is curled up like a baby, shaking, his hands over his eyes. The troops in the back are worse. They've been on edge for months, ever since Samael left and Hell went balls up. Whatever this is, it's broken the weak ones. There's a line of them in the road behind the truck. They went out to feel the rain and never bothered getting back in. We could go back for them but what's the point? The ones that haven't shot themselves already are sawing on their throats or wrists. Black blood flows in the gray rain. The second Unimog moves slowly, trying to avoid the bodies.

The truck stops. Elephant Man puts his head on the steering wheel. I know what this is. The memories flow like poison from a cobra bite but I'm still here. Eyes still open. The fire burns my gut but it doesn't kill me. It's familiar. An old friend you never wanted to see again but still someone you know. I pull Elephant Man from the driver's seat and shove him into mine. Slide behind the wheel and hit the accelerator. This is the ring that's supposed to put the final nail in my plain pine coffin? Regret? Memory? I spent eleven years down here dining and dancing to bad memories and regret. I've had my shots for the memory, measles and rubella regrets. I'm fucking immune. Okay, not immune. My hands shake and my throat's dry but I thought Hellions would laugh off three-hanky flashbacks. Instead they're crying like a school bus full of little French girls whose ice cream all melted.

Half a mile on, the clouds break. The rain fades to a drizzle and sputters out. A few minutes later the second truck pulls up behind us. Geryon points to a stand of bare trees.

"Henoch Breach is at the top of the next hill. We should rest here for a few hours."

"Okay by me."

After we've pulled into the trees and everyone is out of both trucks, I do a quick head count. We haven't even reached Margaritaville and already lost a little over half our troops. The "fuck this shit" human part of me wants to turn around right now and head back to Pandemonium. What do I care that Samael promised these demonic knuckle draggers to scare the monsters out from under their beds? Then the Lucifer part of me pipes up. No matter what, I can't look weak. Like a pathetic mortal. If I'm going to ride this out and stay alive, then I'm king high ballbuster. I took on God and almost did the old man in. A few grumpy horns and hoofs types and a petting zoo full of rabid Pokémons? I'm Satan. I can deal that and play "Smoke on the Water" while getting a lap dance on a runaway train all at the same time.

Some of the soldiers unload supplies from the Unimogs. Food. Guns. Ammo.

The nearby trees are bare. The whole glade looks dead. The trunks of the trees are twisted up to branches that look like snakes made of finger bones. Soldiers gather fallen limbs into a pile to start a fire.

"Why don't you send up a fucking flare and let the monsters know we're coming?"

They stop and look at me.

Devil in the Dollhouse

"No fires. No camp sing-alongs. No square dancing. Have something to eat and drink, quietly. When we ring the doorbell on that castle up there, it would be swell if it was just a little bit of a surprise."

Without a word they do what I say. Toss the branches aside and settle around the trucks, passing out cans of food rations and bottles of Aqua Regia.

"I want to thank you."

I didn't notice Geryon coming up beside me.

"You had no reason to save me. I'd told you the story. You didn't need me anymore but you saved me all the same."

"Don't worry. It wasn't anything personal. I just don't believe in leaving my crew behind."

"All the same, I owe you my life."

Elephant Man comes over with a bottle of Aqua Regia. He hands it to me and I take a pull. Pass it to Geryon.

"So tell me the rest. What does the city of traitors have to do with all this?"

Elephant Man goes back to the other troops while Geryon and I settle on a log passing the bottle back and forth. The booze helps me forget that we both still smell faintly of Hellion shit.

"It doesn't even have a name," he says. "Lucifer didn't want to give them any cause for pride, so he gave them a place but no identity other than as a land for the shame of the lowest among us."

"I thought that used to be me. Nice to know there was someone even more fucked up. So what does being a traitor mean down here? I mean, you're fallen angels. Doesn't that make all of you a bunch of traitors?"

Geryon half turns his head toward me then away again. I guess it's not worth the argument.

"The early days after the fall were hard. Some didn't survive the fall itself. Others went mad. There were murders and suicides. Lord Lucifer, Samael, gathered the fallen and just as in Heaven, he became our leader. He urged us to build and create our own civilization. One to rival even

Heaven. He saved us. Still, with all that, there were some who refused to follow."

"Because he fucked things up so badly during the war?"

I pass Geryon the bottle and he shrugs.

"I'm sure they told themselves they had reasons, but it was really simple greed. Some had escaped Heaven with weapons and riches. Enough, they thought, to mount a new war. Lucifer knew this would destroy us, so he attacked them first. The ones who survived he exiled here."

I can't help but hum a couple of lines from "Town Called Malice."

"What did they do all the way out here?"

"Through the tunnels they lived in they mined the mountains. They grew spices and created rare potions from local plants. In short, even in exile, our Lord made them earn their keep."

"Is the town still there?"

By the trucks the soldiers have broken up into small groups. Good. We did the same thing after a bad day in the arena. It's not something you think about, it just happens. You fall into the orbit of friends and familiar faces. You don't even have to like each other. You just have to be there to remind each other that you survived and that this is real. I'm sure there's a scientific name for it. The old fighters just called it Tea Time.

Geryon says, "No one knows if the town exists anymore. Hell has fallen apart so badly since Samael left and with the beasts on the road, we're the first visitors out this far in years."

I take another hit off the Aqua Regia and recork the bottle. This isn't the time to drink as much as I want to.

"I guess one way or the other we'll know tomorrow."

"I hope they're all gone," says Geryon. There's an edge to his voice I haven't heard before. "One set of monsters is enough."

"Amen to that."

NIGHT AND day are kind of abstract concepts out here in the hinterlands. Hell exists in a kind of perpetual bruised twilight, but in Pandemonium

DEVIL IN THE DOLLHOUSE

and other towns there's an agreed-upon cycle for morning, noon, and night. Out this far the only difference between 12 A.M. and 12 P.M. is a slight color change in the sky. Still, after eating everyone sacks out. A lot of the troops fall asleep. There are guards posted but this far out all they'll probably see are desert rats and sand fleas.

Around what I think might be midnight, the trees start to move. It begins with a rustling. It sounds like wind but I don't feel anything on my skin.

The camp comes awake around me. The troops heard the sound too. Hellions look around for the noise, the breeze, or whatever, as puzzled as I am.

The first scream comes from deep inside the dead grove, followed by another on the edge. One of the guards, a big bastard with a revolver grenade launcher slung over his shoulder, disappears into the trees. Whatever is happening, he doesn't die all at once. There's a dull thump and a grenade explodes in the middle of camp, scattering soldiers and weapons high into the air. A second later another grenade goes off right above the treetops, lighting up the grove. That's when we see the trees moving.

They come apart like ripping cloth and fall to the ground in a tangle of branches and blasted trunks. They writhe and then crawl. A second later they're on their feet running at us.

Guess what? They aren't branches and they weren't trees, thank you very fucking much. They're bodies, as dry and rotten as week-old roadkill. They were wrapped around each other in a frozen graveyard embrace and we woke them up. There's hundreds of them closing on us, and more in the distance.

The firing starts before any of them make it into camp. The sound of piss-scared soldiers blowing clip after clip on full auto fractures the air and numbs my ears, but it doesn't do much else. It sure as hell doesn't slow the roadkill. They charge into camp like a bone-and-gristle Mack truck, mowing down rows of heavily armed and severely motivated soldiers.

I pull out the na'at. Extend it to its full length. Keep the Freud jokes to yourself. Sometimes a killing stick is just a killing stick.

It doesn't take much to stop each individual roadkill. They're not much more than mummies with an attitude. Their teeth are sharp and their talons are long but you can slice them up like buttered toast if you have a sharp blade. I wish I could explain that to the idiots with the guns.

The scene reminds me of L.A. when a load of High Plains Drifters—that's zombies to you—were running extremely amok. Bullets didn't slow them either and even if they did, how do you know which one to shoot when there are six or seven on top of you ripping you to pieces? That's how these brainless bone sacks win. They wear you down until it doesn't matter how many of them you kill. All it takes is for a few to swarm you and you're gone. Short of flamethrowers, nukes, or a bunch of trained Drifter killers, the best strategy is nature's simplest: run like you're a zebra at a waterhole and a pride of lions just showed up with ketchup and silverware. But where do we retreat to? No one is going to follow me into the rain ring and there's no forest to hide in anymore.

I shout, "Up the hill. Get your asses to Henoch Breach."

I grab Geryon. He's a scholar, terrified and useless in a fight. I stuff the hem of my coat in his hand.

"Hold on to that. Keep your head down and keep moving. If you fall I'm not coming back for you."

I circle the long way around the grove, keeping clear of the trucks and the close-in fighting. Anyone penned in there is going to die. At least in the open there's somewhere to run to. I twist the na'at grip until it's like an extra-long broadsword and start hacking my way through the roadkill blizzard. The bad part is that there's a lot of them. The good part is that they're dumb and the ones I don't kill forget me as soon as I pass, zeroing in on the doomed assholes playing Last Stand at the Alamo in the trucks.

Groups of soldiers fall in behind us as we work our way up the hill. Now that their ammo is gone, they're using their rifles like clubs and making a lot more headway than before. Halfway up the hill I look back at the clearing and I can't even see the trucks. They're completely covered around and on top by roadkill.

Devil in the Dollhouse

It's a long way up the hill. Henoch Breach is like a cross between a gothic mansion and an old cavalry fort. The mansion look fooled me into thinking it was a small place but it turns out it's more of a fort, which means big and a lot farther away than I thought. With every few yards we gain, we're losing soldiers. I still feel Geryon hanging on to my coat.

After what feels like an hour, we're finally at the Breach's big double front doors. I don't know how many roadkill bastards we've killed on the way up but it isn't enough. There's a shuffling mob maybe a minute down the hill from us. I don't want to kick the door in if I don't have to. I don't know if there's anything inside to barricade it with once we're in. But the windows are sealed tight behind metal bars. Around the side I find a fire escape leading up to a single door three floors up. I extend the na'at into a billhook and get the curved part of the blade onto the ladder and pull. It swings down in a shower of dirt and rust. I have no idea if it will hold our weight and not a lot of time to do an OSHA inspection. I shove Geryon up the ladder and head up after him.

The door at the top is solid. It takes three good kicks to get it open. Plenty of time for the first of the roadkill to catch up with us. I shove Geryon inside and pull in a couple of soldiers behind me.

It's dead black inside. I can't see a thing. The first screams hit us as Henoch's last booby trap catches up with us. Why didn't Geryon know about the trees? Is this whole thing a setup? If it is, does that make him a suicide bomber or just another loser caught up in the hit on me? I'm going to hurt a lot of people and ask a lot of questions if we get out of here alive.

One of the soldiers cracks a handful of glow sticks. I grab a couple and lead the way deeper inside the Breach. More soldiers are stumbling in but the roadkill is just a few seconds behind us now.

There's no way I'm running upstairs and getting trapped on the roof. I start down a wide grand staircase, heading for the front door. With any luck we can wait for most of the roadkill to come in upstairs and flank them by going out front and down the other side of the hill into Lucifer's traitor town. The only kink in this plan is if some of Henoch's freak beasts show up, but I haven't seen or heard a peep from them and it sure doesn't smell like anything has been living here in a long time.

We never make it to the front door.

We hit a series of hallways on the main floor. They twist and turn in on themselves and it doesn't take long to lose track of which way it is to the front door. I stop to get my bearings. Geryon is behind me. He's pale, holding his side like he's about to cough up his lungs. There aren't more than six soldiers behind us anymore. We're at a crossroads. All four hallways look exactly the same and then it hits me. We're not in normal hallways. The main floor of Henoch Breach is a labyrinth.

"Why have we stopped?" asks Geryon.

"We're lost. I'm trying to figure if I can get us back to where we started."

"Is that a good idea?"

The screams from behind us make his point for him.

"I remember someone once told me that in a maze the trick is to keep turning left and eventually you'll get out."

"Is that true?" Geryon asks.

"I don't know. I never tried. And maybe it's the way to get to the center and not out."

Geryon slumps. Puts his head in his hands. None of the soldiers have weapons anymore. They're ripped and bitten and bloody, and they're all staring at me like lost kids at the zoo. I say the first thing that pops into my head.

"Try the doors. Maybe there's a window or a place to hide and figure a way out."

That gets them moving. We head in different directions down all four corridors from the crossroads, rattling and kicking at doorknobs. They're all locked but there's nothing else to do. We keep trying one door after another. Finally one opens.

"Here," I shout. "I found one."

I push open the door with the glow stick held high. The room is empty. On the far wall is a barred window. I head for it. Three steps in

Devil in the Dollhouse

I hear a crack and the floor gives way beneath me. The last thing I see is Geryon's shocked, scared, stupid face as I fall.

MARTIN DENNY wakes me up. It's "Quiet Village," all birdcalls and tropical piano chords. Someone is pulling me from the floor and setting me on a bar stool. Carlos the bartender is the first thing I can make out clearly. Then plastic hula girl. Palm trees. I'm in the Bamboo House of Dolls.

"Maybe you've had enough for tonight?" Carlos says and turns to someone on my right.

"What do you think? Too much or just enough to take advantage of?" comes a female voice.

I turn and Candy is right beside. She kisses me. My head hurts and I'm as dizzy as the Teacup Ride at Disneyland.

Candy does a mock frown.

"Uh-oh. Too much, it looks like. Maybe we need to get you home."

"Home?" is all I can get out.

Vidocq comes over. Puts an arm around my shoulder.

"You remember home. The lovely Chateau Marmont. It's just a few steps away. Come. We'll take you from all this, *le merdier*. You'll never have to see it again."

"Never again."

They pull me to my feet. Candy, Vidocq, Allegra, and Kasabian. He has arms and legs. A complete body. He wags his finger in my face.

"You never did know when enough was enough."

I look at Candy and my heart breaks all over again, just like it did when I lost Alice.

"I'm sorry to say but I know exactly when enough is enough."

I pull the black blade from the waistband at my back and slice Kasabian's head off. It rolls across the floor like a sweaty basketball. I whirl and stab Vidocq in the eye. Pull out the blade and shank him in the heart. Then I do the same to Allegra and Carlos.

"Stark. What are you doing?"

They're screaming and they don't stop until they're in pieces on the floor.

I turn and look at Candy. She backs away, her hand held up to me. Bumps into the jukebox and freezes.

"It's me, baby. What are you doing?"

I'm dizzy and nauseated.

"Doing just what you said. Getting myself away from *le merdier*."

I flick out the na'at but I can't go for her. I lunge and put the blade into the jukebox. Denny sputters and dies. I turn and hack the bar in half. Swing again and slice through the bar stools. Vault the bar and start in on the bottles. I take out a row of booze with each swipe of the na'at until I'm ankle deep in the stuff. Back over the bar, I push a candle over. The booze goes up in one big *whoosh*.

I'm feeling it now. That old arena feeling, where nothing feels better than something breaking under the na'at or my hands. Candy backs against the far wall. I stab it over her head, pulling out big chunks of plaster. I hack at the windows and floor. I slice apart the pillars by the door and the whole thing collapses. The decorations over the bar are burning and patches of the ceiling glow cherry red. Once it catches we all go down together.

"Right, Henoch?" I yell.

I hack at the beams in the walls. They start to sag. I hack at the floor until it starts to buckle beneath us. The ceiling catches. The air is sucked out of my lungs as all the oxygen in the room cooks off. I look at Candy. I pull out the black blade to throw through a window. She knows a flashover is coming.

"Enough."

She screams it over the sounds of the flames. I don't have to throw the knife. The window cracks. The air explodes, enveloping us in flames as thick as molasses. Then stops. The room goes black.

"Enough."

It's not Candy's voice. It's a man's.

DEVIL IN THE DOLLHOUSE

"What in Lucifer's name is wrong with you?"

Light slowly comes up. I'm standing in a dimly lit stone room with an old man. Splintered pillars and support columns lean haphazardly against the walls and across the floor.

"You mean my name, don't you, Grandpa? I'm Lucifer."

Henoch Breach has wet rheumy eyes set in a sagging face. Scraggly white whiskers that might be the remains of a dead beard. His teeth are black and crooked, like fallen dominoes. He's dressed in robes that probably looked regal about a thousand years ago. Now they look like a gaudy bath mat in a Tijuana flophouse. He looks around the room.

"Look what you've done to my home."

"What was I supposed to do? No one told me there was a ring inside the house. Only this one wasn't suffering. Did you really think the 'it's all been a dream' gaff was going to work? Does anyone ever fall for it?"

He laughs and it breaks down into a wet cough. He finds a chair in the wreckage, rights it, and sits down. His voice is surprisingly deep and strong.

"You'd be surprised. Offer mortals or angels what they really want and the first thing they'll give up is doubt."

"Not me. Not down here. Doubt is my best friend. Doubt that I'm stuck here. Doubt someone like you is going to off me."

"I have no interest in offing you any more than you have in offing me."

"You just murdered a hundred of my troops."

He shakes his head.

"They're not your troops. They're Lucifer's troops and you're not him. You might have the title. You might be hiding that you wear his armor under that coat but you're no more Lucifer than the other one."

"How do you know, Henoch?"

"I'm not Henoch, you young fool. There is no Henoch. I'm Lucifer. The *first* Lucifer."

On any other day I might not believe something like that. Today is different though.

"If you're the real Lucifer then the guy I know as Lucifer is Henoch?"

He leans his elbows on his knees and shakes his head.

"I told you. There is no one named Henoch. Henoch is the town. I'm Maleephas. And before you ask any stupid questions, yes, I said I was Lucifer. Remember that the Lucifer you know was once Samael. Just as you…"

"Stark."

"As you, Stark, are now Lucifer."

I hear something from above. I can't tell if it's screams or someone singing "Close To You."

"What's happening to my people?"

"I assume they're being slaughtered just as anyone who comes here is slaughtered."

"Why? What's so special about this place that everyone has to die if they come near it?"

Maleephas shrugs.

"You'll have to ask Samael. He built it. He made the city. He constructed the road. He made the rings you passed through and the Vorosdok that attacked your men. If you've been in Hell for any length of time you've probably noticed that he's quite clever and has a good sense of suffering."

Is this another illusion? Am I talking to myself or does the roadkill have hallucinogenic saliva and they've bitten me and are tearing me apart?

"Why would Samael do any of that?"

Maleephas stands and crooks a finger for me to follow him.

We go down a corridor with windows that look out over the front of the Breach Roadkill and dead soldiers are spread out in all directions.

"Don't feel badly," says Maleephas. "This is his doing. Not yours."

"Why? Why would he build this? Why are you here?"

He opens his arms wide, turning in a circle. He laughs with more strength than I thought he had in him.

"Because this is Hell. The first Hell. The first after the fall. The one we made together and he took and then abandoned."

DEVIL IN THE DOLLHOUSE

Maleephas looks out the window. A few last roadkill wander up the hill. A lot of them are missing heads, arms or legs.

"What stories do they tell about me now? That Henoch Breach is a rebel Hellion's hold? What do they say about this Hellion?"

"That he's crazy. That he slaughters travelers along his road. That he fucks snakes and rats and makes monster babies that do his dirty work for him."

He grips the bars and presses his face to them.

"At least I'm colorful in this version. These myths about the place, they change over time. Very few in Hell recall what really happened in the early days. Remember what I said about offering beings what they really want? Why would they want to remember that this world began with a betrayal as thorough as the one in Heaven?"

"You're saying that you and Samael were bosom buddies and he turned on you. Why? Why would he care about taking over this shithole?"

"For one thing he likes power."

"So do you, if you were Lucifer."

"Touché. The difference is that I had doubts about the argument with Father. He didn't. When a group of us tried to go back, well, you see the result."

The little gears clank in my brain. I look out the window.

"The roadkill that attacked my men. They're Hellions, aren't they?"

Maleephas nods.

"The ones who wanted to return with me so we could throw ourselves at God's feet, hoping to receive his infinite mercy. What they received was what you saw in the grove. I received this prison."

I take out a Malediction. Light it and offer it to him. He takes it and sniffs, hands it back to me.

"It smells awful. Is that what you do in Pandemonium these days? Pollute yourselves with that?"

"We have all kinds of pollution. You should try Aqua Regia. Or there might be some unicorn salad left in the truck if you want to try it."

He shakes his head.

"Such a stupid world we made together. It was going to rival Heaven but it turned into more ruin."

"You know what's funny?" I say. "Guess where Samael is these days."

"I'm afraid I've lost my appetite for games."

"He's back in Heaven. He had doubts about the argument too. At least the part about the war. He's back upstairs trying to make it up to the old man."

A smile spreads across Maleephas's face. He leans against the wall and chuckles.

"And it only took how many eons and another fool to play Lucifer."

I puff the Malediction and think.

"Maybe it's not as bad as you think. I thought Samael was playing me for a chump when he blew town and left me this job. Maybe meeting you is what's it's all been about. Maybe he couldn't face you or maybe he knew you wouldn't want to see him. Maybe I'm here to blow up the myth. Let you out and remind everyone what really happened here."

He turns his eyes toward me.

"Do you think he's really that compassionate?"

The Malediction burns my throat in a good way.

"Weirder things have happened."

Maleephas comes over to me, using his hand to fan away the smoke. He whispers.

"You know what I think? I think he did send you. But not for the kind of compassion you mean."

I feel the knife slip under the bottom of the armor. Maleephas drives it in two, three times, twisting the blade and holding it in place.

"I think he sent you here as a sacrifice. He's gone and is giving Hell back to me. I'll burn Pandemonium to the ground. Henoch will be the new Hell and this will be Maleephas Lucifer's palace."

He pulls out the blade and pushes it back up under the sleeve of his robe. I fall to my knees. He kicks me. It is a small thing but already bleeding and stabbed, it still hurts.

DEVIL IN THE DOLLHOUSE

"If it truly is so easy for Father to forgive Samael, then he was right and I was wrong. We'll prove them both wrong by creating a brand new Underworld. The hills outside of Henoch are rich in gold and silver. We'll build an entire city of precious metals, so bright it will blind the archangels and over time they'll come to worship us."

"Fuck you, Mally. You're as dumb as the twerps that fall for your picture show. You've started believing your own fantasies."

He stands over me.

"Whatever Samael's intentions, I'm about to become Lucifer again. The armor protects you but not from everything. This athame is quite potent, even against Lucifer."

"I know. I stabbed him with one myself."

He brightens.

"Did it hurt?"

"Yeah."

"I'm so glad to hear that."

"One thing," I say and swing out with the black blade. I never put it away, just held it back against my arm like a polite, stupid son of a bitch. The knife catches Maleephas just above the right ankle. He falls over backward, leaving his foot behind and spouting black blood all over the floor.

I grab a set of the window bars and pull myself up. As soon as I'm upright, Maleephas throws his knife. I'm too hurt to get out of the way. The blade kicks up a spark when it hits Lucifer's armor and bounces into the ceiling. I extend the na'at into a spear and return the old man's favor by pegging him to the floor through the gut.

"You're not Lucifer. I am," he says.

"The difference between us is I don't want the job. Normally I'd offer it to you but that little trick with the knife was annoying, so all you get is a big steaming plate of fuck-all."

"What are you going to do to me?"

He looks scared, which is pretty funny because I can barely stand up. Just to keep up appearances I drop the Malediction by his head and crush it out with my boot, letting my heel graze the side of his face.

"Maybe I'll just leave you there like a butterfly stuck in a display case. Bring bus tours out to see you. Print maps to the star's home and put your face on mugs and T-shirts. How does that sound?"

"Kill me. If you have any mortal mercy left in you, kill me. Or are you fully Lucifer now? Should I worship you and beg your indulgence? Please, great and awful Beast of the Abyss, give me the gift of oblivion."

"Shut up. I'm not going to kill you. But I'm burning this place to the ground. I'm leaving you and your knife here. You can crawl away into a hole in Henoch. You can burn here or you can kill yourself. It doesn't mean jack to me. But I'm not doing Samael's dirty work or yours."

I pull the na'at from his stomach. Maleephas groans and rolls onto his side. I cut through the bars over the window with the black blade and crawl outside. It hurts so much I almost faint when I drop to the ground. I cut a long strip of cloth from my coat and press it against the wound in my belly. I couldn't fight off a Vorosdok kitten right now but I don't think I'll have to. The few pieces of roadkill still alive are laid out on the ground like a truck ran over them. I think when I put the na'at into Maleephas the Vorosdok went down with him.

It's quicker down the hill than it was up. Not running for your life through an army of brainless Hellion zombies will do that. When I reach the nearest Unimog, I pull enough bodies out of the cab that I can get into the driver's seat and start the engine. I head up the hill, steering the truck over every Vorosdok body I can see. I stop the truck outside Henoch Breach's front doors and a couple of corpses get to their feet. I pull the na'at. The dead men are Geryon and Elephant Man.

"Playing possum? How did you get outside?"

Geryon shakes his head.

"I have no idea. After you disappeared, we ran down corridors at random. I don't know what happened to the others. I think we were just lucky."

"Well, get your lucky asses over here. Take a couple of jerry cans of gas and toss them into the Breach."

Geryon frowns.

DEVIL IN THE DOLLHOUSE

"Why?"

"Because I met him. Maleephas. I know the whole story."

Geryon walks over to me. I hand him one of the heavy cans.

"You met him? He's still here?"

"Who do you think gave me this?"

I lean back so he can see my wound.

"Since you knew he was there, that means you know the story you told me is total horseshit."

He shakes his head.

"No, it isn't. It's a myth. You have no idea how ugly the early days were here. We needed to forget all this and when we did, we needed something to replace it."

The old man in the basement had it right. Give people what they want.

"It's over now. This place and the story. Both of you. Toss those cans or I'll do it and toss you in with them."

Geryon and Elephant Man push open the doors and throw the open cans inside. I pull a couple of road flares from storage, spark them, and throw them into the dark. The gas explodes, knocking me flat on my ass. Elephant Man helps me to my feet and walks me to the truck. He pulls out the rest of the bodies from the cab and helps me into the passenger seat. Geryon gets in and sits on the little jump seat between us as Elephant pulls the rest of the roadkill and dead soldiers out and leaves them on the road.

"Is it just us?"

Geryon nods.

"It seems that way."

Elephant Man brings the jerry cans of gas from the second Unimog and secures them in the back.

"I'm not looking forward to going back through the rings," says Geryon.

"I'll bet you a dollar they're not there anymore. Why would they be? Maleephas is probably dead and the Breach is burning. The hoodoo that hid them is probably gone too."

"I hope so."

I sleep most of the way back. I'm a fast healer, so the wound has stopped bleeding by the time we can see the lights of Pandemonium. Elephant Man stops the truck to pour fuel from one of the cans into the tank.

"You're intent on telling the people the truth about Henoch and Maleephas when we get back?"

"Damn straight."

"I wish you wouldn't."

"Hell is a wreck. Forgetting who and what you are isn't how you start putting things back together."

Geryon claps his hands together.

"Lessons in ethics and morality from Sandman Slim. Who would have thought?"

Geryon pours a shot of Aqua Regia into a glass and we drink together. He pours a shot into another glass for Elephant Man when he gets back.

"In many ways this has been a disheartening trip," says Geryon.

"Which part? The hundred dead guys or Maleephas and me wrecking your fairy tale?"

"The hundred are a tragedy. The rest is your fault."

I sit up. The wound makes me wince.

"What's my fault?"

Geryon nods past me.

"That."

I look at Elephant Man. He's slumped against the door, the glass of Aqua Regia still in his hand. I pull my knife and hold it to Geryon's throat.

"You poisoned him to keep your secret? Did you slip me some too? Trust me, I can take your head off before I go down."

"I would never kill you, Lord Lucifer. And you are Lucifer now. You defeated the Henoch, the evil one, and his beasts and I'll sing your praises to all of Pandemonium. Hell needs a brave and glorious Lucifer if it's to rebuild."

Devil in the Dollhouse

"But I'm going to tell everyone the truth," I say, but even as the words come out I know in some weird way I'm not.

"You'll tell them what I tell you. I didn't poison you. I just gave you a little memory draught. What's happened will fade and be replaced with the myth I'll repeat to you on the way to Pandemonium."

I want to stab Geryon but the knife gets very heavy. My hands drop to my lap. Geryon pushes Elephant Man's body into the back of the truck and gets into the driver's seat. He starts the engine and drives us into Pandemonium.

"Henoch Breach lies on the edge of a town with no name. A town of traitors," he says.

"No. That's not true. I'll remember. I'll tell them."

"No. You won't. Henoch mated with beasts and they terrorized travelers on the road."

I start to say something but the words won't come out. I try to picture Maleephas in his dingy robes but I can't hold the image. I try to remember the Breach, the labyrinth, and the fake Bamboo House of Dolls. But even now I can feel it all slipping from me like water down a drain. I try to hold on to the memories but I know that by the time I finish this sentence they'll be

CANDY AMONG THE JADES

Candy awoke early and crept out of bed carefully so she wouldn't wake up Stark. She took her clothes into the kitchen and dressed quietly. The last thing she did on her way out of Max Overdrive was leave a note next to the coffee so Stark couldn't miss it.

> Morning babe.
> Auntie Bi is in town and I'm going to see her and maybe (probably) party with some of her Jade pals. I might (probably will) be out late.
> xxxx
> you know who

Downstairs, she took some money from the cash register and caught a cab to Bel Air, wishing the whole time that she could steal cars as easily as Stark. Her stomach was full of butterflies and she wished she could show up at the mansion in something more impressive than a Yellow Cab. Maybe a Rolls Royce or even one of those old muscle cars Stark liked. But here she was stuck in the back of a taxi feeling like a child on her way to the principal's office. She knew the day would come when Auntie Bi Routhav'n would come calling—it had been years since she'd seen her—but she didn't imagine the audience would weigh on her so much. No. That was a lie. She knew exactly why the matriarch of all the Jades was in town and the thought of seeing her again made Candy feel cold inside.

The ride to Bel Air felt endless. Thankfully, the cabbie wasn't the chatty type and didn't try to engage her in conversation. Still, she saw him glance at her in the rearview mirror a few times, probably wondering why some little punk in dirty jeans, boots, and a too-large leather jacket was creeping into Bel Air so early in the morning. Maybe she was some billionaire's daughter who stayed out late partying and was trying to sneak home before daddy cut her out of the will. *If only it was that simple,* she thought. Candy looked at her hands and ran a hand through her hair wishing she'd been able to take a shower before leaving but knowing at the same time that no matter what she did she'd still feel ugly and off-balance.

Finally, they arrived at the address. At the bottom of the driveway, a tall gate barred their way. Four Jades Candy had never seen before were on guard duty. The sight of them was both exciting and frightening. She loved how they radiated power and how the driver hesitated before pulling the cab up to the gate. But Candy was also nervous when the guards looked at her exactly as they looked at the cabbie—as an outsider. Someone who didn't belong there.

"You want me to drop you here?" said the driver. Candy knew that he understood how unwelcome he was. But she said, "Wait a minute," and rolled down her window. One of the guards approached her.

"What do you want?" said the guard, a head taller than Candy and almost twice as wide, her arms thick with muscle.

"I'm Candy," she said. "Auntie sent for me."

"Give me your hand."

Candy stuck her hand out the window and in one swift motion, the guard pulled her knife, slit Candy's thumb and smeared the blood on

Candy Among the Jades

a piece of red and gold paper she pulled from her pocket. Taking out a lighter, she set the paper alight. It sizzled and sent out sparks like a firecracker. The guard nodded slightly and handed Candy a tissue, which she wrapped around her bleeding thumb. With a wave of her hand, the other Jades moved into position and opened the gate for the cab to pass through.

"You sure you want to do this?" said the cabbie quietly. "I can turn this thing on a dime and we're gone."

Shaking her head, Candy said, "No. I've come this far. Take me the rest of the way."

"I'm not sure I want to."

Candy leaned up between the seats and held out all the cash she had. "Take it."

The cabbie quickly counted the money. Then, without a word, he drove them through the gates and up the circular drive to the mansion. What Candy saw disappointed her. The place was a typical southern California new money Spanish colonial sprawl, not a typical place for high Jades to reside, even temporarily. They had better taste in opulence, but Candy thought, *this is L.A. Nothing is old here. Nothing has real importance or history unless a movie star died there.* This massive, forgettable space was probably the best the Jade court could find that was both reasonably attractive and secure. The moment she stepped out of the cab the driver took off, leaving Candy in front of the house feeling small and as fragile as a bird.

She went up to the front door. There was no bell, but before she could knock the door opened for her. She felt a brief surge of happiness when she saw Rinko standing there. They had been lovers for a time while Stark was stuck playing Lucifer in Hell. But the happiness at seeing her didn't last long when she recalled how badly it had ended between them when Stark returned. For a while, they were able to balance their relationship with Candy seeing them both, but it all came tumbling down when Rinko gave her an ultimatum: her or Stark. Even with her affection for Rinko, Candy had never responded well to ultimatums. So, she left and moved in with Stark for good. It was nothing she thought about often, but standing here now, so vulnerable, it all came rushing back to her. She waited in the doorway until Rinko stepped aside saying, "Don't stand there like an asshole. Auntie isn't coming down to see you. Come inside."

The inside of the mansion was as unimpressive as the outside, full of faux antique furniture and dull paintings of dead people and faraway landscapes. But something did excite Candy. In the foyer, a dozen Jades milled around. Some were going through on business, but others had clearly come there to get a look at her—the lost lamb of the family. So many women. So much power in one place. Some of the Jades smiled, a few sneered, and others just stared at her with the blank look of bored visitors at a zoo. None of them would meet her eyes. Neither would Rinko when she turned to her. "I feel like the newest monkey in the exhibit," Candy said.

Rinko glanced at her and said, "You should be so lucky."

All the evasiveness and staring was getting old and Candy's annoyance began to overcome her fear. "So, what now?" she said.

"Come with me," said Rinko and walked away.

Candy followed her into an empty parlor off the foyer. Rinko said, "Wait here 'til someone comes for you."

As she left, Candy said, "It's good to see you. It's been a long time." Rinko closed the door without a word and left her alone.

Candy walked around the room looking at the furniture and knickknacks, trying to find something interesting to occupy her mind. There was nothing but the same boring garbage the rich always seemed to have to impress each other. What did catch her attention was an old mirror. It was a real antique, and the silver backing on the glass was coming off in places making everything within its frame look worn and a little sad. Candy stared at herself. She pushed her hair back a little and squared her shoulders. It didn't help. She still looked as out of place as she felt. Shaking her head she thought, *I should have dressed up. But I wanted to be myself. Show Auntie and the others that I can just be myself and still as good as any of them.*

CANDY AMONG THE JADES

Her stomach felt funny again and she turned away from the mirror. *Maybe I should have worn a dress.*

When half an hour passed, Candy knew she was being left alone to throw her off balance. To get her focus back she sat on a large easy chair with her back to the mirror and did a series of breathing exercises and meditations she'd been taught in childhood. But she hadn't closed her eyes for more than a minute when the door opened. *Of course it did,* she thought. *They've been watching me this whole time. When they saw me breathing they came for me. Centering myself is the last thing they want.*

Rinko waited at the door with two other Jades Candy had never seen before. They wore long formal dark green and black robes. *More guards,* she thought. Neither woman looked particularly dangerous on their own, but Candy knew what kind of weapons they had under their robes, so when Rinko said, "It's time," she stood and went to the door. But she didn't rush about it. She wasn't about to look anxious in front of these three. Her anger was returning. *Good,* she thought. *Anger is more powerful than fear. Use it.*

The walk was a short one, just across the foyer to a large dining room from which most of the furniture had been removed. All that remained were a few chairs and a tarnished suit of armor in the far corner of the room. The few remaining chairs were in a row facing Candy. Auntie's handmaids, she knew. Or more guards disguised as maids. Auntie herself sat on a large, dark mahogany chair with carved filigree along all the edges. Her dress was expansive layers of dark green and black brocade and her white hair was in a bun held in place with what looked like two sharpened steel chopsticks—in reality ancient Jade throwing weapons. But it was the woman's face that Candy couldn't take her eyes off of.

The woman's cheeks and forehead, which had been deeply lined before, were far past that now. Her skin was furrowed with such deep lines they reminded Candy of the cracked bed of a dry desert river. She looked ancient and delicate, though Candy knew the second of those things not to be true. If Auntie looked delicate it was because she wanted to. Candy recalled what she'd been taught from an early age, "For a Jade, to be underestimated is our first and greatest weapon."

Muscle memory kicked in and Candy curtsied for Auntie before she even knew she was doing it. She hated herself for doing it so automatically and knew how comical she must look bending for the old woman while in leather and jeans. At least no one laughed and she was grateful for it. When Auntie crooked a finger for her to come closer, Candy took a few steps forward until Auntie held up a hand for her to stop. Close enough, Candy understood, that she could be heard easily, but far enough that an attack was impossible.

"Who are you?" said the old matriarch in a deep, resonant voice.

You sent for me, you old biddy, thought Candy, so she simply said her name.

"No," said Auntie. "Who *are* you?"

Candy knew what she wanted to hear. She'd learned it with her fighting classes. "I am myself. Wholly, inviolate. Neither slave nor chattel to be bought and sold, and duty-bound to no one but myself and my sisters."

"And where are you from, child?"

With all her heart, Candy wanted to say "Fresno," but she knew none of this bunch would have a sense of humor, so she said, "Nowhere. Everywhere. From the steppes and the wastes where we were enslaved to the cities where we were second wives and serfs. We are from ourselves because only we are a home."

Auntie thought for a minute and said conversationally, "Have you ever traveled along the old Silk Road?"

For the first time, Candy smiled and spoke as herself. "I've hardly been out of California, Auntie."

"You should go. You recite the words well enough, but you have no understanding of their meaning. If you could taste the dust and feel the wind and stones beneath your feet where we were once bondswomen, you might have some sense of who you really are."

Angry now and tired of old rituals, Candy started to say something when Auntie cut her off with a question. "Why are we Jades?"

CANDY AMONG THE JADES

She refused to give the right answer. "We're born Jades. There's nothing we can do about it."

The handmaidens whispered to each other until Auntie said, "Quiet." She looked at Candy and repeated the question. "Why are we Jades?"

"I don't know. Because diamonds are a girl's best friend, but they're so expensive."

Candy heard a shuffling behind her. The door guards had come closer.

"You have one final chance. Answer foolishly again and there will be consequences. Why are we Jades?"

There are two guards behind me and who knows how many of the maidens are armed too, Candy thought. She didn't heal like Stark and she had no weapons, so she made a face and answered, "Because of the old emperors."

"What about the emperors?"

"They bought and sold us as guards and warriors for our weight in jade."

"So, you do remember something of importance."

Candy shifted her hips, ready to fall and roll if a blow came from behind. "Why am I being quizzed on such childish bullshit?"

Something moved in the air, but Auntie raised a hand and Candy was relieved when nothing hit her.

"It's not your place to question me," said the old woman. "I choose what is appropriate and what is not because I don't speak for myself, but for all Jades. Do you understand that? You are not here to answer to me, but to every one of your sisters around the world. It's their judgment, not mine, that will decide your fate."

Nervous again, Candy looked down at the antique carpet and dug her heel into it. "I said what you wanted. Emperors bought and sold us. What else do you want to hear?"

"Emperors," said Auntie. "Kings. Autarchs. Fools and pimps. In short, men. They have sought to control us for themselves for millennia.

They did control us—for a time. Until *Nocte Rubri Cultri*. Do you even remember its meaning?"

Candy nodded. "The Night of the Red Knives. When we killed our enslavers, took to exile, and became our true selves," she recited.

"We were never bought and sold after that," said the old woman. "When we worked for men, it was for a price. We controlled our own destiny."

Her anger rising again, Candy said, "Then *you* controlled it. Or some older Auntie. Look at this place. Maidens. Your personal goon squad. We've never really been free."

Auntie slammed a fist down on the arm of her chair hard enough to crack it. "Hush, child!" she shouted. "We've been free of the control of men for centuries. But now to many in this world we are seen as mere Lurkers. Just another freakish species begging for acceptance from our betters—the men who rule this stupid world. For protection, we must become more powerful and control them through any means necessary." The old woman leaned forward in her chair and stared into Candy's eyes. "What is the most powerful way to control a man?"

"Fear," she said, refusing to give Auntie what she wanted.

"Don't be stupid. Say the word. How do you control a man?"

"Hide the TV remote?"

Auntie raised her chin a fraction of an inch and something slammed into Candy's lower back. She collapsed to the floor. She looked up at the guards over her. No sympathy there.

"How do you control a man?" shouted Auntie.

"Buy him pizza."

The guards didn't wait for Auntie's orders this time. They closed on Candy and kicked her in the back and stomach until the old woman waved them off.

"Don't be stupid, child. We both know you'll give me the correct answer in time. Do it now and save all of us so much trouble."

Candy looked back up at the guards. This time they had knives out.

"How do you control a man?" whispered Auntie.

"Goddammit," Candy said.

"Say it."

"No."

"Why not?"

"It's horrible."

"Yes. It is. That's why we speak of it so seldomly."

"I don't know what you want from me."

"That's obvious. Just say the word. If you're incapable of saying it, you're no use to anyone and one of your sisters will cut your throat right now."

Candy looked back up at the knives. This wasn't a bluff. She felt afraid again, as she had been as a child when she'd stepped out of line and had been beaten or locked in isolation for some infraction of Jade rules. That lost feeling came back to her at the thought of dying on the floor right there, right now. Just disappearing from the world and her friends. From Stark. She couldn't allow that. Candy pushed herself up onto her knees and took one deep breath before saying the word.

"Love."

Auntie clapped her hands together. "Yes. Love." She gestured for the guards to help Candy from the floor and move back by the door. "Such a simple thing. You loved your friend, Doctor Kinski. Didn't you?"

Still not steady on her feet, Candy said, "I did."

"That was foolish. We sent you to him to make him love you, not the other way around."

She shrugged. "I didn't mean it. It just happened."

"Then, if you loved him why didn't you carry out your assignment?"

Thinking about Doc Kinski brought a few tears to Candy's eyes. "I couldn't."

"Couldn't or wouldn't? It was the simplest thing in the world. All you had to do was open your legs for him and have his child."

"I couldn't."

"Why not?"

"I didn't love him like that. I loved him like a father and he loved me like his family."

Auntie slammed her hand down on the arm rest again.

"Your feelings have no place in these matters. Look at you, whimpering like a man about your poor, poor heart. You had your orders. History turns on these decisions. Do you have any concept of how powerful the offspring of a Jade and archangel could be?"

Candy bent her back, feeling where the blow had fallen, taking strength from the pain. "I didn't want to. That's all there is to it."

"Worse than not completing your task with Kinski, now you've fallen into the trap of love with someone worse. The monstrosity, Stark."

"Yes. I love him. You can cut me or kill me and it won't change that. I love him."

Auntie tut-tutted. "I would never truly hurt or kill you. You are a Jade and I know that means something to you still."

"It does."

"And you love your Auntie and your sisters?"

"I do. So much. You don't know."

"A bold claim for one who's displayed such contempt today."

Wanting to curse the old woman, instead Candy found herself saying, "I'm sorry, Auntie. How can I make it up to you?" She stood stunned for a moment, but knew what she said was true. She wanted forgiveness.

"What makes you think you're worthy of the chance?" said the old woman.

Candy shrugged. "Maybe I'm not. I know what you wanted was important, but I just couldn't. But you can give me something else."

Auntie's gaze went to someone across the room. "Should I, Rinko? Is she ready for another test? Is she worthy?"

Rinko shook her head. "Ready? Maybe. Worthy? Definitely not."

"Perhaps," replied Auntie. "Still, we must learn to forgive even those who've strayed far from home and duty. Very well, Candy. You can still be welcomed back to your true family."

CANDY AMONG THE JADES

"How? Tell me," Candy said, hating herself for the joy she felt at being able to get back into the old woman's graces. She knew she'd been trained for this every bit as much as she'd been trained for combat, but it didn't stop the feeling of wanting absolution.

Auntie leaned back in her mahogany throne and looked down at Candy. In a deep, calm voice she said, "Kill the monstrosity."

Candy froze. "What?"

"Kill him or we will. He's corrupted you and he must pay for it. And you must pay for your part in this. You have until dawn tomorrow to decide. You'll stay here with us in a room you can think in. Come to me in the morning with your decision," said the old woman. She raised her eyes to the guards. "Now take her from me."

The guards took each of Candy's arms, led her upstairs to one of the guest rooms and locked her in.

SHE LAY on the large bed for a while wondering if this was real or if she was high and on a very bad trip. But the pain in her back and the look in Auntie's eyes when she'd ordered Candy beaten told her that everything was real. All her Jade training and the bonds she'd formed felt poisonous to her. Auntie controlled her so easily because she'd been raised to be controlled. Furious with herself for succumbing to it, she felt herself turning—going Jade—and she punched holes in the walls until her knuckles bled. But it got her nowhere so she relaxed, doing the breath and meditation exercises she'd started downstairs. There was a pitcher of water on a side table. Candy drank two glasses and sat on the edge of the bed when a dark thought hit her.

What if this was all her fault and Auntie was right? Was she so weak she was ready to betray her sisters for a *man*? A killer at that. Maybe she deserved the beating and all the rest of what she'd endured to bring her to her senses. *I've betrayed everything I was taught to love,* she thought. *First with Kinski and now with Stark. Is Auntie right and I'm a child? A bad child? It feels like I've always been one and now it's finally catching up with me.*

Candy closed her eyes and pictured Stark in bed, his head twisted at a strange angle. It would be so easy and quick. He'd never see it coming. He'd already caused her so much pain. Making her love him and then disappearing into Hell to help another woman. What did she owe someone she'd known for what? Months? She'd been a Jade forever and would die one. Tears came back to her. How could she betray everything she'd been born to?

Getting up for more water, she staggered a few steps. Candy poured a glass and sniffed it. She couldn't detect anything, but she felt drunk and sleepy. It was early in the day, but she could barely keep her eyes open. *I'm dosed,* she thought. *They fucking roofied me. Why?* But the question was meaningless right then because as soon as she made it back to the bed, she was unconscious.

WHEN CANDY came to, it was dark out. She'd slept the whole day and into the evening but wasn't sure how late it was. There wasn't a clock in the room and when she patted herself down, she realized someone had taken her phone when she was unconscious. She went to the window and tested the bars that crossed them. They were sunk deep into concrete and she couldn't move them a bit. Besides, it was a two-story drop onto a stone walkway. The window was useless. She went to the door and tested it. Someone had changed the ordinary home door for a metal one with hinges sunk into stone and a steel lock that only worked from the outside. She was stuck and she knew it. There was no way out. Nothing to do but wait for dawn when Auntie would call for her.

Candy lay down on the bed and hated herself for thinking even for a minute of hurting Stark. Being drugged didn't excuse it. She'd been looking for an easy way out and the easiest was blaming herself and allowing herself to be manipulated into something she knew was wrong. She wished she could talk to Doc Kinski. He knew all about the head games people played with themselves. She missed him so much. And Stark. She missed him too. Part of her brain was frantic with trying to figure a way out of the room while another was calm, assessing the situation like a warrior. Like a Jade. Finally, she knew what to do.

AT DAWN, she heard the lock to her room turn. Candy stood by the bed with a heavy chair leg tucked under her jacket.

"It's time," said one of the guards. She was one of the two who'd worked her over during her interview with Auntie. Candy came forward quietly, a whipped dog on its way to its master. But at the door, she faked a cramp, grabbed the chair leg and smashed it into the side of yesterday's guard's head. The other guard pulled a knife and tried to slash her, but Candy did the unforgiveable—she went Jade, sank her shark teeth into the guard's arm and tossed her across the room. Before the first guard could get up Candy picked up the chair leg and brought it down onto the woman's back the way she'd done to her the day before. She left both guards where they lay and crept along the floor to the staircase.

The mansion was strangely quiet. She still held the chair leg for the fight she anticipated below. But nothing happened. There was no one around. She listened for shuffling feet or weapons being drawn—the sounds of an ambush. But there was nothing. The building was empty. The two guards upstairs might have been the last two Jades inside.

Oh shit, she thought. *They never trusted me. Everyone has left to find Stark. They're going to swarm him.*

Candy ran outside still ready for a fight, but it never came. If the other Jades were in hiding, they were doing a masterful job of it. But nothing happened. Candy walked along the driveway still uncertain, checking a couple of SUVs the others had left behind. The first one was locked, but the second wasn't, and the keys were in the ignition. She jumped into the driver's seat, gunned the engine, and tore around the circular driveway. She didn't need any more proof that the Jades were gone than the front of the mansion where the gates were open and unguarded. The two Jades who'd come for her were probably assassins they'd left behind. *You should have left more, Auntie,* Candy thought. *You trained me and so did Stark. Two was never going to be enough.*

She sped east from Bel Air, heading into Hollywood, running lights where she could and dodging pedestrians where she had to. She got into a fender bender with a Tesla in West Hollywood, but sped around the shouting driver, dragging his bumper behind her. The thing finally fell off around Fairfax Avenue. Traffic jammed up by the Chinese Theater and she was tempted to jump the curb and drive on the sidewalk, but it was too crowded, so she just jammed between smaller cars, running lights all the way to North Las Palmas where she dumped the car on Hollywood Boulevard. She ran the rest of the way to Max Overdrive on foot, holding a crowbar she found in the back.

Like the mansion in Bel Air, the street was strangely quiet. Candy had expected a whole phalanx of cars and vans and Mac Overdrive in flames. But there was nothing. It was just another anonymous Hollywood street deserted this early in the day. Still, she didn't lower the crowbar until she was inside the shop. She heard footsteps from above and crept up the stairs quietly.

Where she found Stark shirtless in the kitchen making coffee. He smiled when he saw her. "Hey you. Did you have fun with your Jade pals? What's with the crowbar? You need to change a tire?"

Still ready for an ambush, Candy remained at the top of the stairs, listening. Stark looked at her. "You okay?"

"Yeah. Did you see anyone around here today?"

Stark grunted. "Yeah. This morning, at the crack of fucking dawn, your pal Rinko stopped by with a note for you. She really doesn't like me. For a minute, I thought she was going to stab me with the damn thing. It's on the table."

Candy set down the crowbar and tore open the envelope. The note was written in a neat, formal hand that she recognized instantly as Auntie's.

During your audience yesterday, your fate became quickly clear. You've made your decision and are beyond redemption. You have failed your

CANDY AMONG THE JADES

sisters utterly. But unlike the men who held us in bondage, we are merciful. Neither you nor the monstrosity will be harmed, but you are no longer a Jade. You are cast out. Alone. This decision was yours. Not mine or your sisters. Do not attempt to contact us.

There was no signature. Nothing but the short, cruel verdict. Candy read over the note several times, then wadded up the paper and the envelope and threw them into the trash with the coffee grounds. She sat at the table without saying a word. Stark brought her a cup of coffee and sat down across from her at the table.

"Are you all right?" he said.

Candy nodded and rubbed her temples, trying to wipe away a headache from the drug she'd been dosed with. "I'm fine. Just tired."

"You girls must have tied one on last night."

"Yeah. I guess we did."

"How's your aunt Bi?"

Candy laughed. "The same as ever. Going on and on about family. Wanting me to come home. In fact, she insisted."

Stark sipped his coffee and said, "I know the feeling. *You never call. You never write.*" He hesitated for a moment before he mumbled, "What are you going to do?"

It touched Candy to see Stark so suddenly vulnerable. She leaned back in her chair and stretched. "Nothing. Not a damn thing. Auntie was right. I made my decision a long time ago. I am home." She put her head down on her crossed arms.

"You look beat," Stark said. "Come on. Let's put you to bed."

He led her to the bedroom and tucked her in under the covers, but before he could go back into the kitchen Candy grabbed his hand. "Forever?" she said.

"What?"

"Us. Forever?"

He leaned down and kissed her forehead. "'Til the wheels come off, baby. And we're grinding axle."

Candy hugged him and lay back down. "That's all I wanted to hear."

"You sure you're okay?"

"Perfectly. Now go drink your coffee. I like listening to you rustle around in the morning."

"Then I'll be extra noisy," he said but Candy didn't hear him. She was already asleep.

Copyright Information

"Ambitious Boys Like You" Copyright © 2015 by Richard Kadrey. First published in *The Doll Collection*, edited by Ellen Datlow.

"The Secrets of Insects" Copyright © 2016 by Richard Kadrey. First published in *Children of Lovecraft*, edited by Ellen Datlow.

"Razor Pig" Copyright © 2020 by Richard Kadrey. First published in *Subterranean: Tales of Dark Fantasy 3*, edited by William Schafer.

"A Trip to Paris" Copyright © 2021 by Richard Kadrey. First published in *When Things Get Dark: Stories Inspired by Shirley Jackson*, edited by Ellen Datlow.

"A Hinterlands Haunting" Copyright © 2019 by Richard Kadrey. First published in *Echoes*, edited by Ellen Datlow.

"Suspect Zero" Copyright © 2013 by Richard Kadrey. All rights reserved.

"Black Neurology—A Love Story" Copyright © 2020 by Richard Kadrey. First published in *Come Join Us By the Fire*, Volume 20, edited by Theresa DeLucci.

"Flayed Ed" Copyright © 2020 by Richard Kadrey. First published in *Come Join Us By the Fire*, Volume 20, edited by Theresa DeLucci.

"A Sandman Slim Christmas Carol" Copyright © 2021 by Richard Kadrey. First published on Patreon.com, December 20, 2021.

"The Air Is Chalk" Copyright © 2019 by Richard Kadrey. First published in *Wastelands: The New Apocalypse*, edited by John Joseph Adams.

RICHARD KADREY

"The Tunguska Event" Copyright © 2008 by Richard Kadrey. First published on The Infinite Matrix.

"Horse Latitudes" Copyright © 1992 by Richard Kadrey. First published in *Omni, Best Science Fiction One*, edited by Ellen Datlow.

"Snuff in Six Scenes" Copyright © 2020 by Richard Kadrey. First published in *Final Cuts: New Tales of Hollywood Horror and Other Spectacles*, edited by Ellen Datlow.

"What Is Love but the Quiet Moments After Dinner?" Copyright © 2022 by Richard Kadrey. First published in *Screams from the Dark: 29 Tales of Monsters and the Monstrous*, edited by Ellen Datlow.

"Devil in the Dollhouse" Copyright © 2012 by Richard Kadrey. All rights reserved.

"Candy Among the Jades" Copyright © 2023 by Richard Kadrey. Appears here for the first time.